Falling for My Brother's Best Friend

Falling Series
Book 2

Laura Eagan

Rouge Point Books

Chapter 1

Abby

"If you don't wrap it up, I'm going to leave you," I yelled at Jessica in as loving a tone as I could muster while she ate the face of her boyfriend of the month. Boys had swooned over her since we were thirteen.

We all knew why.

She had been an *early* grower. Her chest developed before any other girls in our grade, and it became an automatic bullseye for all the boys to aim at.

It continued through high school and all four years of college. I couldn't count how many drinks guys had bought her, or how many dates she had been on in the last four years. Meanwhile, in my last year of college, I went on one date from fall until spring.

My *senior* year of college—the year that was supposed to be everyone's prime in the dating world—was wasted on getting a 4.0 GPA. While Jessica was on dates at nice restaurants, I would be on study dates at the coffee shop with Rebecca, Tonya, and Kelly. *I guess there's always time to find guys.*

It was going to pay off, though. My only goal this summer

was to get a teaching position at a great school, and since I had no experience, my college record was the only thing to put me ahead of others.

I started scrolling on my phone, because what else was I supposed to do while she and some guy were sword fighting with their tongues?

Immediately in my feed, there was a picture of three of my other best friends on their way to the cruise ship. I sighed. Rebecca, Kelly, and Tonya had begged me to join them, and I would have loved to. But just the thought of a cruise ship rocking up and down in the sea made me want to hurl. My parents had taken me and my brother Kyle on a cruise when we were younger, and I did *not* have a good time.

Rebecca said she would buy all the Dramamine and sea sickness bracelets in Texas if it would help, but I knew they wouldn't.

Every other post I saw was a picture of a friend showing their goodbye-for-the-summer selfies, or some of my brother's friends' graduation photos.

Speaking of Kyle—I couldn't wait to see him again. My brother went to school near where we grew up, and I went more than a few states away. We hadn't seen each other since Christmas, and though he could be aggravating in a brotherly way, I missed him.

He and his friend Jacob were driving home the next day, so momma hen was going to have both of her chicks back in our childhood home on the same day. Actually, it was kind of like three baby chicks, since Jacob had basically always been part of the family. We three had been especially close. My brother was a year older than me, but he was held back, so we ended up being in the same grade for a lot of our time in school. At the same time, Jacob was also held back because he was struggling with the death of his mom. He and Kyle weren't really friends before that, but they were the only two people in their grade who didn't advance, so they stuck together from then on. They were always hanging out at our house.

In fact, I was pretty sure they were the reason I wasn't so great with boys in the dating realm. Kyle had always been so protective and wouldn't let any of them near me. I rolled my eyes at the memories of boys being too afraid to ask me to prom out of fear of my brother. *Or maybe they just didn't want to ask out Abby the geek.* Then the one who *did* ask me turned out to be a piece of human garbage.

My phone was losing battery life fast as I scrolled, and my charger was broken. I was tired of waiting. So with a slight fury, I put my palm in the middle of the steering wheel, ready to yell some obscenities. Before I pushed down, Jessica turned my way and started walking over with her boy toy watching her longingly, praying that he could keeping swapping mouth bacteria with her.

Jessica opened the passenger door with a loud *creak* and sat down. *Yeesh, I need new everything. New phone, new charger, new car. I need money.*

"Sorry I took so long," she said. "They never take it well when I let them go."

"How many of those have you had this year?" I asked. Jessica had been a cheerleader in college, so even though we were friends from the same smallish town, she had her own life separate from me. A party animal compared to a bookworm.

"Ha! Too many to count. It was fun, though."

I arched an eyebrow at her.

"Hey now, don't look at me like that. I'm just having fun. Guys can sleep with a bunch of girls and they're praised for it. But we sleep with, what, more than two guys in a year, and we're sluts? It's just such bullshit, you know?"

Do I know? No, Jessica, I sure don't. Not at all.

"Oh yeah, I know," I lied. "It's like, I'm considered a prude if I don't have as much sex as a guy, but then they say I'm a whore if I want to bang one out with someone without officially dating!" *Am I doing this right? Do I sound like I know what I'm talking about?*

Jessica looked at me and smiled. "I'm so glad you came out of your shell this year, Abby. We have a long road trip ahead for me to get all those juicy deets you've been hiding." When we were in college, our different social circles made it so that we didn't see each other too much. It was an arrangement that worked for us. But when we would go home for the summer, it was like we were back in high school, and we were best friends who hung out all the time. Who knew what Jessica was going to do now that college was over? I didn't think she even knew.

I opened my eyes wide. "Well, my stars, you know a proper lady never kisses and tells," I said in a thick country accent. I laughed along with her, but I cried a little on the inside. I had lied to Jessica a couple of times that year.

I know. I'm the worst. I hated lying. But I always made sure it served a higher purpose the few times I succumbed.

After her constant dates became a routine, I had started to be embarrassed that I didn't have the same experiences. It was like she was winning, and I was a competitive person.

So I may have lied a little. I pretended like I was going on a date a few times throughout the year, but I was really only going to the coffee shop to study. There had been one real date during my Junior year, but it only made my trust issues worse.

This guy in my class took me to an Italian restaurant and then a movie on a Friday night. We kissed at my doorstep, and he asked to come in, but I said no. It was late, and I didn't want to do anything on the first date. He looked disappointed but kissed me again and went on his way. Over the next few days, he wouldn't answer my texts. Then while I was walking to class that Tuesday, I saw him holding hands with another girl.

It probably ended up that way for the best. I didn't think I had time for guys. I needed to focus on school.

And that theory may have been correct, because Jessica's final GPA was abysmal. I, on the other hand, worked my ass off in high school to earn a full scholarship, and I wasn't going to let any boys distract me from my goals, even if it meant I was behind the curve, so to speak.

Surely me sacrificing a social life in college will have been worth it, I thought. I was ready to start my career, just like my friend Rebecca and I had planned out. My job search to find an amazing school to work at would begin as soon as I got back home. I wanted to be the best teacher I could be, and I wanted to find a school where the kids would be motivated to learn.

So my goal that summer was to get hired by the perfect school first, and then maybe I could focus my attention and energy on having a love life for the first time.

Chapter 2

Jacob

Billboard after billboard passed the car window, and I rewrote them in my head almost without thinking. It had been my favorite game with my mom when I was younger—trying to come up with better copy than the lifeless ads we drove past.

Bored of listening to my best friend talk to his girlfriend for hours, I opened up my investing app. I scanned all the companies on my watch list, looking for the patterns, and then I saw it. On a whim, I bought twenty thousand shares of some security-analytics company in Florida and watched its price. After a few minutes with my eyes glued to the screen, I sold. *Boom. Just made fourteen thousand dollars.*

"All right, babe. We're exiting. I'll talk to you later," Kyle said. "I love you too, sweetie."

I looked over at Kyle, waiting for him to end the call. His eyes darted over to me.

"Honey, you know I love to call you that, but I'm not alone right now," he whispered.

Well, *now* my interest was piqued. I quirked an eyebrow, and his cheeks turned rosy.

"Of course I love you, Mel, I just—"

Uh-oh. I could hear Melanie getting upset with him. Not like that was anything new.

"Okay, okay. I love you too...my little cookie dough," he said, looking like a defeated general surrendering to the enemy. She said something back, and they ended the phone call.

"Wow," I said.

"Don't start."

"Cookie dough? Your *little* cookie dough? What does that even mean? What does that represent for her? Or was it for *you?*"

What unspeakable things have they done with cookie dough?

"Ugh, please just stop," he begged.

"You know I'm not going to give up until you tell me. Or maybe I'll have to enlist your parents or Abby to help me find out. Your mom might think it's cute, but your dad..."

"I don't know what! Jesus. We made cookies one night, and I jokingly called her my little cookie dough, and I guess she liked it enough to force me to call her that ever since," Kyle replied. "Every time we get off the phone together. Every. Time."

"Oof. I'm sorry, bud. But why were you even on the phone with her? You said goodbye in person when we left like a few hours ago, and then you guys talked most of the way here. It's been a really fun ride for your passenger."

"Hey, man, she likes the sound of my voice, I guess." He laughed. "And you can give me dating tips when you actually get a girl."

I laughed too, but it hurt a little bit. I'm sure he didn't mean it to be hurtful.

I had never had a girlfriend. Up until half a year ago, I weighed three hundred pounds, and the ladies generally stayed away from me. After my mom died, I ate my feelings. I was overweight growing up in middle school, high school, and most of college. I was sure there were girls that would have dated me, but I knew most of them wouldn't. So why would I have tried?

Kyle and I had been roommates all four years of college, and his metabolism was finally slowing down halfway through our senior year. He came back from Christmas break determined to lose weight, especially after he got back to campus and his girlfriend asked him if he'd had eight Christmas dinners instead of the one.

I had cracked up, which was unusual since it was Melanie who'd said it, but Kyle had turned straight to me and said, 'What are you laughing at? I'm going to need a spotter.'

Thus began our workout regimen. I didn't have much hope. I had tried working out before, to no avail. So why would this time be any different?

But it *had* been different. Kyle had gotten us into cooking healthy food. He'd banished my precious carbs from the apartment. We'd bought athletic watches so we could compete with each other for steps. The loser got to run two laps around the track while the other watched and enjoyed a couple of beers. We'd ridden stationary bikes in the gym, lifted weights, and cut soft drinks from our diet. We stopped going out and chugging beers so frequently.

And it had worked. I'd had a lot more fat to lose than he did. At first, when I didn't see any results, I'd gotten disheartened, as usual. But once I started losing it, I lost it fast.

I'd first noticed it in my face and neck. Then I'd noticed my man boobs were getting smaller. My legs had started looking toned.

One day I had taken off my shirt in front of the mirror and

gasped, "Is that an ab?"

Just the one, though. No other abs. No six-pack. But a month later, I'd had two, and then four, and now...Kyle joked I could wash clothes on my abs.

I was a changed man, and it felt great. Best of all, my grades hadn't suffered with all the extra time working out.

Kyle looked over, maybe noticing my silence was because of his jab.

"Have you heard anything else from that girl you hooked up with? Katie? She has been posting some hot-ass pics of herself on Instagram lately," he said.

Now it was my time to say, 'Ugh.'

"Nope. I texted her, but she never responded."

A lie. *She* was actually the one who had texted *me*. Katie had come up to me after class one day toward the end of the semester to talk. We had realized recently that she grew up about an hour from my small hometown, but we hadn't talked much after that. So on the last day, she'd asked if I wanted to go get a drink and then gave me her number. I had just stared at her with my mouth slightly open for a few seconds.

Is this what happens to guys who work out? I'd thought.

We'd met up, the night had gone great, and we'd walked back to her place. Her roommate had been out of town. We'd sat on her couch, put on some TV show that I don't even remember, and then had an eventful night together.

She'd texted me the day after, saying she'd had a great time and would be interested in hanging out again, but for some reason, I couldn't bring myself to text her back. She'd texted me again a couple days after that to check in and see if I had gotten her previous text, but again, I'd ignored her. I didn't even know *why*. I couldn't explain it, other than the fact that I had trust issues. My life was filled with girls lying to my fat ass to make me feel better or leaving me for a better-looking guy. It was hard for me to trust people.

I looked out the window and hoped I would learn how to find someone I would be comfortable with. Or at least someone to fuck more than once. I was going back to my hometown, and no one was going to recognize me. Maybe some of those girls from high school would forget Jake the Cake and see the shredded man I had become.

"What a bitch," Kyle said.

"Nah," I said. She didn't deserve that. "It is what it is."

"Oh well. Forget her. You're going to get back home, and girls who never looked at you before are going to drop their panties as soon as you walk in the room. Just wait. You're going to get whatever hot babe you want."

I smiled. I had never had that option before.

"And hey, man, have you done any more thinking about that business idea I told you about?"

I shifted in my seat. Kyle had told me the other day of his grand plans of starting a home renovation company once we moved back to our hometown. He said it would be the perfect way to find a career that wasn't forced on me by my dad. I'd told him I would think about it. And I hadn't really done much thinking yet.

The thing was, I didn't feel the rush or anxiety to pick any career...because I was already rich. When I was in high school, one of my teachers had shown us this new investing app called Wealth Jump, which eliminated fees for day trading that would otherwise make it too costly for someone to start investing. It also had an option where you begin with fake money in your account, and you could practice trading with it to see how you would do with real money. I made some stupid decisions at first. But then I read as much as I could on the internet and quickly got the hang of things. My fake money grew by one thousand percent over a couple of years.

In the last month of high school, I received a bunch of money from family for graduation. *Then*, my dad told me my mom's parents had given me a trust fund, which would be available to me as soon as I started college.

So, I made the extremely risky decision to invest *all* of it. My dad would have killed me if he knew. My mom and her parents probably would have too, if any of them were still alive.

Because of my smarts and a lot of luck, I turned that million into over twenty million dollars over the last four years. The market bottomed out right before I invested, and then it made a quick recovery. I was most likely the richest person at my college.

The thing was, *nobody knew*. None of my friends, not even Kyle, and not my dad. I'd kept a low profile about it. People changed when they knew you had money. I used to think that I would be open to people about my income—that it was corporate greed that convinced employees not to discuss their earnings with each other. But then, when I finally had a lot of money, I understood. If people knew I had money, they would ask me for it. To solve their financial problems, to start a business, you name it. And the ones who wouldn't ask might still see me differently. So I made an effort to make it seem like I had no money. I worked a desk job at the college's bursar's office, trading stocks while I sat there doing nothing. I didn't even have a car. I either rode my bike, took Ubers, or rode with Kyle.

So, in Kyle's mind, I was a poor street rat, and he was giving me an opportunity to start a career. But, just like my dad wanted me to follow in his footsteps to become an attorney, and I said no, I didn't want to renovate houses either.

The problem was I had no idea what I *did* want. I had all

the money I could ever need. Now I just needed to find a job I was passionate about.

"Yeah, I've thought about it. I just don't know how much value I would offer," I said.

"Psh, I'll teach you everything you need to know. I mainly just need a second pair of hands. As well as someone else to help me secure a loan from the bank." He looked over at me with a big boyish grin on his face. "We can do this, man. Get a loan, buy a few houses, renovate them, and put them back on the market, all while having full time jobs. We'll be swimming in cash in a few years!"

I laughed. "All right, man, get the business formed and draw up a business plan, and then I'll see." Kyle was a guy who talked about big plans more than executing them.

He tapped on the steering wheel, looking triumphant.

God, I needed to work on just telling people I wasn't interested. But I cared too much about not letting them down.

What Kyle didn't know yet was that I was not planning on staying in our little town. I had a shit ton of money and wanted to travel. Maybe I'd be a nomad and just travel Europe and Asia for years. One thing was for sure—there was no reason for me to hang around.

Chapter 3

Abby

Driving all day was never fun, and it was even worse when you had to do it again the next day. Jessica and I were lucky enough to know someone who lived a little more than halfway where we could crash. We ended up arriving pretty late, but having a home cooked meal of banana pancakes made being in the car all day worth it. We left pretty early in the morning because I didn't want to be on the road at night again. It always scared me a little.

"So, what are you going to do while you're home?" I asked Jessica. I was trying to prod her to think about what she was going to do with her life. She let her grades suffer and really only thought about being a cheerleader and having fun. She barely got her degree.

"Hmm, I'm not sure. I'll text our friends from Elmwood, probably. I'll let you know if anyone comes up with anything. What about you?"

I was not very sure either. All I could think about at the moment was sleeping in my childhood bed again.

"First goal is to find a teaching position somewhere, and

then there are a couple books that are recommended for new teachers, so I'll probably get started on those."

Jessica gave me a pained look.

"Abby. We're not even back home from college yet, and all you can think about is homework? *School's out for summer!*" she sang. "Relax a little. Enjoy the time. Find another guy to spend your time with. Just have fun."

I laughed. "And where do you expect me to find a guy in our town? The supermarket parking lot?"

"Hey, don't knock it till you try it," Jessica said with a wink. "What about Tony? You always had a crush on him growing up."

Oh, Tony. The hottest boy in Seguin, Texas. Who didn't have a crush on him?

A muscular track and swimming star with brown eyes and long brown hair perpetually flopping over his forehead. I'd joined the girls' swimming team just so I could see him in those Speedos they put on guys that left nothing to the imagination. Then, without meaning to, I'd ended up breaking a couple of swimming records at my school junior year—all to impress Tony.

I crushed hard on him for four years, though I never did anything about it, of course. One year, I spent too much time in science class staring at him and daydreaming about the kids we would have and all the beach trips we would take. It was the only B I ever got.

Worth it.

"I don't even know if Tony is in town, and it's not like I'm going to—"

"Yep, he's here," she said, scrolling through her phone. "You should send him a message."

"Oh yeah? Saying what? 'Hey, Tony, it's Abby from high

school. Want to go get ice cream or something one of these nights?'" I said, rolling my eyes at her.

"Yes, that's perfect, actually." She looked at me so seriously.

"Jess, why would Tony ever say yes? He probably has a girlfriend, who is either a model or Emma Watson. And if he doesn't, then he's probably only interested in dating the cream of the crop."

"Abby, *you* are the cream of the crop. You've changed so much since high school, like a caterpillar turning into a butterfly. Plus you've started wearing makeup, you started running every day to keep in shape, and that push-up bra will definitely give him something to notice. I bet he'd hit on you if he saw you in the street."

"Well, hopefully we'll both be walking down a street soon, and I'll let you know how it goes."

I looked her way with a smile and noticed she was holding my phone, typing something.

"Umm, what are you doing?" I asked.

"Oh, I'm just making sure I don't have to wait for the off chance of you two walking on the same road."

I heard the sent message sound.

"Jess! What did you just do?" My heart was beating faster.

"I just relayed a message from my friend who's too nervous to do it herself."

Oh. My God. I can't believe she did this, and I can't do anything about it because I am still driving on the interstate.

"What did you say?" I asked, pretty aggravated.

"What you told me to—'Hey, Tony, it's Abby from high school. I'm about to be back home from college. Want to go get ice cream or something one of these nights?'"

I can't. Can't. Can't believe her! This is so embarrassing. He's probably going to screenshot it and send it to all his friends.

"I can't believe you just did that. I may hate you now," I told her. I mean, of course I didn't really hate her. But what the hell was she thinking?

"No, you love me, and you're going to love me more when he says yes!"

I rolled my eyes and stared straight ahead at the road.

I mean, it would have been pretty amazing if he was single and decided to go out with me. But it was Tony Catalano. He never really noticed me in high school. He probably had no idea who had just messaged him.

Still, I could remember what our fake children would look like. Brown hair, brown eyes. We would move to the beach. Tony would teach them surfing, and I would teach them how to sit in the shade of a beach umbrella while reading a book. And all the kids were going to be swimming prodigies, since Tony and I were both talented at it.

"Are you going to be a lifeguard during the summer again?" Jessica asked, changing the subject.

"That's the plan," I said, remembering my lovely little job. My dad had owned a local swimming pool club for the last seven years and suggested I try it out for a summer job. Being on the swimming team had given me the skills to be a lifeguard. I mostly just sat there all day, getting a tan if I wanted, and told kids to not dive in the shallow end. I had never had a drowning scare yet and hoped I never would. The money was not amazing, but I didn't really need much. I would be moving in with my parents, paying no rent and not paying for much food, until I found a job.

* * *

A couple hours of driving later, we finally exited. When you've been gone from home for so long, those last minutes after you exit the interstate were always the worst. They took forever to get through, too. They were exciting, but my body always felt drained, greasy, and tired.

I sure *hoped* I wouldn't see Tony on the street any time soon. I looked like a hot mess.

I dropped off Jessica at her house and helped her bring her stuff inside. Her mom basically crushed us with hugs, then offered me cookies and pistachios, her two favorite things.

Of course I took some cookies.

We all said goodbye, and I headed home, which was just a few minutes away. There was still daylight out, but the sunset was producing some beautiful colors dancing across the sky. Hints of light purple and orange. I hoped I remembered to take a picture once I got out. It was a beautiful painting I never wanted to forget.

I pulled into the neighborhood and was hit with the usual nostalgia. Mrs. Berry's flowers were all busy and blooming. There was that house with the basketball hoop still rusting away in the driveway. And Mr. Marshall was cutting his grass, which he did *every* day. He was missing some things in his head, but he had his own kind of charm.

I turned down my street, and my hands were sweating. I didn't know why. *Just the nerves of being back home, I guess.*

It was going to be great. I felt so excited to see my parents and brother again. I couldn't wait for a big bear hug from Jacob or to see my old friends.

But living on my own in college had been nice. No parents to tell me when to clean something up or having to approve if I went out somewhere. Getting in late without having to worry about being super quiet. There was so much freedom.

It was going to be nice to have home-cooked meals again, though. Those last four years had seen perhaps a bit too much boxed macaroni and cheese—though I'm not sure if a limit existed. Same with my laundry. I hated having to bring all my clothes down the elevator to the communal laundry room and then lug them back up. Everything being on the same floor, and not sharing a washer and dryer with strangers, was going to be great.

As I approached the house, I saw my brother's car with the doors open. He must have just gotten home. I craned my neck to see if anyone was outside.

When my eyes landed on the man walking through my front door, I nearly forgot I was still behind the wheel. He was wearing gym shorts and a muscle shirt, the kind where the sides of the pecs were exposed. And oh my, were they *exposed.*

He had short, brown hair and the sexiest arms I had ever seen. The kind that could easily pick me up by my waist and twirl me around. I was starting to get tingles in certain places, which did not happen very frequently. *Who is this Greek god and why was he in my house and can he stay for dinner and does he need to share a bed?*

He saw my car rolling in front, caught my eyes, smiled, and waved to me. *He's smiling at me. Oh, honey, I've got this one in the bag. Watch out, you sexy hunk. I'm gonna make you mine whether you like it or not.* It was like the heavens had answered my prayers of finding love this summer and dropped some beautiful stranger right on my doorstep—a reward for all my hard work in college.

I looked him over again, and there was something familiar about him. *Wait a second. Oh my God, I know that smile.* Jacob? There was no way. This guy could have fit inside of the old Jacob.

My car was slowly rolling forward to park in front of my house, but I couldn't take my eyes off of him. Jacob had always been my favorite of my brother's friends. He was like another big brother to me. But I was never attracted to him.

But I was *definitely* attracted to him now. *Shit, I can't be thinking these things about him. He's like family. Why is he waving those sexy arms at me? I wonder what he did to lose so much—*

Suddenly, I heard a crunch. *Oops.*

Chapter 4

Jacob

Oh no!

As I was waving to Abby, her car kept rolling until it knocked over the trash can, which toppled over and spilled some of its contents. She abruptly slammed on her brakes and put the car in park.

I rushed over to her and opened her door.

"Abby! Are you all right?" I asked, as I instinctively put my palm to her cheek. I didn't know why. It just felt right.

Her skin was soft and warm against my hand, and I wanted to keep it there forever. But I immediately snapped out of it and offered my hand to help her out of the car.

She took hold of it and looked up at me.

Wow. This was strange. I had never *seen* Abby like this. I didn't know if anything had changed, but I had a feeling in the pit of my stomach that I had never felt around her. She had always been like a little sister to me. But at that moment, my blood was rushing to a certain place, and there was nothing brotherly about the way I was feeling.

I gently pulled her hand up so she could stand outside the

car. She seemed dazed and confused. But it was just a trash can. Surely she wasn't so transfixed on accidentally knocking it over, though I was sure she was embarrassed.

"Hey, Jacob. I, I don't know what happened."

"Well, I'm pretty sure you just ran into your trash can," I said with a laugh.

She gave me a look that said, *Thanks for the dad joke, bud.*

God, I couldn't stop staring into her eyes. She was *gorgeous.* I'd always thought she was cute enough, but I had never *felt* anything when I looked at her. Her hair was up in a ponytail, and she was wearing some comfortable shorts that left most of her long legs bare. And then I trailed my gaze up to something I *definitely* hadn't noticed before—two somethings. *There goes my blood rushing to a certain somewhere again.*

"Hopefully I didn't break it."

"Well, if it's broken, then we can just throw it in the trash," I said, trying to get her to laugh.

It worked.

She giggled and smiled, and I felt on top of the world that I was the one to make her do that. *What the fuck is going on?*

She looked down at her hand. I followed her gaze and realized I was still holding it. They were clasped together perfectly, like they were made for each other. *Like magnet to metal, it would take a force to break us apart.*

"Whoa, what did you do, you klutz?" Kyle emerged from the house, seeing the damage.

We both immediately let go of each other's hand. We had the car blocking his view of us, so he likely didn't see anything.

"Why was the trash can already on the street?" Abby asked.

"Mom thought it would be good so we could throw away any trash from the car," Kyle replied. "I don't think that's the problem, though. Maybe you need some glasses. Or this is just more evidence that you shouldn't drive in general." I knew it was just a joke, but something awakened in me that wanted to punch him in the fucking face.

"Maybe you need some glasses," she repeated in a mocking tone as he rounded the car.

That made Kyle laugh. "Come here, little sis." He stepped toward her and embraced her. "How was your drive? Other than the recent drunk and disorderly conduct?"

She rolled her beautiful eyes. "Too long," she said. "How was yours?"

"Oh, it was fine. Short as usual."

"Short for one of us," I said. "He was talking to Melanie the whole time."

"Oh, have you two not seen each other for a bit?" she asked.

"Nope, they saw each other this morning," I cut in. "His *little cookie dough* just needed some extra love." Kyle's face turned red.

"His what?" Abby asked.

"Jacob, I'm gonna kill you," Kyle said.

"He calls her his little cookie dough in private. She calls him her little oven," I said.

Abby busted out laughing. Hearing her laugh sent a tingle to my stomach, like little butterflies flying around, happy that I could make her laugh. *Are butterflies just for girls? What about moths? Yes, there we go. Abby sends moths flying around my stomach.*

"So if she's the cookie dough and you're the oven, does that mean she's the pitcher and you're the catcher?" Abby asked. She bent over in laughter before she had the words completely out. I snorted. Kyle's face turned redder with each second.

"She does not call me her oven," Kyle said furiously, his face baking like the oven he was.

"But the cookie dough part was true?" Abby asked, tears streaming.

As she was laughing, Kyle looked at me like he was going to get revenge by flicking my sack.

"What happened? Is everyone all right?" Their mom came rushing toward us. "Abby, are you okay?"

"I'm fine, Mom. I just got caught off guard," she said as her mom gave her a hug tight enough to squeeze the breath out of her.

"How did you not see a big trash can in front of you?" her mom asked.

"I...was distracted. I, uh, saw a squirrel on top of the roof and was trying to figure out what it was doing up there."

Interesting. I was pretty sure she was looking straight at me when she knocked it over.

"Okay, well, come here, darling," she said as she gave her daughter another full hug and a kiss on the cheek. Then she kept one arm around Abby and put the other around Kyle. "It's so good to have both of my babies back."

Seeing her love for them made me smile, and I wished I had that kind of relationship with my dad. The kind I used to have with my own mom.

"Get yourself in here, Jacob. You're part of the family too," Mrs. Kathy told me as her hands motioned me toward them.

I put my arms around Kyle and Abby, and we all had a group hug. It felt so nice.

What felt *especially* nice was my arm around Abby. A feeling went through me like I wanted to...I don't know, protect her, put both of my arms around her. Something more.

Grabbing her shoulder sent a warm feeling through me. And I don't know if I was just imagining it, but I felt her lean into me.

"Okay, Mom, can we stop this silliness? We still have some unpacking to do," Kyle said.

I wished he hadn't said that. I could have stayed in that group hug forever.

"Sure, sure, sure, take away this loving moment from your mother who hasn't had all of her kids in one place in six months," she said, half joking, half serious, with her eyes a little misty. "Is anyone hungry?"

"I'm starving," Abby said.

"Yeah, I could eat too," I said. Perhaps I was just seeing what I wanted to see, but I swore I could see the corners of Abby's mouth go up.

"Great. Well, I'll go inside and heat up some hot dogs and chili while you all finish unpacking. Jacob, will you be able to stay to eat? Or do you need to get back to your place?"

She knew that I preferred her house over my own. But I appreciated her letting me choose.

"Of course I'll be able to stay, Mrs. Kathy," I replied without hesitation.

"Wonderful. Well, make sure you three work up an appetite. Shouldn't be hard after picking up that trash in the street!" she said with a laugh. She gave each of us a kiss on the tops of our heads before walking back inside.

Kyle looked at Abby and me and said, "Okay, should we finish unpacking my car, and then we can move it and get Abby's car in the driveway so it's closer to the door?" Always the efficient one, Kyle was.

"Sounds good to me," she replied.

"Now, Abby," Kyle started, "I think there's an empty trashcan in the garage, so I could drive your car up if you want. You know, in case you have a vendetta against disposable containers or something."

"Oh har dee har har, very funny," Abby said, rolling her

eyes in that way she'd always done. But I had never thought she was cute when she did it. Until today.

"Well, I just had a long drive and didn't pee at Jessica's for some reason, so I'm going to go use the little ladies' room real quick."

I watched her as she walked away. With each step she took, her lower cheeks gave the slightest jiggle. Her ponytail bounced as well, and I had the thought about pulling on it while I—

"What are you looking at?" Kyle asked, with one of his eyebrows raised.

Shit.

"Oh, nothing. I was just thinking about something."

"Uh huh," he said. "Well, let's get back to work so we can eat as soon as possible."

He started walking toward his car. I followed him, but all I could think about was how grown up Abby looked.

She had always been shy when we were kids, focused on school. I had never really seen her as anything but my best friend's sister. But *now...*

We finished unpacking Kyle's car, except for my stuff, which we were planning on doing later when he dropped me off.

Abby moved her car into the driveway, and we started on hers. When it was nearly empty, I looked over at her and noticed she was sweating a little. As I looked at her, a bead of sweat dripped from the base of her neck down into her cleavage, which was heaving up and down from her slight panting.

I thought about what would be under her shirt, and I could feel myself getting hard. *Pull yourself together, man!* It was legitimately like I grew up in a monastery and had seen the bare skin of a woman for the first time in my life. *What was she doing to me?*

I quickly looked away and tried to think of something—

anything—else. I was wearing gym shorts, and they wouldn't hide anything like a pair of jeans could.

I stopped growing, but I still had a slight bulge, so I turned away from them and made sure my shirt was covering it as much as possible.

"All right, kids!" Mrs. Kathy yelled from the front door. "Dinner is ready!"

"Perfect timing," Kyle said as he picked up the last box in the trunk. "Jacob, can you close it?"

"Yeah, sure," I said. Abby was coming back outside, probably to see if there was anything left. As I reached up to close the trunk, my shirt lifted up and exposed my skin above my shorts. My abs were definitely showing, but more worrisome was that my bulge would be noticeable to anyone who thought to look at it.

I closed the trunk and looked at her. *Shit.* She was definitely looking downward. Then she caught my eyes and blushed a bit.

"Is that everything?" she asked with a crack in her voice.

"Yep, I think so," I said, wondering if dying from embarrassment was possible.

"Great. Great. Cool cool cool cool. Well. Um. Let's go eat." She awkwardly pivoted toward the house. *Well, this isn't how I imagined tonight would go.*

Again she turned around and walked away, giving me a great view. The way her butt moved was mesmerizing, and I imagined her long tan legs wrapped around my waist as I laid her back on her kitchen table.

Jacob. STOP.

Why was I thinking these things about Abby? She was like family. I had known her since middle school. I shouldn't have been thinking those things about her.

One, she would probably be disgusted at the thought of us together.

Two, Kyle would kill me. Or at least break off our friendship. If I had a sister, I wouldn't want my best friend dating her either.

And I couldn't risk Kyle shunning me. He and his family were the only family I felt comfortable with.

These were just subconscious thoughts because of male biology. I could turn them off if I wanted to.

Just put them away and don't think about her like that again.

Abby had gotten cute, and she was all grown up now, but she was not the one for me.

She couldn't be. I would just have to stay away from her as much as possible.

Chapter 5

Abby

"Great, you three finished just in time," my mom said. "The hot dogs are over there. I lightly toasted the buns, and I whipped up some of my quick chili to top them with. Be sure to help yourself, grab some cheese and onions if you want, and Jacob, make yourself at home as usual."

"You don't have to tell me twice, Mrs. Kathy," he said.

I looked at Jacob and was reminded of all the times he had been in our house. His mom had passed away when we were in middle school, and the loss had turned his dad into an iceberg. Instead of being twice the parent that he needed to be for Jacob, he worked longer hours instead. Jacob only had their maid to keep him company for a short time after school before she went back to her own family. His dad would get home when Jacob was getting into bed.

So, our place had always been like a second home to Jacob. He had already been a little heavy, but after her death, he'd put on a lot of weight. I was pretty sure my mom prepared too many hot dogs today, thinking he still had the same appetite.

Maybe he does with all his new muscles, I thought.

Kyle went ahead and served himself first, and I waited for Jacob to serve himself, but he motioned for me to go ahead of him. *What a gentleman.* He tried having my mom serve herself before him as well, but she wouldn't have that. We all sat down at the table and dug in.

I scanned everyone's faces to see Jacob and Kyle devouring their food, and my mom was just looking at us and smiling. She was pretty famous for her quick chili.

"It's so good to have all of you back. Seeing you three at the dinner table brings back so many memories," my mom said.

"Don't get all gushy on us again, Mom," Kyle said.

"Well, I can't help it. You will understand one day."

"Not anytime soon, I hope," Kyle said. "No babies for me." My mom rolled her eyes.

"It's good to be back, Mrs. Kathy," Jacob said. "The chili is delicious. Thank you so much for making it."

My mom smiled. "Well, thank you. Make sure you get yourself some more. I made plenty."

I went to take a bite out of my hot dog, and some chili spilled down my chin. I glanced up to see Jacob looking at me, and he was smiling.

I blushed a little. I didn't know why. Jacob had seen me do *way* more embarrassing stuff before. But then again, he had never looked this hot.

"So," my mom started, "what were each of your favorite things to have happened at school this year?"

Kyle swallowed his bite of food. "I think I'm going to miss being in the football stadium the most. We had a great season last year, and being in the student section singing and cheering with thousands of others all in sync was amazing. I get goosebumps just thinking about it."

"Oh yeah?" I asked with a smirk. "Your favorite part wasn't Melanie? She must not be that special. Maybe she's the oatmeal raisin cookie dough instead of the chocolate chip." Jacob sounded like he was going to choke on his hot dog.

Kyle squinted at me, picked up a piece of shredded cheese, and threw it in my hair.

"Kyle!" I shrieked.

"That's what you get." He picked up another piece of cheese.

"Hey now," my mom said. "No throwing food at the table. And no throwing insults either, Abby. Sorry you had to see that, Jacob."

"Oh, don't worry, Mrs. Kathy. We know I've seen worse."

"What about you, Jacob?" my mom asked. "What was your favorite part?"

"Hmm, I don't know. I'm going to miss so much. I'm going to miss the friends I made that all went in different directions after graduation. I'm going to miss the quiet mornings walking to campus and just sitting on a bench looking out over the open green fields thick with fog. That peace and quiet was so nice. I'm going to miss the relationships I had—"

He coughed a little.

Relationships? I hadn't known Jacob was in any relationship. Although it didn't surprise me with how sexy he had gotten. *Oh my God, Abby, get a hold of yourself.* The thought of him dating another girl sent a sting down my spine. There was no good reason for me to feel that way. But I did.

"Sorry, I think a chili flake hit the back of my throat at the wrong spot," he recovered.

"Wuss," Kyle said.

Jacob rolled his eyes. "Anyway, I'm going to miss the relationships I had with my professors. They talk to you like you're a human being. If you take the time to ask them questions, or go to their office hours, they get to know you and like you and help you out. And not just in class, but in life, too."

Well, he was hot before, and now he's straight-up sexy. A warmth traveled down to my lower belly. I loved that he appreciated his teachers so much, since that was what I was going to be. It suddenly got pretty hot in the kitchen.

"What was your favorite thing they taught you?" I asked.

He looked at me with those piercing green eyes, and I could see the corners of his mouth go up a bit.

"It's hard to think of the best piece of advice, but the one that comes to mind was something you hear every now and then, but for me, it didn't really stick until one of my business class professors was talking to me one day. He basically said don't be afraid to try something out. If you try something and do poorly, or fail, it's not the end of the world. For the ones who don't try again, it was the end of a tiny part of that person's world, in a sense. The ones who fail and don't try again never get what they want. They take the easy way out so they don't get hurt. It's something I try to remember, but I'm not perfect at implementing it."

"Well, that's something I agree with wholeheartedly," my mom said. "What about you, Abby? What was your favorite part?"

"I really liked my course load. I really just focused on my classes and poured myself into my work."

"Boring," my brother said.

"Well, I think it's wonderful that you took your amazing education opportunity so seriously, sweetie," my mom said. "But there is more to life than just studying. Especially when you're in college." She winked.

Oh God, here it comes. The question I always dreaded.

"Did you meet any boys during your study breaks?" my mom asked.

"Ooh, yeah, Abby, tell us about your boys," Kyle said with a smile. He was smiling because he knew there was none to talk about.

I noticed Jacob giving Kyle a little mean mug before looking at me curiously.

"No," I said. "No boys to report. I have more important things on my mind than becoming someone's uncooked dessert."

Jacob spit up his drink as soon as the words left my mouth and started laughing and banging his fist on the table. Kyle was giving me the look that said, *Don't you say another word.*

"Hey, Mom," I started. "Do you think you can make some cookies tonight?"

"Um, sure," she said. "Though I'm a little confused as to— Kyle, so help me God, if you throw that piece of onion across the table, I will take away your car keys for a week. Your dad and I still pay the insurance, so don't think I won't do it." Kyle was half sitting, half standing with his arm cocked back, and slowly set himself back down.

Uh-oh. That was the side of Kathy we didn't like to see.

Kyle was red in the face looking at me, but Jacob was smiling at me.

I felt butterflies in my stomach again. *Why are you guys fluttering around like this? Great. I'm talking to imaginary butterflies now.*

Jacob is off limits, I reminded myself.

Besides, there was no way he'd want a girl like me. There were just too many factors for why a relationship wouldn't make sense. He was hot now and probably had girls way more experienced than I am lined up to date him. He wouldn't want to waste his time on sweet little innocent me.

He looked at me like a sister and nothing else. He had basically lived here in high school. We studied together all the time. And I was pretty sure we had both seen each other in our underwear before. There were never any feelings between us. But I bet that would be a different story if I saw him in his underwear right now...

Final reason, Kyle would kill both of us. He had always shooed guys away from me, no matter how good or bad they were. There was not a chance in hell he would be okay with me and Jacob being together.

But there was nothing to stress about. It was simply never going to happen.

Still, it sure felt good to make him laugh.

Chapter 6

Jacob

When most people were back in their beds at home after being gone for a long time, they might feel comfortable. They might feel like they could sleep again. But I wasn't able to.

As I lay on my back with my hands clasped behind my head and looking up at the glowing stars that were still on my ceiling from when I was a kid, all I could think about was how cold this house had seemed ever since my mom died. Like someone had turned the thermostat all the way to zero and left it there forever.

She had been amazing. She'd never *needed* to work because my dad made enough money with his own law firm, but she had anyway. She'd taught kindergarten at the elementary school I went to. To have her as my teacher had been a special experience most people didn't get. Teaching had been her passion because she loved helping children learn. She would volunteer to stay after school to watch over kids as they waited for their parents to pick them up. And she was able to do all that and be so great at her job while *still* giving me all the love and attention that I could ever ask for.

My dad used to be okay when she was alive. He actually used to smile from time to time. They would have date nights, and I would go spend the night at Kyle's. They would get so dressed up and go to a fancy restaurant, and sometimes they would get their own hotel room and have their own time together. I didn't care because it always meant I got to hang out with Kyle.

When my mom got breast cancer, she was the most optimistic one out of all of us. She said it would all work out. Like everything always had.

She lived her life like nothing changed. She still gave me all the love I needed, she still taught her classes, and she still stayed after school to care for other kids. She just needed someone else to help watch the kids while she took frequent trips to the bathroom.

She finally wasn't able to do all that in the last few months of her life. Toward the end, she was in hospice for three days. And even though she was dying, in pain, and likely worrying about what would happen to me and my dad, she was always smiling. She was still trying to be the support that I needed. That my dad needed.

In her final moments, I held her left hand, and my dad held her right, and we listened to "Somewhere Over the Rainbow," by Israel Kamakawiwo'ole. It was her favorite song, and she would always listen to it nine times at home. When it started playing for the ninth time, her face relaxed, her hands released their grip, and, finally, she exhaled her last breath.

I had sobbed as I shoved my face into her leg. I looked up at my dad to see tears rolling down his cheeks as he put his hand on the side of her face. It was the only time I'd seen my dad cry. And I hadn't seen him smile since.

After she was gone, he and I had a strange relationship. I knew he loved me, but he always seemed to love his work more. Most days in high school, I would come home, and he would still be at work. I would either have to fix my own dinner that the maid had cooked a few hours before and left in the fridge or, more often than not, I went over to Kyle's house and had dinner with his family.

They really were like my family, with Kyle being my brother, Kathy my second mother, and Abby my sister. And that was why I needed to get rid of these thoughts going through my mind about Abby. Seeing her yesterday did something to me. I'd never really thought about her in *that* way before, but I guessed her being twenty-two now and wearing clothes that showed off her skin instead of the sweatshirts and sweatpants that I had been used to all those years changed things. I shifted in bed, thinking of what it would be like to have her lying next to me.

But I had to stop. Anything between us would have been weird—surely she looked at me as a brother as well. Plus, probably both Kyle and his dad would have something to say or scream if I ever tried anything.

"Jacob!" my dad yelled from downstairs.

Here we go. Barely home for twenty-four hours and he was already going to get on me about something. I sat up on the edge of my bed, took a deep breath to prepare myself, and stood up to head downstairs.

Part of the reason why our house felt so cold was because it was so big. We didn't need all of that space. Never had. The only thing that helped keep it warm and alive was my mom, and she hadn't given off her light for about a decade now.

I walked down the stairs. My dad put his briefcase down and walked over to the bar to pour himself some whiskey. We had barely spoken to each other since I got back the previous night.

"What's up, Dad?" I asked. He looked over at me with his cold expression, as usual, and took a sip of his drink.

"So, what time are they picking you up?" he asked.

"They should be here in a few minutes," I said. I had hoped they would get here before he got home.

"Well, since you're about to go enjoy yourself, I hope you got some work done today. Or am I the only one who's not a lazy ass in this house?" In my mind, I rolled my eyes. I wouldn't dare do that for real when he was looking at me, though. Especially if he had a drink in his hand. It was awful that I still cared what this piece of shit of a father thought. I hoped one day I had the strength to tell him what I was really thinking.

"I weeded the garden in the backyard. That took a couple of hours."

"Oh, a couple of hours?" He took another gulp. "What did you do for all the other hours? Or is a couple hours the new standard workday? I wish I would have known before I worked a full ten hours today." He threw back the rest of his drink and poured himself another. *God*, I hoped they would come soon. "Look, I know you just got done with school, but you don't have summer vacation anymore. Now starts real life. You're an adult. And if you are going to live in my house, eat my food, and use my electricity, then I expect you to at least keep busy. I don't want to make you pay rent or pay for groceries. But I do expect you to keep busy. And if you can't find yourself a job, then I will gladly find one for you. You can always come work in my firm as a paralegal."

Over my dead body.

How to explain to my father that I probably made more money last week than he did? *I should just move out. I would* have moved out in a heartbeat, but my mom's memory kept me there for the time being. Plus, he was never here, and these interactions were rare, *and* I was a cheap-ass trying to hide my wealth from everybody. Maybe I would start looking for a place after a couple of months if he proved to be too much of a problem. I would have to get an actual job, though, unless I wanted to let people know how I've been making my money.

"Or, since I can practically feel your disdain for working in an office, your uncle could always use an extra hand in the oil field." He smirked.

I rolled my imaginary eyes in my head even harder. Uncle Gary was insane. He'd once tried getting me to catch a rattlesnake with a burlap sack when I was a kid.

The blood inside me boiled. "You've heard all the shitty stories he's told us over the years. All the injuries, and the heat exhaustion. Are you really suggesting I go do that?" Why did I even ask him? Of course he did. It was a great way to get rid of me.

"No," he said. "That's why I'm giving you an opportunity to find your own job. I just don't want you sitting around with no direction. Hell, you have a business degree. But what are you going to do with it? Go get your MBA next? Or, if you are going to become a corporate attorney like you talked about in high school, you need to study to take the LSAT. Which you really should have taken already, because now you're just going to be idle while you take the LSAT and then wait to get in somewhere. You should have made the mature decision and taken it while you were still in school."

A car horn sounded outside.

Thank God. Saved by the beep. "Is there anything else we need to discuss?" I asked my dad. It wasn't the homecoming I wanted, but it was what I expected.

He took a swig of his drink. "No. I think I've said everything I need for now. Go have fun playing games instead of focusing on becoming a man. Speaking of which, maybe one of these days you'll earn enough money to buy your own car." He turned around and walked toward his office. I turned around and headed out the door.

I walked up to the car, and the driver's window rolled down. Mr. Mike was driving. This guy meant so much to me. Any good qualities I had that weren't given to me by my mom could all be traced back to him. After she died, he took me in as his own and treated me like a son. Everywhere my father failed in raising me, this guy had filled in. I was more afraid to betray or disappoint him than anyone in the world.

"Hey, Mr. Mike!" I said. "How are you?"

"Good, good. I'm good. It's great to see you again, my dude." We fist bumped, and I smiled. Kyle groaned in the backseat at his dad saying, 'my dude.'

I opened up the back door and saw Kyle sitting in the other window seat. Abby sat in the middle with an empty seat right next to her. My heart rose in my chest a little. My eyes met hers. She was looking at me with a smile on her face. Her hair was straightened, she was wearing a teal tank top and some jean shorts that were once again tempting me with her sexy legs. They looked so smooth and silky and all I could think about was kneeling down in front of her and spreading...*Oh man*. I needed to stop thinking about that or else my pants were going to rise.

I sat next to her, closed the door, and put on my seatbelt. When I leaned over to put it in the buckle, I could smell that she was wearing perfume. It smelled so good that it was almost like I could taste her. *The things I would do to be able to taste her...to nibble on her neck.* Abby seemed a little tense and took in a big breath.

Kyle looked over at me and performed three exaggerated

sniffs. "Are you wearing cologne?" he asked. "To bowling night? You think you're going to find a girl and fall in love while we're all eating chicken wings?"

I opened my mouth to say "no," but my second mom beat me to it.

"Oh hush, Kyle. There could be plenty of cute girls at the bowling alley. It would be a great place to meet somebody. You could learn a thing or two from Jacob and try to find a nice girl."

Kyle wrinkled his brow and said, "I already have a nice girl."

She turned her head toward the back. "Oh yes, darling, that's right. I must have forgotten," she said. Mrs. Kathy be throwing shade.

This back-and-forth was great and all, but it was extra hard to concentrate on anything at the moment. Abby's bare legs were up against mine, and with each bump in the road, the sensation of her smooth legs rubbing against me was increasing my heart rate. I was powerless to stop myself from setting up a tent in my pants. I was even starting to sweat a little, and it wasn't because of the temperature outside.

Then she looked at me, with that beautiful face, those gorgeous eyes, and those delicious lips, and asked me something. *What do you want, my angel? I'll give you anything*, I thought. Hmm, now she was looking at me like I was dumb.

"What?" I asked because I had been too distracted by her beauty to hear what she said.

"I said, did you do anything fun today?"

"No, not really. I just stayed home, unpacked, and decompressed."

It was technically a lie, though. At least until this moment. Something special was happening *right now*. Against my will, I was forming a hard crush on the only person I shouldn't be crushing on. I just needed to not be touching her anymore, and hopefully that would break the spell she had over me.

It wasn't long before we were pulling into a parking spot at the bowling alley. I didn't want the car ride to end. But I needed it to end.

I also needed to somehow fix the hard rod in my pants without anyone seeing, or else I was going to have a lot of embarrassing questions to answer. I opened the door, faced outwards, slid out, and used the door to block everyone's view while I did a quick tuck. I smiled, quite sure that I had completed my mission with enough stealth to go unnoticed. But then I looked up to see Jessica, with her phone in her hands, looking straight at me with her eyebrows raised. I stood in my spot, unable to move, wide-eyed, not knowing what to say, when Abby got out of the car.

"Hey, Jess! We could have met you at the door," she said.

"Oh, that's okay," Jessica said. "I didn't want to stand by the door all by myself and look like a loner. Plus, I was able to take in the sights in the parking lot."

My whole body tensed because I was ninety percent sure she meant she'd just seen me adjust my Washington Monument. Thankfully, though, her attention wasn't on me anymore.

"Hey, Kyle," she said. "Long time no see."

The way she said it sounded like she was flirting. She was also dressed like she wanted to pick up guys rather than go bowling. She was wearing a short yellow dress that showed enough of her legs and breasts that most of the men tonight were probably going to be a bit distracted from bowling their strikes. *Someone should probably hand Jessica her ball tonight, so she doesn't have to bend over to get it.*

"Ugh, don't be gross," Abby said as she locked one of her arms through Jessica's and marched to the doors.

"What was that?" Kyle asked. I shrugged. Mainly because Kyle wasn't the kind of person who needed anymore stroking of his ego.

Mr. Mike stepped out the car and said, "Son, if you couldn't get that hint, I don't know if there's any hope for you." He patted Kyle on the shoulder and headed inside once Mrs. Kathy walked up to his side.

The bowling alley hadn't changed my whole life. It could definitely have used some sprucing up. It had its regulars, but some marketing and a renovation would have gone a long way.

The man behind the counter put my size shoe on the counter. I went to reach for my wallet, but Mr. Mike put his hand on my wrist.

"My treat," he said.

"Thanks, Mr. Mike. But you don't have to."

"I know, Jacob. I want to. You kids go get set up in lane ten, okay?" We all nodded and walked over. We were lucky for the time being and had our two-lane section totally to ourselves.

Before long, Mr. Mike and Mrs. Kathy walked back from the bar with a pitcher of beer and some cups. Abby was busy putting everyone's names into the system.

"Would everyone like a glass?" he asked.

"Sure!" we answered in unison.

He poured the ladies a glass first, and then one for me, him, and Kyle. "So, how are things, Jacob? How's your dad?"

"He's the same, unfortunately," I said. I could feel everyone feeling sorry for me, and I hated it. I was soon regretting telling the truth and creating a gloomy atmosphere for the group. I should have just put on a smile and lied for everyone else's sake.

"Well, that's too bad," he said. "I know I'm glad to see Kyle and Abby back home, and you as well. I'm sure he's glad you're back, even if he can't express it."

"I don't know about that. I think you give him too much credit. We've barely talked since I got back, and our only topic of conversation was him grilling me that I needed to get a job. Or he'll have me go work in the oil field with my Uncle Gary."

"That's too bad," Mr. Mike said. "Any idea on what you want to do?"

I took a sip of beer. "Nope. I didn't think it was such an urgent matter. I was hoping to relax a little after graduating. But he's pretty adamant about me finding something if I want to stay under his roof." Once again, I felt bad not telling everyone I wanted to just go travel and leave everything in this small town behind.

"Well, I hope you find something," Mr. Mike said. "Let me know if you need help, and if you have any interests in any particular fields, and I could ask around." I knew he meant it.

"Thanks, Mr. Mike," I said.

"Thanks for being polite, but you're old enough to just call me Mike from now on."

I laughed. "I'll try my best, but in my head, you'll always be Mr. Mike."

"Same here, Jacob. Just call me Kathy. You're a grown man and make me feel too old when you put that Mrs. in front my name," Mrs. Kathy said.

I shook my head. "Now, that's going to be really hard for me. But I'll try that too if you really want."

Mr. Mike took the pitcher and topped me off. "Well, besides looking for a job, do you have any plans for the summer?"

"Nope, that's about it," I said. As soon as the words came out of my mouth, I knew I sounded like a deadbeat. Part of me wanted to share my investing success with them, but I didn't want it to change their view of me. And I wanted to keep my wealth a secret. I wasn't really comfortable talking about money.

"Well, I don't know if Kyle has already mentioned it, but we're taking a trip down to the beach this summer. You should come if you're able."

"Oh, wow. That would be amazing." I had so many fun memories of that beach condo. Waking up to the sounds of seagulls, not a care in the world. I would walk to the shore with a chair and a book. Take midday naps in the hammock on the balcony. Sit on a floating tube in the water to soak in the sun. The place was truly an escape from the world and its problems. My mind shot ahead a few weeks, dreaming of the possibility of going. Scenes of Abby in a bikini running down to the water flashed before my eyes. I tried to shake the image from my mind, but it kept coming back. *Wrong thing to be thinking while talking to her dad, dude.* "I would love to. But we'll see if my boss at whatever job I get is going to be okay with me going on vacation right after starting."

"Oh, yes, that's true," Mr. Mike said. "But the invitation is still out there."

"Oh thanks, Dad," Kyle said. "I'm glad you're inviting my friends without asking me. What if I wanted to invite someone else?" He grinned.

"Well, Jacob is basically family, so I don't really need to ask you, do I?" he said with a smirk. It was nothing new to be treated like a son by Mr. Mike, but after the brief interaction I'd had with my dad earlier, it felt all the better.

"So," Abby said to the group, "how are we going to divide into teams? Boys against girls?" She sat down next to me, and, once again, feelings were stirring up in me that she had never made me feel before.

"Sounds great to me. I love winning," Kyle said.

"Yeah, yeah, yeah. We'll see about that," Abby said.

And so our game commenced. Abby, Jessica, and Kathy played against me, Kyle, and Mike. Jessica went up first. I could feel half the men in the bowling alley turn her way as she walked up to the lane. Even Kyle stopped texting his girlfriend to look at her. She ended up knocking down eight pins, but I barely noticed. I turned to Abby. "So, what will you be up to this summer?"

I wanted her to say, 'Hanging out with you, silly.'

"Oh, I'm probably going to lifeguard at the pool like usual. At least while I search for a job. I've been doing it forever, and it's easy work. Plus, it can be pretty cool when your dad is your boss and lets you off of work easier than other bosses might."

I was pretty sure Abby had been swimming before she learned to walk. She had always been great at it, and she had won more than a few competitions in high school.

"Did you ever end up joining the swim team in college? I'm sure you would have killed the competition."

She blushed and looked down at her feet. "No. I thought about it, but I didn't want it to affect my grades."

I scoffed. "You're one of the smartest people I know. You definitely could have done both." She smiled, and it sent all the good feels down my body. She leaned over and bumped her shoulder into mine.

"Well, thank you. But it's too late to know now."

I looked up to see that Kyle had bowled a spare. He seemed pleased with himself as he walked back to the bench. Even though there was open space elsewhere, he sat right next to Jessica.

It was Abby's turn next. She got up and started picking out her bowling ball. As she did so, she bent over, and I got to see her ass. *And wow, what an ass.* I had to pretend that I was looking at something else, though, because I didn't want any of her family to see me staring.

But as she walked down toward the lane, I couldn't help myself, and I took another peek. The way her jean shorts hugged her body, and the way her legs lifted her cheeks up and down with each step, was casting a spell on me.

Mr. Mike cleared his throat. "Jacob." I jumped in my seat. *Fuck.* Had he seen me staring at his daughter's ass? Of course he had. *Fucking fuck fuck. There goes my invitation to the beach.* "I have a crazy idea. You don't have to say yes, and it's not the most rewarding work or best paying for a college grad, but if you need just a regular old job so your dad gets off your ass, why don't you come work at the pool this summer? It's our busiest time now that everyone's out of school and wanting to relax, and I could use a pool hand to help around the club. I could teach you how to take care of the pool with the chemicals and brushing the sides. And I'll need help on the inside, too. Possibly as a bartender some days as well. No fancy drinks or anything. It's all simple."

Well, holy shit. I stared at his daughter, and instead of giving me a warning, he offered me a job to spend more time with her. I guess he didn't see me drooling at her after all...

I opened my mouth to give him an answer, but he cut me off.

"Like I said, you don't have to be polite or feel obligated, but I wanted to offer you the opportunity. Just let me know in the next few days."

"Thanks, uh, very much, Mr. Mike. I'll definitely let you know." He moved his glass of beer toward me.

"Cheers," he said. We clinked our glasses. I took a sip and looked back at Abby again as she was trying to make a spare. My eyes again drifted lower than they should have. She lifted the bowling ball to her chest, took a breath, and went to take a step, but she paused and turned around.

I didn't know why I made my next move. It would have

been completely normal for me to be looking at her, since she was taking her shot. I should have just looked into her beautiful eyes and smiled at her. But I got nervous she would catch me looking at her butt, so I looked away, and my eyes unfortunately fell on the first two things they saw—which were attached to Jessica.

Chapter 7

Abby

"Now you have fun today," my mom said with a wink as she handed me a brown bag with a sandwich, chips, and some fruit. I wasn't sure why the wink was necessary.

"Thanks, Mom. I will." I tried to sound chipper, but she knew me too well.

"Is something wrong, sweetie?"

"No, I'm good," I lied.

I got into my car, turned the key in the ignition, waved goodbye to my mom at the door, and backed out of the driveway. For some reason, she had a big smile on her face. Maybe she was just happy I was home.

Since it was just the beginning of summer, the weather wasn't scorching hot yet, so I rolled down my windows to enjoy nature's air conditioning before work.

I couldn't pin down what I had felt the other night. I didn't know what I had expected. But I felt let down. *I guess that's what happens whenever you create expectations. You're only going to set yourself up for disappointment if you expect people to act a certain way or to do certain things.*

Bowling night was a tradition in our family. We did it at least one night a month. And it was normal for Jacob to be there, since he had basically been a part of the family my whole life. That was reason number one why I shouldn't have ever had any feelings for him in the first place. It was a non-starter.

But how could I not think about the possibility? It's our brains' duty to think of any situation and do a pros and cons analysis, even if it was unattainable.

Jacob had always been such a great guy. He had always been funny and always looked after me, even when Kyle wanted to play pranks on me. But I had never thought of him that way with how close he was to my brother.

Now, though. Now he was a tall, domineering, ripped hunk of meat that I kept imagining picking me up and tossing me on the bed as if I were as light as a pillow. I was not a super confident person, but going to college and growing up had made me mature at least a little bit, I thought. Because of this growing confidence within me, I was interested in trying to get him to notice me as something more than just Kyle's sister. I thought I had felt a spark between us on our first day back from college.

So, for the first time ever on bowling night, I put on perfume. I made sure to put on a cute outfit that would accentuate my features and show some skin. I *wanted* him to stare at me.

For once, I was happy sitting in the middle seat, when usually Kyle and I would rock papers scissors for the "bitch seat." But that night I wanted to sit right next to Jacob. I had smelled his cologne and wondered if he'd put it on for me. I couldn't remember him *ever* wearing any. During the ride, our legs had brushed up against each other. And instead of consciously pulling my legs inward like I normally would have, I let them stay.

He didn't move his leg, either.

Touching him like that, and having those thoughts, was a completely new feeling, and I was getting an itch between my legs that I wanted Jacob to scratch.

I had been a bit annoyed with the amount of boob that Jessica was showing, but it wasn't that abnormal. She was just usually a bit more conservative on bowling night.

The night was going great at first. Everything was going normal. Jacob and I sat next to each other, and once again, I thought I felt the sparks between us. But then, all of my cautions were validated when I got up to bowl.

Jacob and I were having a nice little conversation before it was my turn. I had gotten up and thought I would entice him by bending over extra low to pick out my bowling ball. I got six pins on my first roll, and I was up there mentally preparing myself for how I was going to knock down the other four. I turned to see my mom, my dad, and Kyle looking at me. But Jacob's eyes were on something else.

Jessica's. Damned. Boobs.

I turned back around, took a frustrated breath, and shot a gutter ball. I walked back to our seating area, and Kyle was laughing, so I punched him in the arm. Then I sat next to my dad to avoid Jacob. I could see Jacob looking at me out of the corner of my eye, but I didn't want to look him in the eyes at that moment. He was cute as hell, but how could I trust him? Hell, why trust any man? *They're just going to cheat on you, eventually*, the voice in the back of my mind told me.

One of the reasons I was so hesitant to date a guy in college was because my senior year high school boyfriend cheated on me during prom night. I was alone on the dance floor and couldn't find Patrick anywhere. Someone told me they saw him walk outside with another girl from my class. I saw his car shaking...and commence the tears. Ever since that night, it had been hard for me to trust a man.

So, the last few days had not been amazing. I hadn't been depressed or thought the world was going to end. I had just been disappointed. I had some urges that were obviously stupid. *Of course he's not into me. Of course he's into Jessica. Like everyone else.*

It was okay. Thinking of Jacob as anything more than a friend was a mistake. At least I learned it quickly.

I didn't blame him for looking at her. She had always been pretty, and her sexual confidence went through the roof after our first year in college. So Jacob was seeing this new side of her for the first time. He was a guy, after all. I was just dumb enough to hope he would look at me instead.

As I pulled my car close to the curb and made a complete stop at the end of the driveway, I took a deep breath before beeping the horn a couple of times. He opened his door immediately and jogged over to the car. *Man, was he staring out the window or something?*

He got in the car, sat down, and said, "Thanks so much for giving me a ride."

Oh, right. Surprise for me. Right before Jacob had zeroed in on Jessica's goods, my dad apparently offered him a job at the same place I work. So, my plan of distancing myself from Jacob went the opposite way. Now we were stuck together.

"Yeah, no problem. Your house is close by and on the way, so I can always give you a ride to and from work, if you want." *Ugh. Why the fuck did I offer to do that?* Sometimes my kindness killed me.

"That would be great," he said, flashing a smile that was going to make it hard to ignore him every day.

"Why don't you have a car?" I blurted out. *Wow, Abby,*

rude much? "Sorry, I didn't mean that to be rude. It's just that I was pretty sure your dad could afford to help you buy one?"

"Yeah, he could probably buy a car dealership if he wanted to. But he said he wants me to buy my own car. That it'll build character. I thought about getting one in college, but I didn't really need one. With my bike and my college shuttle bus, I got everywhere I needed to. But now, I guess that can be a goal for me."

"Ha, it might be hard to save up for a car with this job. It doesn't exactly pay very well."

"Yeah, that's true. But it's something for me to do. And I'll be in good company," he said as he turned to look at me. There was that damned smile again. "But I could make money doing other things, too."

"Oh yeah? Like what?" I asked.

"Well, I've been designing logos the last few years, just for some supplemental income. And because it interests me."

"Logos for..."

"Businesses and organizations."

"Well, why don't you do that instead of this?" I asked. Again, that probably sounded rude, like I didn't want him to work with me. I loved Jacob, like a brother. But I was afraid I might start to love him as something else if I had to spend all day every day looking at that smile.

He laughed. "Eh, with this job, I'll be out of the house and in the sun. And it'll keep my dad off my back. Not that he's that happy with me working this job, either. I don't think anything would make him happy, though."

He looked out the passenger window. It pained me to see him like that. I always knew from secondhand stories from my mom how tough Jacob's dad was on him, especially after his mom died. But he never really talked about it himself. At least not to me. Kyle was his best friend, which was how my mom heard everything. I didn't remember Sarah too well. But my mom said she was an amazing woman that would volunteer all hours of the day if she could. She was a devoted teacher, a loving mother, and a great wife.

Cancer really sucks. It had always been a fact of life that everyone died, but it was hard to know which was the best way to go. Was it better to get diagnosed with a disease like she did, where she knew the end was coming, and she could take time to say goodbye to her friends, her family, and take care of whatever she needed to? While at the same time having to see everyone be sad when they visited her, or cry, or feel sorry for her?

Or was it better to go quickly? Something like a car accident that could end it all in an instant. But then the abruptness of it might be worse for your family, who never got the chance to say goodbye.

I didn't know which was better, and I was pretty sure it would be hard for anyone to give a great answer. But I did know that, in this moment, more than any other time I've spent with Jacob, I felt really sorry for him. I just wanted to give him a hug.

Jacob turned his face back to me. "So, what's my first day going to be like?"

"Um, I'm not exactly sure. I'm one of the lifeguards, obviously, so I mainly watch over everyone all day and sit in my shaded chair. Sometimes I teach swimming lessons. But you will be the pool boy. You'll have to scrub the sides to get any algae or debris off them and keep everything spotless. You'll need to learn how to put in chlorine and other chemicals to keep the pool clear and clean. And you'll have to skim leaves out of the pool, and other disgusting things that people might leave behind."

"Other disgusting things?" he asked with a laugh. "*What other disgusting things?*"

"Oh, I'm sure you heard horror stories from Kyle back when he had your job. It could be anything. From somebody's cigarette blowing in, to somebody's chicken wing they decided to bring in the pool after ignoring the signs saying no food allowed, and occasionally...poop. From kids and adults alike." I looked over to see a horrified expression on his face.

"Oh my God. What did I get myself into?"

But he said it with a big smile on his face.

"It's not too late to end it. I could turn around and drop you back off." *Which would probably make sure I don't fall in love with you.*

"Nah," he said. "I'm pretty happy with the situation I've got going." He turned to stare out the window again.

I wonder what situation he's talking about. Just having any job to get out of the house and avoid working for his uncle? To be a pool pooper scooper?

Chapter 8

Jacob

When Abby and I arrived at the Country Club, Mr. Mike's truck was already there. I knew he always went in pretty early to set up every day. But Abby and I didn't need to be there until eight in the morning.

I wasn't going to lie. It was nice not having a car at the moment if it meant riding with her every day. It had been her mom's idea.

It hadn't taken me very long to tell Mr. Mike that I would accept the job. I did it that night at the bowling alley. The pay was lower than I should have been aiming for at my age, but I had money covered. This was an excuse to get out of the house and see Abby more. After I accepted, Mrs. Kathy mentioned that Abby could pick me up each day. I'd smiled at the thought, but when I looked at Abby, she only smiled weakly. I had hoped she would be more excited. Had my eyes betrayed me and driven a distance between me and Abby?

I hadn't meant to look at Jessica's chest. It might have been the worst thing my eyes had ever done. But it wasn't like I could bring it up without making things weird and giving away my attraction to Abby. Not yet anyway. But maybe I was looking too much into it. Maybe she was upset over something else.

The weather was perfect for my first day. As soon as I got out of the car, I didn't stop moving. Mr. Mike showed me how to clean and treat the pool and arrange the indoor and outdoor furniture. I kept taking pictures with my phone so I could refer to them later, and he laughed. Said something about "millennials."

Then he brought me inside and showed me around.

"And this here is Pat," Mike said.

Pat, a short guy in his late thirties, held out his hand. "Pleasure to meet you!" He shook my hand vigorously.

"Likewise," I said.

"This is Jacob, our new pool boy. Pat is the manager of the club. He's been with us about four years. If you have any questions, either find me or him, and we'll get you the right info," Mike said.

"Yep, I've about done it all. Started as a pool boy myself when Mike's son, Kyle, quit and went off to college," Pat said.

"And the pool has been cleaner ever since," Mike said wryly.

I finished the tour inside, including the kitchen and behind the bar. Kyle always talked about his different responsibilities while working here in high school, but I never really grasped all the behind-the-scenes work that went on. I should have visited this place more when I was younger, but I avoided swimming pools at all costs back then.

It was a pretty big place. It was surrounded by a wrought-iron fence and palm trees. The main recreation pool had a shallow end for the kids and a deeper end for the adults. Its deepest was only eight feet. On one side of the pool, there were a bunch of white lounge chairs interspersed with umbrellas for people to pop open—or, more likely, call me over to open for them.

* * *

Before I knew it, it was the end of the day, and I was vacuuming in the main entertainment area around the couches when Pat walked up to me.

"Hey, it's Jacob, right?" he screamed over the noise.

I turned off the vacuum.

"Yeah. Hey, Pat. What's up?

"I'm done cleaning behind the bar. I can finish this up."

"Oh, okay. What do I do next?"

"Go do a walk around outside and pick up any trash. There is a dustpan and a trash grabber for you to use if you want. Or you can just get a broom. And if you want them, some disposable gloves are over there under the sink."

I decided I *did* want them after hearing Abby's little rundown in the car this morning. I walked over, grabbed the gloves, dustpan, and a broom, and made my way outside. I hadn't been outside in a few hours, and I was glad to have an excuse to go back out. Abby was still in her usual spot, sitting in her elevated chair looking over the pool. We were closing soon, but there was still a mom and her kid in the shallow end.

Abby was as hot as ever, wearing a traditional red one-piece lifeguard suit. It wasn't traditionally as "sexy" as a bikini, but somehow, she *made* it seem sexier. Plus, the bottoms of those one-pieces still left little to the imagination.

That morning when we'd opened the gates and let the first people in, she went ahead and got ready. I tried not to look. But it was an automatic reflex. She took off the shirt she had on. My heart started thumping against my chest. Then she took off her shorts, revealing those sexy swimmer legs that I never knew I liked so much. She started climbing up to her chair, and I got to see her ass move in a way that was so pleasing to the eye.

Man, I've got to get a hold of myself. I was obsessing over her. It was already bad that I was staring at this girl I had known for so long. But what was worse was I knew her dad would eventually catch me drooling at his daughter, if I was already doing it this much on the first day.

I circled the pool, picking up a paper cup here, a wrapper there, some pickles that I guessed someone didn't want on their burger.

I sneaked a peek at Abby. The mom and her kid were getting out of the pool, so Abby took out her book again. I started daydreaming about what it would be like one day if she and I were the only ones left after work. Maybe I would take off my shoes and socks, jump in the pool, and wave her over. She would giggle and say, 'But there's no lifeguard on duty!' I'd finally get her in, take her hand, pull her toward me, put my hands on her waist and pull her closer still. I would look into her beautiful eyes and take her in as long as I could help it before my lust forced me to kiss her soft lips. I would trail my hands down—

"Hey, loser!" I whipped around, and Kyle was standing behind me. *Holy fuck. That would be even worse than Abby's dad seeing me staring at her.* Kyle would probably kill me. I had to learn how to control myself, but I couldn't help it. I was smitten with her.

"Hey, dude. What are you doing here?" I asked. My face felt red.

"Oh, you know, just seeing how my best bud was liking my old job," he said with a smug grin.

"Well, no poop in the pool yet. So I've got things going for me."

"Oof. Yeah, those were always rough days."

"Those? It happened more than once?"

"Oh yeah. Some people in this world are fucking disgusting, dude. Others just have an accident. I'm just glad I don't have to deal with it anymore." He looked around the pool and then up at his sister and back at me. "The question is, why are *you* dealing with it?"

Fuck. Had he caught on to me that quickly? On my first day? "I needed a job, man."

"Yeah, but this? You have a business degree. Even if your plans are to do law school or go get your MBA, you could do so many other jobs in the meantime that would pay way more. And you wouldn't have to be working in the sun all day or be picking up people's trash. It doesn't make sense. I thought you were smarter than this."

"Yeah, yeah, I know. What can I say? I guess I was just lazy and accepted the first opportunity thrown my way. It should be pretty low stress, which you know I like." I smiled, trying to play it cool. "But listen, man, I don't want to be caught relaxing on literally the first day of my job. So..." I picked up a piece of trash.

Kyle laughed. "Sure thing. I'll see you later, man." Kyle waved at Abby and yelled, "Hey, loser!" She didn't even look up from her book, just slowly raised her middle finger at him and smiled.

He left and walked away. I thought of what he asked me.

Of course, I couldn't tell him the *real* reason I picked this job over getting something in the city that could pay much more. The reason was right behind me.

I tried to sneak a peek at her one more time, but as I looked up, our eyes locked for a split second before she returned to her book.

Chapter 9

Abby

"You're doing great, Matthew. Keep kicking."

"I can't," Matthew said.

"Yes you can. I know you can. Just a little bit longer, just like the other day. You are the strongest swimmer I've ever taught, so I know you can do it!" I said with a smile. When someone received the right encouragement, it was amazing what they could do.

Matthew smiled and mustered up the strength to kick harder for a little longer. I was supporting the front of his body by holding his arms up and walking backwards in the shallow end of the pool.

Giving swimming lessons was my favorite part of the job, because the rest of it was kind of boring. Most of my day was spent just sitting in the chair and looking out at everyone. If there was at least one person in the pool, I really wasn't supposed to be reading, or on my phone, or distracted by anything. Which was a *little* harder those days with Jacob in my line of vision flexing his muscles while scrubbing the pool or lifting furniture. Too bad he wasn't the lifeguard, so I could see *him* with his shirt off every day.

Focus, Abby.

I especially needed to be cheered up today. This girl I went to high school with, Heather, came by the pool earlier and chatted with me. She was also in the market for a teaching position. I told her my plans of applying to Franklin Middle, and she told me not to even bother. She had apparently talked to the principal at the International School, one of the ones on my list, and he laughed at her, saying she was just out of college and had no experience. He told her she would need to put in the time before landing a school like his. So ever since then, I had felt sad and defeated. I was rethinking everything.

Giving swim lessons brightened my mood a bit, though. I guessed it was the teacher in me. In fact, teaching swimming lessons here when I was in high school was how I realized I wanted to be a teacher in the first place. When I was thinking about what I wanted to do with my life, and where I wanted to study to achieve it, I had to think of what interested me. The main thing that kept popping up in my mind was instructing others how to swim. I didn't want to do swim lessons forever, though. So I thought teaching would be a great career—making the younger generation better and all that. And I loved working with kids so much, especially the little ones. So that's why I was aiming to teach anywhere from pre-K to sixth grade. It was going to be hard not to snatch a lovable one up and take them home with me, though. I *loved* kids.

Like this little guy right here. Matthew was cute as a button, and he was a hard worker who just needed to be pushed every now and then. His mom and dad were divorced, and when his dad was there, he never put his drink down long enough to watch Matthew swim.

I definitely wanted kids of my own one day. At least two,

but maybe even three. I didn't care about the genders, but I thought it would be great to have at least one of each. And whenever I finally did find the right man, he was going to be the kind that would stay outside and watch his son practice whatever sport he's playing.

"Keep going, Matthew!" Jacob yelled.

Matthew smiled and kicked even harder. I felt a tug on my heart. Would Jacob be a great dad one day, since he had a father that had never really been involved? Or would it be harder for him to be a good dad because he didn't grow up with it?

Why was I even thinking of that? I waited patiently for my brain to answer that question...*nothing*.

I don't know. I just couldn't get him out of my head when I worked with him every day. Even the other day I had trouble when he was doing some not-so-sexy work. Just picking up trash. He would turn away from me and bend over to pick something up, and all I could see was his butt, which looked *fantastic* in shorts. I wished he hadn't accepted this job because my life would probably have been easier.

Then, in the middle of me appreciating his cute butt, my brother walked into view. I was kind of glad he did, though, because it was yet another reminder that I needed to stop having those stupid thoughts.

Jess kept telling me I should reply to Tony. It had taken him a few days to reply after she texted him from my phone, but to my surprise, he said he would love to meet up and get some coffee or lunch. High-school me would have died on the spot reading that message, and there was still something pretty alluring to it. But, for some reason, I didn't feel the excitement that I thought I would.

"Okay, Matthew, you're in the final stretch. Just a few more seconds. Five! Four! Three! Two! One!"

Matthew relaxed his legs and stood up. We were in the super shallow end of the pool, where it was only two feet deep.

"Great job, dude!" I told him and put out my hand for a high five.

He slapped my hand, and then he came in for a hug.

Oh, my heart. My ovaries were *screaming*, and who did I look up to see other than that tall, chiseled hunk of a man standing over me with his hands on his hips and the biggest grin I had ever seen?

What if the feelings that kept coming up weren't *that* strange? What if this was meant to be? My heart skipped a beat at the thought of it.

"Jacob, his lesson is over. Can you go inside and tell his dad?" I asked.

He still had the goofiest grin on his face, which ended up making me smile even more. "Yeah, sure thing."

After a minute, Jacob came back out, shrugged, and said, "I told his dad he was done, but he said to just let him play on his own a little longer."

I shook my head. "Some people," I said. Shit like that got my blood boiling. A good dad would have come out as soon as he heard his kid was ready. No, a good dad would have been out there with us the whole time.

I looked to my left and noticed my dad walking toward us. I hoped I could find somebody just like him one day. He had to be one of the greatest fathers in the world.

"Hey, you two. I'm going to head out a little early. I trust y'all can close the place without me?"

"Yeah, Dad, no problem," I said. There wasn't anything to do around closing time that we would need him to stick around for.

"Good deal. I'll see you later tonight, darling. See you tomorrow, Jacob," he said with a pat on Jacob's shoulder before walking away. As soon as he was out of earshot, Jacob turned to me.

"Well, fuck me," he mouthed so Matthew wouldn't hear.

Gladly, my brain screamed. Ugh. I must have been crushing hard.

Why was he so nervous? "What's wrong?" I asked.

"We have to close up by ourselves! Everyone else is gone!"

"So? You've been working a few days now. I think you can tell it's not that hard."

"Yeah, I guess you're right."

"I know I am," I said with a wink. Oh, well, fuck *me*. He was going to think I had a crazy eye twitch or something. Winking had never been my forte.

His eyes got as big as an owl's, and then he looked away.

"Uh, I'll, uh, I'll go start cleaning up inside," Jacob said, already walking away. "Maybe Matthew's dad will come out if I run the vacuum close to where he's watching TV!"

I giggled, thinking that it was nice to know he and I were on the same page about Matthew's dad. But why did his eyes get so big? Why did he get so awkward?

I looked down at Matthew, and he was playing with his toy boats, being suspended by his arm floaties. He was trying to have fun, but he was obviously lonely. I wished his dad would come outside and spend time with him.

"Hey, buddy, I need to get back in my chair. You stay in the shallow end, okay?"

"Okay, Miss Abby," he said in the sweetest voice. I got out of the pool and into my chair.

I looked back toward the clubhouse and saw Jacob, and all I could think about was how sexy his abs might be, and how I wanted to rip off all his clothes and make babies with him.

What the hell? Babies? *He* had me thinking of *babies before we've even kissed? Great. Now I'm thinking of kissing him.*

But imagine how fun it will be to have kids with Jacob, I thought.

I tried to fight those thoughts, but my armor felt like it was getting rustier and weaker every day I was with him. It was becoming uncontrollable. My mind unwillingly drifted off into a daydream.

We're on a swing hanging under an oak tree next to a lake with nothing but the stars and the moon lighting our surroundings. His arm is around me, his thumb sliding back and forth along my shoulder. My head is leaned into his neck. He kisses me on the top of my head. I look up and bring my lips to his and we breathe into each other and our souls combine into one.

He puts his hand near my belly button, and his fingers inch closer toward my center. I moan into him, my body squirming, wanting, needing him to touch me. His fingers find their way to my panties and go under them. I dig my nails into him, both loving and hating his teasing at the same time. I want his fingers to be on me, in me.

The sound of the big glass doors closing woke me up from my fantasy. I felt angry at whomever just stopped me from getting a made-up orgasm, but I looked up to see that it was Jacob. Surely I wasn't daydreaming for that long. He shouldn't have been done cleaning inside yet.

He looked up at me and waved, and my whole body turned to Jell-O. He had a smile on his face. Who was that for? He walked up to a table by the pool and took off his shoes and socks. I gave him a puzzled look, and his grin just got bigger. He took off his shirt, revealing his hard-cut abs, his toned chest, and his large biceps. He looked like a Spartan coming home after battle to take his prize. I squirmed in my seat. *Does he think what he's doing to me is funny?*

I shut my mouth quickly when I realized it was hanging open. Was he playing a joke on me or something? Acting like he was going to relax when there was work to do? I didn't care what his abs looked like. Okay, yes, I *did* care, but I didn't want to have to stay later because of him goofing off.

He turned his back to me, showing me all the muscles in his upper shoulders, and all of my temporary anger disappeared for a moment as I imagined my hand gliding over each one of them. He turned toward me again and took his sunglasses off, squinting like a newborn puppy. He started walking toward me, and I swallowed hard. Was I still daydreaming, or was this real life?

Instead of walking to me, however, he went straight for the diving board. He stepped up and went to the end, putting his toes on the edge.

Is this asshole for real? He was going to go swimming on the job just because my dad left? I exhaled a defeated breath. Poor work ethic was apparently a huge turnoff for me.

And there he went. He dove majestically into the water, making himself wet and me completely dry. I was not looking forward to having a conversation later with him that slacking off at work affects everyone else.

He swam toward the shallow end of the pool. He had pretty good form for never being on a swim team like I was. It was definitely a turn on. He reached the shallow end and stood up, wiping the water away from his eyes and brushing his hair back. It was hard to be angry at him when he looked like Poseidon just coming back from the gym. Then he did something that made my heart melt into my stomach.

He walked over to Matthew and started talking to him, but I couldn't make out what they were saying. Matthew smiled and handed Jacob one of his toy boats. Jacob took the boat and floated it on the water, acting like there was nothing more interesting in the world. All of my anger disappeared, and feelings deeper than lust emerged for him. Feelings I never thought I would have, or could have, for him.

Matthew took his boat and made shooting noises toward Jacob, who dramatically jumped and flew back as his boat was sunk. Matthew giggled and paddled after him, shooting more missiles. Jacob picked up another one of Matthew's submarines so that he had one in each hand, turned around, and started chasing him. Matthew screamed in delight and splashed away through the shallow water.

He's good with kids. It made my insides all mushy. I guessed having a crappy dad didn't matter. Maybe it would make him a better father to his own children, since he knew how *not* to be.

I put my book away and spent the rest of my workday watching them play with boats before a round of Marco Polo. I was glad Jacob wasn't doing his job.

Chapter 10

Jacob

I was having the time of my life. "Marco!" It was a shame his dad didn't want to switch places. His loss, my gain.

"Polo!"

The sound came from my right. I jumped in that direction, blindly waving my arms about, but I got nothing. I stood up. "Marco!"

"Pol—"

"Matthew! Let's go!" his dad barked. I opened my eyes and saw him standing at the edge of the pool, his arms folded, face hardened.

"Dad! Come play!" Matthew said.

"Get your ass out of the pool this instant. You should have gotten out at five. That's when I told you I wanted to leave."

That language directed at a kid so young filled me with rage. "Not like there's a clock out here for him," I said before I knew what was coming out of my mouth. *Cool it, Jacob. You're at work.* But I couldn't help myself. His dad narrowed his eyes on me.

"Excuse me?" he asked.

"If you wanted to leave at five, you should have come out to tell him. He's a kid. How was he supposed to know?"

"I don't think I fucking asked you, dipshit," he replied.

"Watch your language around your kid, man." He looked like he would have fought me if he didn't care too much about getting his clothes wet.

"He's *my* fucking kid, and I'll talk how I want to talk around him. Who the fuck do you think you are to tell me how to deal with my kid?"

"I'm just a guy who also has an awful father." I heard Abby gasp in her chair.

The dad's face was redder than an apple. "Come say that to my face, asshole. And Matthew, get out of the fucking pool, right now!"

Against my better judgment, I walked to the pool steps in a hurry to see if this guy really wanted to make first contact. He pulled up his sleeves and clenched his fists. It wasn't until I stood up on level ground with him that he realized how much bigger I was. He was tough when he was looking down on me in the pool, but I saw his determination waver when he had to look up into my face. His fists turned white. I clenched mine and was ready to answer his punch with nine of mine.

"Jacob, no!" Abby screamed.

The dad looked to her and smirked. Him setting eyes on her sent a fire through me that made me want to leave him with a feeding tube. He turned back to me.

"Do you work here?" he asked.

Shit.

"I do," I said.

His grin grew wider. "Well, it was nice to meet you, Jacob. I hope you have better prospects, because I doubt the owner will like it when he hears you threatened me while on the job, in front of my son, no less. Come on, Matthew."

"But Dad, my toys," he pleaded.

"Leave them." The dad turned and walked toward the parking lot. "I'm getting in my car and leaving, so you better be in it!" I turned to Matthew and saw tears welling up in his eyes as he was trying to dry off. I bent down to get to his level.

"Don't worry, dude. I'll gather up your toys and save them for the next time you come, okay?"

His eyes were closed as he nodded while wiping away the tears streaming down his face. I related more to this kid than he would ever know.

"I had a lot of fun today, Matthew. I can't wait until our next rematch, but you should run along. Don't want to make him any angrier."

He gave me a miserable little smile and nodded again before jogging away. I stood, looking in their direction, reminded of my own upbringing. At least he still had his mom, though.

"You shouldn't have done that," Abby said, walking up behind me. I didn't want to be angry at her too, but I felt like telling her off for not backing me up. "But I'm glad you did it," she finished.

The truck pulled out of its parking spot, and I turned around to face Abby. She was closer than I thought she was, and she just looked so beautiful. I thought about pulling her in and kissing her right here. But that was probably the adrenaline talking. I was also only wearing a loose bathing suit that wasn't very good at hiding anything, so I needed to get my mind off of her for now.

"Thanks. Hopefully I don't get fired," I said.

"Yeah. We'll see what my dad says. At least you have a good witness to support you," she said with a wink, which looked more like a contact lens was coming out of her eye. But that just made her more adorable. "What?" she asked.

Oh shit. I didn't realize I was just staring at her with a big stupid grin on my face. "Nothing," I said.

"Well, as much fun as that was, we should start cleaning up."

I nodded. She walked to her chair and put her clothes back on. *My least favorite part of the day.*

I walked to my towel and dried off. As I bent down to dry my legs, I felt like eyes were on me. I stood up and looked at her, but she was looking somewhere else. I put my clothes back on and walked inside to do my closing duties.

First, I vacuumed inside. Depending on how busy Pat was behind the bar for the day, he would usually offer to finish vacuuming while I grabbed the mop. After that, I needed to prep some food items for the next day and then take the trash out. Outside came next.

I walked out by the pool and thought of what needed to be done. Straightening the chairs, picking up any trash, and taking care of the pool. These were part of Abby's closing duties as well, but I liked to help her out.

Before I tied up the last trash bag, I usually went to each skimmer around the pool. They were the suction filters that collected anything from floating leaves, to trash, to spiders or frogs. They were hard to open, too. It wasn't about strength. It was about finding the right way to jiggle them. I had been getting better, but sometimes I still had trouble, especially with the one I was walking up to.

I bent down to take the top off, and what do you know? It was jammed. I wiggled it. I tried to turn it as I pulled, but it wouldn't budge. I was ready to go rent a jackhammer from Home Depot.

"Does the big strong man need some help, as usual?" Abby asked. I loved hearing her call me strong. I'd love to pick her up and lean her against a wall to show her how strong I *really* was.

"I got it!" I said, though I didn't even believe myself.

She walked over, and the closer she got, the more entranced I felt. I was fairly certain she was a witch to have that much power over me. She stood over me, waiting for me to make some progress. "It's extra difficult today," I said. "Must be the humidity."

"Uh-huh," she said. "Here. Let me."

Defeated, I stood up and let her try. She got down on one knee, giving me a perfect view of her cleavage. *Maybe I need her help for every skimmer.*

She put her fingers in the slot, did her magic jiggle, and pulled.

Nothing.

"See, I told you," I said.

"Hold on." She pulled harder and jiggled some more.

Nothing. Frustrated, she got into a squatting position so she could use her leg muscles to pull up on it. She pulled hard, did her jiggle, and it popped off!

Pulling it as hard as she did, her whole body came up with the force. She lost her footing, screamed, and started to fall into the pool.

My superhero senses were on high alert, though, so I leaned forward and grabbed her with both hands. I pulled her into me, saving her from the pool. She dropped the skimmer's top as I held her close to me. This was the closest we had ever been. Her chest was against mine, and our centers connected.

Time stood still. She looked up at me with those beautiful puppy eyes. *This is it. This is the perfect moment to kiss her.* I felt like she wanted it. God knew I wanted it. I couldn't let this chance pass me by. She felt it too and closed her eyes as I leaned in.

"You two okay? I heard a scream," Pat yelled.

Suddenly, time was no longer still. It was actually moving pretty fast.

Abby pushed me away as her face turned redder than a Valentine's Day card.

"I'm fine! I just slipped. Thanks!" She quickly turned around and didn't meet my eyes. I stood in place like an idiot, trying to process what had just happened. Pat closed the doors and went back inside.

She was definitely all for it, right? Or did I read that wrong? She was waiting for me to kiss her. I was certain of it, but I couldn't help but feel embarrassed at being pushed away like that. I guessed it was only natural.

I got back to work on the other skimmers, and in another half hour, I was in Abby's car on the ride home. It was a silent ride, which rarely happened. She didn't even bother to put some music on.

She stopped the car in front of my house, and I tried to catch her eyes, but she was looking straight ahead. I was hoping maybe to kiss her here, now.

"Well, thanks for the ride, as always," I said, trying to get her to look my way.

"Yep, no problem. I'll see you tomorrow," she said, still staring straight ahead.

"But we're both off tomorrow..." I said.

"Oh, duh, of course. You know what I mean. See you next time." She stubbornly avoided eye contact.

I got out and closed the door. She immediately took off down the road.

Huh. I had thought we'd both felt a connection back at the pool. But maybe not. I would have bet my entire bank account that it was going to keep me up all night, though.

Chapter 11

Jacob

Well, it didn't keep me up all night, because I was tired as shit, but almost kissing Abby was the only thing I could think about last night. I kept remembering how right it felt—how right it would be. How perfect she was, how beautiful she was, how funny she was, how much I loved being around her. It would be stupid for us *not* to get together.

But then I started thinking about what that would mean. Would her parents approve? I thought so. They had always loved me like one of their own. But maybe the thought of me dating their daughter never crossed their minds as a possibility.

Would Kyle approve? *Fuck no, he wouldn't.* Which was the whole dilemma. Kyle had been my best friend for more than a decade. Throughout that time, I had made friends and lost them. It was just a fact of life that you lost touch with the majority of people as you grew up. Life took everyone in different ways. But then there were the few, or in my case the one, who stuck around forever.

Someone smart once said, if you had been good friends

with a person for seven years, that you would be friends forever. Kyle was the only best friend I had, and I felt like this could be something that would destroy us. There was no way he would be okay with me dating his sister.

I didn't want to lose anyone else. I was close to my mom, and she was gone. I was close to my dad before she died, but he became and stayed a miserable person ever since her passing. *If I fuck this up and lose Kyle, I might lose his whole family.*

I couldn't be infatuated with a girl that would cause me to lose the only loving family I had left. My relationship with Kyle was tried and true. Nothing could break us apart, except for me betraying him somehow.

Maybe I was just meant to be a bachelor all my life. Though I might as well become a priest, because the only girl I wanted to do anything with was Abby. *The way I held her needs to happen a million more times.*

I didn't know what to do. I wanted her, but for now I was just going to have to not act out on it. Maybe over time I could sneak in questions to Kyle to see if he would be cool with one of his friends ever dating her.

His ears must have been burning, because a few minutes later, I got a text from him.

Kyle: Hey man, come over to my house. We need to talk.

Oh fuck. Did Abby tell him I tried to kiss her? Did I read everything wrong? Were my nightmares all coming true?

I texted him back.

Me: Yeah, I'll be there in a bit.

. . .

I grabbed my house key and my wallet and walked over to their house.

On the way there, I was sweating, and not because of the heat. My armpits were much sweatier than they should have been, and I kept having to dry my hands off on my pants. Not only was I nervous about Kyle finding out my feelings for his sister somehow; but if Abby told him, then that meant she *didn't* think about me in the way I thought she had. That would be the most upsetting thing about all of this. If that was the case, I would probably just quit the job at the club and skip town tomorrow.

Even though I didn't really need any job. I had enough money in the bank to retire tomorrow. But I liked the secrecy. The anonymity. It was nice to get genuine reactions from people. *Rich people never really know who their true friends are, and they don't know if the person they fall in love with was truly into them, or their money.*

I felt that growing up. Some people hung out with me because they knew my dad was rich. If Abby, or anyone else, developed feelings for me, I wanted to know they were really into *me* and not my bank account.

As his house came into view, I hoped he remembered how strong our friendship was. Now it was up to me to decide whether I was willing to risk that friendship for his sister or not.

I took a deep breath and rang the doorbell, ready to accept my fate. But then I learned I wasn't ready, because when the door opened, all I saw was an angel. Abby was smiling when she opened the door, but her face turned blank when she saw it was me. It made me feel sick thinking she didn't want me, or worse, that she wanted to be distant from me. If I never dated her, I at least still wanted to be friends with her.

"Hi," I said.

"Hey. What, uh, what are you doing here?" she asked.

"He's here for me, idiot. What do you think? Come on in, dude," Kyle called out behind her.

It wasn't every day you saw an angel roll her eyes so hard. "He's been in a particularly bad mood today." She opened the door and moved back, gesturing her arms toward the inside. "Come on in, good sir."

"Thank you, m'lady." Her eyes widened. "Not that you're *my*, uh, lady. It's, uh, just a uh—"

"Come on dude!" Kyle yelled from the hallway. I walked in, embarrassed yet again. Jessica was on the couch with the television paused on something. It looked like she and Abby were watching a movie. "Hello, Jacob," she waved with a mischievous smile.

I waved to her and followed Kyle to his room. He stood inside with an angry—or was it sad—look on his face. Doorknob in hand, he slammed it shut as soon as I was inside.

He stared at me, taking in deep breaths. *I'm a dead man*, I thought. *At least there are witnesses.* Then his eyes scrunched up, and he lunged toward me in an embrace. He hugged me tightly and then started sobbing. I hugged him back.

"Whoa. What's up, man?" I asked. He cried for a few more seconds, unable to speak. A dozen possibilities were going through my mind. One crazy thought was that he was happy about me and Abby.

"Melanie called me a little bit ago and broke up with me." Disappointment, relief, and elation coursed through me all at once.

Disappointed it wasn't because he was happy for me and Abby.

Relief that he wasn't going to punch me because of me and Abby.

Elation, because I didn't care much for Melanie. But friends needed to support each other.

"Aw, I'm so sorry, man. What happened?" He wiped away tears from his eyes.

"She called me a few hours ago to talk. She was acting weird, so I asked her what was wrong, and she started going off on a tangent about how she thinks we're drifting apart or some shit. Which I told her wasn't true. Then she said she wasn't crazy about the long distance relationship, even though it's temporary and we're only an hour apart...So I told her to tell me the truth, and she said she was seeing someone else and thinks we should break things off. She wouldn't tell me with who. So I just hung up, locked my door, and started crying. I needed someone to talk to, so I texted you. I'm sorry if you were busy."

I put my hand on his shoulder. "Not a problem at all, man."

"I can't believe she did this."

"I can." *Oh, you idiot, Jacob.* Why did I have to blurt shit out like that?

He looked at me with a puzzled face. "What?"

Screw it. There was no hiding it now. And she just did the ultimate betrayal, so she can eat it. "I mean, Kyle, I love you, and I say this out of love, but Melanie was and has always been a bitch. A hot bitch, yes, but a big old bitch. I never understood why you were with her. I mean, again I could understand *why* you were with her, but for anything more than sex? No idea. She's self-centered and mean. She talked down to everybody, including you, but it was like you were blind to it. I mean, dude, she hated ducks. Who the fuck hates ducks? Ducks are fucking adorable." He smiled through his sobs and wiped away more tears. "I know you're hurting right now, but I'm relieved for you, because you dodged a bullet by not wasting any more time on her."

His face was a mix of emotions. I couldn't tell if he wanted to thank me or punch me in the face.

"Why didn't you ever tell me that?" he asked.

"Because that's a really hard thing to do. You have your best friend who is dating a horrible person, but he's happy. You want to tell him he's making a mistake, that he can find someone better, but you know that if you tell him, he's most likely just going to get angry at you for trying to get in the way of his "happiness" he's delude himself into. It's a dilemma all friends face. Like, if your friend was getting married to a horrible girl, do you tell him to call off the whole fucking wedding because of your opinion? That would be nice, but no, you don't, because he has already made the decision, and if you tell him that, you risk your whole friendship. So, you let your friend marry an awful person, and you just try your best to make them happy when you can, because you damn well know they're miserable in their marriage." *Wow*. I didn't know I had all of that in me.

"Damn." Silence. I waited it out, thinking had I talked enough. "Well, could you maybe next time tell me if I'm making a mistake or not? Preferably before I ask her to marry me." He smirked.

I smiled and held out my hand. "Deal," I said. We shook on it.

He looked down at the ground. "Fuck. I need to get out of this house, man."

"What do you want to do? Go to a bar?"

"No. I don't want to drink. I'll probably just get extra sad. Or angry."

A devious light bulb went off in my brain. "What about the park?"

The look of 'Really?' came to his face. "The park?"

"Yeah, I hear they have ducks that like to be fed." I smiled.

He smiled back and laughed. "That's actually not a bad idea. Let's do it."

He turned to open the door, but I put my hand on his shoulder to stop him. "You should probably wait a few minutes before you go out. You don't want Abby or Jessica to see you've been crying." He turned around and hugged me again.

"Thanks man. You're the best," he said. I smiled.

No, I couldn't let anything come in the way of this friendship. *I'm sorry, Abby.*

Chapter 12

Jacob

We played a few rounds of Super Smash Bros. before we walked out of his room. We headed to the kitchen to see if there was any old bread we could use for the park. Abby and Jessica got suspicious of our rummaging. Jessica flipped around on the couch to look at us. She was leaning over toward Kyle. It almost looked like she was trying to show him all her cleavage.

"So, what are you two dorks up to?" Jessica asked.

Not sure we wanted the girls to know we were going on a duck feeding bro-date, I tried to come up with something. "We're just looking for—"

Kyle interrupted. "We're going to go feed the ducks in the park. Do you guys want to join?"

I looked over at Abby, who seemed a little opposed to the idea, but Jessica was like a dog wagging its tail.

"Oh yeah! That sounds like fun! I haven't done that in ages. What do you think, Abby?"

"Umm," Abby shot a look in my direction. "Sure." My heart

felt ten times lighter, and I was thinking this duck date just got much better.

Kyle took out a loaf of bread that looked a little stale. "Okay, let's go then."

"Hold up," Abby said. "I'll go, but not if we're feeding them white sugary bread. It's terrible when everyone feeds them that. It's bad on their bodies and for the water in the park when people are literally feeding them the same thing every day."

I thought it was beautiful she cared about the ducks. Kyle, on the other hand...

"Oh jeez Louise, look at the party pooper over here. Do we need to go to an organic grocery store or something?"

Abby rolled her eyes. "No. We can go anywhere. We can either get corn, or lettuce, or defrosted frozen peas, or oats... They're not that picky."

"Since when did you become an expert on ducks?" Kyle asked her.

"Since my bestie Tonya taught me when we went to the park in college," Abby said. "It's never too late to learn something new, big bro."

Kyle looked at me, like it was my decision to choose his side or hers. But it wasn't even a contest.

"Let's go to the grocery store. Abby can pick out the duck food, and we can pick out some human food and turn this into a little picnic." The heartwarming smile on Abby's face was too strong and made my heart melt.

"Oh yay! Picnic time! I love it," Jessica said, bouncing up and down.

After getting a big blanket, we all got in Kyle's car and headed to the store. Abby and Jessica went off to find duck food and anything else they wanted, and Kyle and I got the human food and drinks. We all met up near the cash register. The girls bought a big tin of oats for the ducks and wine for us. We bought some bread, hard cheese, salami, and green grapes.

On our way to the park, I sat in the passenger seat, and Abby sat right behind me. It was a beautiful day out, and she had her window rolled down. The wind blew her hair back, and she looked like a model in a photo shoot. I kept glancing to my side mirror, unable to control myself. She was just so gorgeous. I wanted to stare at her face every day. One time when I looked, she smiled and waved her fingers at me while keeping her eyes averted. She caught me in the act...but she didn't seem weirded out.

We arrived at the park, and there were a good bit of people out enjoying the weather like we were. Multiple families were feeding the ducks white bread. I looked around at all the bread sitting on the ground and floating in the water, and Abby's duck lesson earlier was making sense. I was glad we got them something different. Soon after Abby started throwing her oats, all the ducks left the other families and swarmed us.

Oh fuck, they are literally swarming us. Kyle and Jessica weren't too crazy about that, so they ran away. Some ducks were assholes—mainly the Muscovy ducks, as Abby had taught me—so the thought of joining them definitely crossed my mind; but that would have meant I had to leave Abby. So I stayed.

As the ducks surrounded us and inched in closer and closer, Abby and I were forced to move nearer together until our whole sides were touching each other. She stayed there, not moving away. She was holding the tin of oats, and we were taking turns grabbing handfuls. I tried to throw the oats far away from us to get the ducks to spread out, but they were so light that they barely fell three feet from us.

At one point, without looking, I reached my hand into the oat tin, but instead of grabbing oats, I grabbed Abby's hand. We both stopped looking at the ducks, and our eyes met instead.

Neither of us pulled a hand away. I took that as a sign, and I squeezed her hand a little harder while caressing it with my thumb. Our eyes were still locked on each other, and she took a deep breath. *God* I wanted to kiss her so badly, but I knew Kyle was somewhere behind us, waiting for us to finish feeding.

I let go of her hand, and she took another deep breath. She pulled out a handful of oats. "I think there's one last grab in there, if you want to throw it," she said. I dug my hand in and threw the oats out. Then I took the tin and turned it upside down to get any last little bits out.

Still surrounded by many different types of mighty ducks, we turned to each other and smiled when our eyes meet. We didn't say a word, but we were communicating. Unless I was a complete idiot, I was pretty sure she was having the same feelings as I was.

We tried to walk toward Kyle and Jessica, but the ducks had created an impenetrable blockade around us, like the Berlin Wall. A Quacker Wall. Abby tried to take a step and walk through them, but they nipped at her bare ankles and didn't get out of the way. She screamed as one bit her. I was two seconds away from punting that duck across the park with my foot, but I kept my cool.

The ducks were getting vicious. They were quacking obscenities at us, angry that we didn't have any more delicious snacks. *I thought Quakers were chill because of the oats they eat...*I turned to Abby. She actually looked a little scared.

"Get on my back," I told her. Her eyes went wide.

"What?"

"Jump on my back, and I'll carry us out of this."

She nodded. I quickly lowered myself. She hugged her arms around my neck and jumped on. I supported her by grabbing the underside of her bare thighs behind her knees. She was wearing short khaki shorts, and I was in heaven. I stood up, and she hugged me tighter. *We should have come to the park to get attacked by ducks much sooner.*

"Ok, on the count of three, let's scream and scare them out of the way," I said.

She giggled. "Okay!"

"One...two...three!" We screamed, and the ducks opened their wings, startled. I took that as our chance and ran away from them. She and I were laughing with every step. I turned around to see if we had cleared them, but instead, they were following us. The fat ones were walking, but the aggressive ones were running and a few of them were flapping their wings, ready to dive bomb us. *Maybe Melanie wasn't completely wrong...*

"Holy shit!" I said as I picked up the pace.

Abby turned back and screamed. "Go! Go!"

We ran past Kyle and Jessica and went straight into the trees. Once we hit the tree line, the ducks stopped pursuing us and went back to eating white bread from the other families. We were both laughing hysterically in the aftermath. I needed to put her down, but I didn't want to, and she hadn't made any effort to get down.

I turned to see Kyle and Jessica coming toward us. *All good things must come to an end*, I thought. "Ready to get down?" I asked. She didn't answer immediately.

"Yeah," she eventually said. As I let her down, my hands slid along her smooth legs and ended up cupping both of her ass cheeks. Both of us paused. Neither of us moved away quickly. But we soon had to, since Kyle was walking up.

He and Jessica finally reach us, and we decided this clearing was as good as any to put our blanket down and start our picnic. Kyle tore open the salami, and I uncorked the bottle of wine. The girls set the cheese up on a platter. Abby realized we needed to rinse the grapes, so she rinsed them with one of our bottles of water. I poured everyone a glass, and we all sat to relax and eat. Kyle sat on my right. Abby sat on my left, and I was having a really hard time not staring at her legs. We were all pretty close together since the blanket wasn't too big.

Kyle guzzled his glass down. I guess I couldn't really blame him, considering what happened to him just a few hours ago. We had two bottles, so it was fine. He drained his last drop and looked at us.

"We should play Truth or Dare," he said.

"Oh goodness. Are we still twelve? Feeding ducks and playing Truth or Dare?" Abby said.

"Truth or Dare is a game for all ages," Kyle said.

Jessica chimed in. "Let's do it!"

I shrugged. "Sure. Why not?"

Kyle poured himself another glass, but he had a very serious face on. "Okay. If we play this, everyone has to follow the rules. If you pick Truth, you *have* to tell the truth! If you pick Dare, you have to do the dare unless it puts you or others in physical harm. No chickening out on either. Got it?"

We all replied "yes" in unison.

"Okay, I'll go first," Kyle said. He turned to me with a sly grin.

"Truth or Dare?" he asked me. I knew Kyle really well, and he could be fucking crazy with his dares.

"Truth," I said. I thought he wanted me to pick Dare, but the growing smile on his face told me he was glad I didn't. *Damn.*

"Okay, I'm going to ask this, because you've never talked about it any time I've brought it up, and I've always wanted to know. Are you a virgin?" I could feel Abby's head whiplash in my direction.

I should have picked Dare and agreed to go fight those six dozen ducks. I was dreading the fact that he asked this in front of Abby. Things had been going so well. What if my answer weirded her out?

I looked around the group. Jessica was on the edge of her seat, and Abby was listening intently, her face blank. I wish I knew what she was thinking.

"No, I'm not a virgin," I said.

"Woo! My man!" Kyle screamed. I looked toward Abby, but her eyes were staring at the dirt now.

"But I might as well be a virgin." Abby looked up at me. "I'm not going to expand too much, but I don't ever think about it fondly." I looked around the group again. Kyle had a puzzled look on his face, and Abby was looking at the dirt again, but with a smile this time. Jessica was looking at Abby with an evil grin on her face. *Is it because she's talked about me?* Or...*Oh no.* Was Jessica going to ask Abby the same question? I didn't know if I want to know the answer to that right now. *But of course I do.*

She started to open her mouth to ask Abby something, but Abby caught it too and asked her own question instead. "Kyle, Truth or Dare?" she asked.

"Hm. Dare," he said with a smile.

"I dare you to walk up to that couple over there, tell the girl, 'Well, you sure seem to have moved on quickly.' Then walk away."

I cracked up.

"What? Are you kidding me? I'm not doing that," Kyle said.

"You *have* to do any Dare that doesn't put you in harm's way," she said, imitating his tone from a minute earlier.

"Yeah, well, that might *actually* put me in harm's way. What if the boyfriend punches me?" he pleaded.

"That is a risk I'm willing to take. I didn't make the rules." God, she was so cute.

"Fuck. Fuck me. Fuck a duck." he said. Kyle took a deep

breath and stood up, leaving his wine glass behind. He walked up to the couple, said some words, and then hurried away. The girlfriend looked confused, and the boyfriend kept looking at her like 'what the fuck?' As the couple walked away, the boyfriend kept shooting looks back at us.

We all laughed as Kyle walked back up. His face was bright red. "That was a good one, sis," he said. She did a little bow in her seated position. I saw Jessica grin toward Abby again. I saw her open her mouth to ask Abby something, but I felt a need to protect her.

"So, Jessica." She and Abby both turned quickly to me. "Truth or Dare?"

Jessica put her hand on her chin. "Hm. Truth," she said.

I went to ask her something, but I realized I didn't actually prepare anything to say. "Uh." In my panic, I decided to be unoriginal and steal some used material. "Are you a, uh, are you a virgin?"

Probably not the best question for me to ask in front of Abby, who was looking at me with a look saying, 'and why do you care?' I wanted to tell her, 'I don't! All I want is you!' But obviously, that wasn't an option. Instead of Jessica answering, Abby spoke up.

"That's a pretty terrible question, Sherlock. Jessica's sex life isn't exactly a secret."

Jessica looked just a tad bit offended. "Well, look at this little know-it-all. You might be surprised by the truth, Abby." Jessica turned to answer me. "I'm still a virgin," she said.

"Bullshit," Abby said, not a millisecond later. "I've personally heard...your activity." Kyle looked at me and wiggled his eyebrows.

"Can a girl only moan from sex alone, Abby?" Jessica asked her.

"You're a poet," Kyle said. If it was a little brighter and the sun wasn't setting, I could swear Jessica just blushed a little. Jessica looked back at Abby.

"I've done everything but sex," she said.

"Butt sex?" Kyle joked. Jessica giggled and playfully slapped his arm.

"I've done everything *except* sex," she corrected herself.

Abby's mouth was completely open. "Wow. I had no idea."

"Yeah, I don't know. I guess I'm just waiting for that perfect guy for the last step, you know? But I still wanted to have some fun along the way." We all nodded, and then she started laughing. "Oh, I'm just kidding, you gullible idiots. Of course I've had sex!"

Abby was shaking her head. "I was seriously about to question everything I knew about you and the universe," she said.

Jessica laughed. "Okay, so my turn. Abby. Truth or Dare?"

Abby made a quick glance at me, then looked down at her hands. "Dare," she said. *What didn't she want Jessica to ask her?*

"Oh wow, Jessica. Make her do something she'll never forget! She's never picked 'dare' *anytime* we've played," Kyle said.

Jessica was thinking. Probably because she expected quiet, innocent little Abby to pick Truth too. "Okay! I've got a good one." Everyone was on the edge of their blanket, especially Kyle. "Abby, I dare you to kiss Jacob for five seconds." My heart stopped.

"What? That's stupid," Kyle said.

"Shh. No judging my Dares!" Jessica told him.

"Um," Abby said.

"No backing out!" Jessica screamed.

"No, pick a different Dare," Kyle told Jessica.

"No. Rules are rules," she told him.

Abby looked at me. I raised my eyebrows. *Do I lean in some or is she supposed to come to me?* I had been waiting to do this for days, and it was going to be literally in front of her brother? The one I had been trying to hide from? I didn't think our first kiss would be like this. But I wasn't going to argue with fate.

"Guys, this is gross. Don't do this," Kyle said. He didn't look so happy about his idea to play Truth or Dare anymore.

Jessica slapped his arm. "Shut up, Kyle. Now, you two, kiss! I'll count out loud, so don't come apart before you hear me say five Mississippi."

This was it. I got to kiss the girl of my dreams in just a few seconds. I wished it were more intimate. I wished no one was watching.

I wished it would last longer than five seconds.

We scooted closer to one another. My heart was pounding in my chest, and I could feel my cock swell when I thought of *all* the places I want to kiss her. Starting with those sexy legs.

She looked nervous. But it was okay, because so was I. We leaned our faces toward each other. Our lips were inches apart. I wanted to grab her and pull her into me. The sunset behind her had turned the sky to shades of bright orange.

"And kiss!" Jessica said. Before I knew it, we both closed our eyes and our lips connected and my soul was sucked out of me. I heard Jessica say 'one Mississippi' in the background, but everything else was muffled out. I wanted to let out a moan to release the feelings I'd been experiencing for the last week, but that would have been too much for Kyle to bear. Her lips were soft, and she tasted like mint. My cock hardened to full strength, and I was very glad we were sitting down, so it stayed hidden.

"Guys!" Kyle screamed. I awakened out of my trance and opened my eyes. Abby's were still closed, but quickly opened as well. We separated. "Jessica said 'five Mississippi' like three seconds ago."

"Sorry," Abby and I both said in unison. We looked at each

other and smiled. Jessica's eyes were wide, and her mouth was popped open.

"I think the wine affected my hearing," I said.

"Yeah, me too," Abby said. She started playing with her hair.

"Uh huh," Kyle said. "Well, I'm nauseous. Let's pack up. It's going to get dark soon." He didn't seem so happy.

I tried to pick up as much as I could while sitting down, so I didn't unveil the giant tower I had been building in my pants. Thankfully, it was quickly getting dark with the setting sun and us being beneath the shade of the trees. I could finally stand with just a small bulge instead of a boulder.

We all walked back to the car. None of us talked much. Kyle wasn't talking at all. All I could think about was when I would get to kiss her next. We drove back to our neighborhood, and he dropped me off. I watched them drive away and then practically skipped inside.

I couldn't wait to see her the next day.

Chapter 13

Abby

Today has been so awful. I was glad it was almost over. It had been awkward. It had been tense. It had been *all* of the things you didn't want after your first kiss with someone you had been crushing on.

When I picked up Jacob this morning, our conversations weren't as easygoing as they usually were. It was like we had to make an effort to speak to one another, and I hated it. Usually we talked so naturally.

While at work, we typically found time to go talk to the other, but he hadn't come up to me, and I hadn't gone up to him, which was strange. It had just been one hell of a day, which was the opposite of what I was expecting.

I thought our first kiss would change our lives for the better. But did it mess everything up because it was forced on us instead of it happening naturally? When was it ever going to happen if Jessica hadn't dared us? Did he even really *want* to kiss me?

When our lips touched yesterday, I both hated and loved

that my brother had to watch it. I cared too much about what he thought, so I hated it. But we enjoyed annoying each other, and he did not like us kissing at all, which was fun. But I wished he and Jessica were gone. Because as soon as Jacob kissed me, I wanted him to rip my clothes off right there and make love on top of the grapes and cheese. It would have been a delicious affair.

When we got back to our house last night, Jessica and I shut ourselves in my room. She said she thought she saw sparks flying and asked what was up with us. So I told her everything, not that there was too much to tell. Just the fact that I was dying to be intimate with Jacob, and that it was torture seeing him every day without being able to act on anything. I swore her to secrecy.

When she left, I got in the shower. My body was begging to be touched, so I lowered the handheld shower head to run water in between my legs and imagined Jacob's hot, naked body getting in the shower with me. We'd wash each other's hair and rub soap on each other. Then he would push me against the wall and make me scream with the touch of his fingers. The water was warm, and the stream hit me in all the right places. It only took me a few minutes to orgasm. Thinking of Jacob... *Jacob.*

I got out of the shower, thinking I had cured myself, but my body was squirming again once I put on my pajamas. So, I went to bed horny. I woke up horny. I picked Jacob up that morning practically drenched down there. Now I was sitting in my chair, watching him clean up, still horny. I looked forward to another shower tonight.

Before I knew it, it was time to go home. We closed up, locked up, and started driving to his house. I attempted some small talk.

"So, anything new with you lately?" I asked. *Like, have you even thought about our kiss? Has your cock been going insane, too? Why haven't you brought it up?*

Well, why I haven't I?

"Um, not really. My dad is out of town for the next week, so life should be more enjoyable than normal." His relationship with his dad always made me so sad. I didn't know what I would do if my father and I weren't as close as we were. "What about you?" he asked.

Oh, you know, just masturbating and coming to thoughts of you touching my body in the shower. "Nope. Same things as usual," I said. *Coward.*

I pulled up to his house. Defeated, I just kept staring straight ahead. "Have a good night. See you tomorrow," I said. Normally, he would have already opened his door to get out, or at least responded. But he had done neither. So I turned to face him, and he was just staring at me, smiling. It made me smile too. "What?" I asked.

He cleared his throat. "Well, I was just thinking. I always enjoy being prepared for the future."

Prepared for the future? Was he thinking about going to grad school or what career he wanted to pursue? Typical guy. Not even thinking and obsessing over our kiss yesterday like I was.

He continued. "And I was just thinking it might be good for us to practice kissing some more. You know, in case Jessica ever dares us again, we should look professional."

I felt my face turn hot, and I didn't think I could hide my stupidly big grin if I tried. I was sure my nipples were about to show through my clothes any second now. "Oh really? Preparing for the future is definitely best. So, when do you want to practice?" I asked.

He leaned closer to me and took his hand to brush my hair behind my ear. "I was thinking right now would be perfect, because I can't wait any longer," he said. His hand went to the back of my neck before he brought my face toward him, and our lips crash together and created fireworks throughout my car. I whimpered. I had been hoping for this moment all day and night. I undid my seatbelt and moved a little closer to him. He popped his buckle too. I could *eat* his lips they tasted so good. His tongue came out and parted my lips, and my whole body melted like butter.

His hand traveled down my neck, grazed the side of my boob, and traveled lower. I made a light moan in anticipation of him going beneath my clothes. Instead, his hand went to my legs and caressed them all around. His lips separated from mine, and I wanted to glue them back to mine. "Your legs have been killing me, Abby," he said. His hand went to the inside of my thigh and slowly traveled up to my center. He didn't touch me in the area I *needed* him to, though. He was being a nice guy, which I really appreciated. I showed him he didn't need to be such a gentleman by putting my hand on the bulge growing in his shorts and grabbed his hard cock. I was so inexperienced with this kind of thing, but my mind had been preparing for this day for a while now. He took a deep inhale and moaned softly for me. He returned the favor and cupped my pussy with his hand, applying pressure with his middle finger. I moaned into his mouth as his hand found its way under my shorts. I squeezed him again in passion.

Beep beep! A car driving by honked at us. The driver looked out the window and yelled, "Woo!"

We both stopped immediately. What were we thinking? My windows were not that tinted. We were in front of his house. We both lived in this neighborhood. This town was not that big. Were we crazy? *Well, yes, because being super horny makes people do crazy things.*

He cleared his throat. "Well, thanks for practicing, Abby."

That's it? That's all you're going to say?! "You bet. Though I think we'll need a few more sessions to get it down just right," I said as I wiped my mouth. I didn't want this to end. My nipples were basically screaming for attention.

He smiled and said, "I'll see you tonight." He opened the door but didn't step out just yet.

"Oh, will you?" I asked, confused.

"Yeah, your mom invited me for dinner."

That was going to be absolute torture. I had to eat dinner with him sitting next to my family? Not able to act out on anything? Why was fate so cruel?

"Cool. Will you need a ride?" I asked, hoping he said yes so we could have a little alone time together. It would be darker then, so hopefully no more cars seeing and interrupting us.

"No, I could just walk. But thanks," he said. What a bastard. Why would he deny extra alone time with me? He leaned across the center console and grabbed the back of my neck again. He pulled me into him and kissed me so deeply that I quickly forgot any reason why I was mad at such a perfect specimen. "See you in a few. I really enjoyed the practice." he said. He got out and closed the door. I waited until he was at the door before I drove off.

Once I was far enough away, I squealed with excitement. Now *that* was the kind of first kiss with him I was imagining. I pressed play on my Taylor Swift playlist and Cruel Summer came on. I turned the volume up, rolled down the window, and let the wind take my hair. I felt like I was on top of the world.

I parked in front of my house and ran inside, trying to go straight to my room.

"Honey!" my mom called out. I stopped in my tracks. This mother of mine was unfortunately too nice for me to ignore her. I turned around.

"Yep?"

"Could you help me with dinner?" It was so hard to tell this woman 'no,' but I felt like I needed to. I walked into the kitchen so I didn't have to scream. The smell of onions sautéing in the pan made me salivate.

"Is there any way Kyle could help you tonight? I was actually rushing to get ready."

"Oh. Well, I can't promise everyone it will taste as good if it's Kyle cooking," she said with a smile. "But I'll ask. Where are you going?"

Shit. I was so bad at lying. I didn't even think of one. "Um, some new place Jessica was talking about. She's on the prowl." I felt awful lying to her. But she would understand.

She laughed. "The way Jessica dresses, I'm pretty sure she can just stand there and be the prey. Couldn't you get ready after dinner?"

You're killing me, mom. "Well, I was thinking I could get ready before Jacob comes over. That way I could give him a ride home after dinner, if he needs one, and he won't have to wait for me to get ready." *Look at me. So smooth.*

My mom cocked her head and squinted her eyes at me. Was that a smirk I saw on her face? *Uh oh.* Maybe I was the opposite of smooth. "Huh. Yeah, okay. You go get ready, sweetie," she said. "Will you be on the prowl tonight as well?"

"Anything's possible," I said with a smile as I skipped back to my room.

"Kyle! Come help your mother mash some potatoes!" I heard her scream as I walked into my room.

I wasn't the kind of person to put on a lot of makeup, but I did like to touch myself up. First, I decided what I was going to wear. I picked out a black top and a white skirt. I put on my deodorant that I had worn since high school that gave off a fragrance of flowers and berries.

My face was mostly done when I heard the doorbell ring.

Jacob always rang it before opening the door, even though my mom had told him a thousand times he could just walk right in. He even had a key to our place. I looked at myself in the mirror, and I looked *hot*. Not even gonna lie.

I headed to the living room, but I had to walk by Kyle in the hallway. We passed each other, and he stopped.

"Why are you all dressed up?" he asked.

"I'm going out with Jessica later."

"Where at?" he asked. If I told him any location, he would probably go there to be an overly protective big brother asshole.

"None of your beeswax!" I said, as I continued walking.

I strolled into the living room and saw Jacob standing at the kitchen table. He was looking fine as hell in a navy polo shirt and khaki shorts. His sleeves were tight around the muscles in his arms. He was concentrated on setting the knives and forks down, but he heard me walk in and looked up. I smiled when our eyes met, and his mouth literally dropped. My mom had her back turned to me, so I did a little twirl just for him. He smiled and shook his head at me.

My mom saw me walk into the kitchen. "Oh, look at you. All the boys in town better watch out tonight," she said as she nudged me. "Here, bring this to the table, and then you can sit down." She handed me the broccoli.

"I'm just going to be there as moral support for Jessica, mom." Jacob was already sitting, and Kyle was walking up to the table. I sped up a little, put the broccoli in the center, and then took a seat next to Jacob. It obviously was where Kyle was planning to sit, but luckily he didn't seem to think much of it as he sat down across from us without a fuss. My dad was hanging with his friends playing poker tonight, so it was just the four of us.

Jacob had his phone out and was texting someone. Who was he texting when I was sitting next to him looking like *this*? I got my answer a few seconds later when I felt my phone vibrate.

Jacob: You look amazing and smell divine. How am I going to keep my hands off you during dinner? This is evil.

I smiled and texted him back.

Me: You'll just have to be a good boy. Save the bad boy for later.

A week ago, I never would have thought I could type something like that. But he was waking up things inside me that I had never felt. His text had me feeling all giddy inside.

I saw him read the text, and he shook his head. I looked down at his crotch and saw his bulge. I rubbed my bare knee against his, and he rubbed back. It was the only way I was going to be able to get through dinner without going crazy. Poor Jacob, though. I saw his cock grow even larger.

My mom brought the roasted chicken to the table and sat down. Everyone started serving themselves. "Jacob, isn't Abby looking beautiful tonight?" she said.

Yeah, I'm not a good liar one bit...There's no hiding anything from your momma.

"Ew. Mom, don't make him answer that. What a weird question," Kyle said.

"Yes, Mrs. Kathy, she does look beautiful," Jacob said. He smiled when he said it, and I was trying really hard not to turn as red as a farmhouse, but I didn't think I was succeeding. I couldn't believe he said that in front of my brother.

"Dude! You all are weirding me out," Kyle said.

"You're beautiful too, Kyle," Jacob said. I snorted. Kyle rolled his eyes.

We all continued to eat and talk about random things. Our jobs, our futures, the normal stuff. All the while, Jacob and I kept sneakily rubbing our legs against each other. When everyone was done eating, my mom turned to me.

"So, Abby, where are you going so dressed up?" she said with a smile. This woman was going to do me like that? She *knew* why. Right? Maybe not?

"I'm not sure where yet. Jessica just said we were going out looking for boys." Jacob's leg stopped moving against mine. I looked over at him, and he had a confused look on his face. I wanted to tell him it was a lie, but I couldn't. I also couldn't text him that info, because it would have been obvious we were texting each other. I nudged his leg a few times, but he pulled his away.

"Well, the girls are hanging out," Kyle said. "You want to go play some video games or go to a bar, Jacob?"

Jacob looked up. "No thanks. I'm actually pretty tired. I think I'm just going to walk home soon."

That was my cue. "Well, I could bring you on my way out to meet Jessica," I said.

"Nah, it's okay. I could bring him," Kyle said. Out of all the moments for him to choose to be nice, why was he offering this time?

My mom stepped in. "Actually, Kyle, could you help me with the dishes? Abby's only done them a hundred times more than you, so it's only fair."

"Ugh. Sure. I was hoping to get out of dish duty, though."

"Thanks, sweetie. Well, Jacob and Abby, you two are free to move along whenever. We'll take care of the cleanup."

Jacob stood up immediately. "I'll see you later, Kyle" They

fist bumped across the table. "Thank you for the dinner, Mrs. Kathy. It was delicious." He bent down to give her a kiss on the cheek and walked out of the house. I had to hurry to catch up. When I walked outside, he was standing by the passenger door.

We got in the car and headed to his house. When I was daydreaming about this moment earlier, I imagined he would be touching me, or kissing my neck, or something. But all he was doing was being silent and staring out the window. My mom shouldn't have asked me that question. Maybe she was trying to help me out and make me seem hard to get or something? Whatever her strategy, it backfired. Or maybe she was clueless. But I wasn't worried.

We pulled up in front of his house and I put the car in park. Before I could say anything, he did. "So where are you and Jessica going out?" There was some salt in his tone.

I rolled my eyes extra hard for him to see. "Are you that dense? Jacob, it was an excuse."

"What do you mean—" he started to ask, but before he could finish, I leaned over and locked my lips to his. He let out a sigh of relief, and I put my hand on his chest. My center felt warm when I felt how hard his pecs were, and then my whole body screamed as I trailed my hand down his rock-hard abs. I landed my hand on his groin and squeezed his package. With each beat of his heart, his cock grew bigger and harder.

"I put makeup on and dressed up for *you*, dummy," I told him. He lunged forward to kiss me some more, but I leaned back. "Do you think we could take this inside? I don't really want our neighbors, or God forbid my family, to see."

He smiled. "Yeah, no problem."

"And...do you think I could park my car in your garage? Who knows if Kyle or one of my parents will drive by and see my car out front? Just to be safe."

"Man, you're smart. Yeah, let me go open it." He closed the

door and practically sprinted inside. I laughed at how enthusiastic he was.

A minute later, the garage door opened, and I drove inside. I put the car in park and looked at Jacob standing in the doorway. A tribe full of drums was beating my chest. I was ready for this. I wanted this. But I had never done anything like this. I didn't even know what we were going to do. But I was going to try not to think too much. I always wanted to wait until I was comfortable with someone. And there wasn't any other guy in the world I was as comfortable with as Jacob.

I stepped out of the car and walked to him. When I reached him, it was like we were animals in heat. He pulled me close and kissed me. Our hands traveled all over each other's bodies, exploring what each one of us wanted to take. I walked him backwards until we were in his living room. We kept going until his calves hit his couch, and I pushed him on it. I quickly climbed on top and straddled him, our bodies moving back and forth against each other. We kissed each other hard, and in our passion, I nibbled his bottom lip. I felt his hard cock pressing against my pussy, pushing into me, undoubtedly angry at all the clothing separating us. I got wet at the thought of putting it inside me.

Jacob slid his hands up my legs until they found their way up my skirt. He grabbed both of my cheeks hard, and I moaned into his mouth. I ground into him, hard, wondering why we both still had all these clothes on. One of his hands found its way under my panties on my backside. It slid down until it found my lips. It was the first time a boy had ever touched me there. I took a deep intake of breath, and I moaned when he started moving his fingers in slow circles. I couldn't concentrate on making out anymore, because it felt too good, so I stuck my face into his neck and leaned forward to give him a better angle. He kissed and sucked on my neck in turn. He was doing it just right, like he was a master, pressing down light on my button and going in slow, slow circles. He heard how much I liked it, and he went faster.

But it was too much faster. "No, no, go slow again," I told him. I hoped that didn't hurt his feelings. Maybe I shouldn't have said anything.

"Thank you," he said. He slowed down.

There you go. "Lighter," I whispered into his ear. He took some pressure off, and his light rotating touch had my body in ecstasy, wanting everything he had to give me. With each revolution, I felt like a steam engine becoming more likely to burst.

He kept rubbing me, slowly building me up. After a few minutes, I let out a high-pitched moan. "Yes, Jacob, just like that. Don't stop," I somehow said. I felt so good that it was hard for me to have any lucid thoughts, let alone saying anything intelligible.

After a few more minutes, I felt myself ready to peak. His middle finger was rubbing my clit perfectly. "Yes, yes, yes," I gasped. I dug my nails into his muscles, I panted, and I cried out in the best orgasm I had ever had. He rubbed me until I moved my center away from his hand. I was way too sensitive for him to do any more.

He took his hand out of my skirt, and I started kissing him ferociously. He pleased me, and now I wanted to please him. I started undoing his belt, his button, and his zipper. I stood up and pulled his shorts off of him. I caught my breath at the sight of his cock trying to escape his boxers. I bent down and pulled them off of him, and I couldn't believe how perfect his cock looked once it flung straight up. I knew I just had my orgasm, but somehow the sight of him had me wet all over again, thinking of it being inside me.

I knelt down, not knowing exactly what I was doing, since I had never done anything like this before. But instinct took over.

His cock was too big for me to fit the whole thing in my mouth, so I grabbed the base of his cock, and he moaned. I started kissing along his length, starting from the bottom and working my way up top. I got to his tip, dripping with his pre-cum, and I licked it all away. It tasted pretty bitter.

"Oh, Abby," he said to the ceiling. His pleasure made me want to give him more. I looked at his tip, and even *that* was so big. I didn't know how far down I could go, but I tried. I opened my mouth and sucked his whole tip. It took up more of my mouth than I thought it would. "Yes, Abby, yes," he moaned.

I looked up at him and could tell he was in ecstasy. It made me so happy to make him feel good. I sucked a bit past his tip and came back all the way up, and he moaned again. I looked at how big was cock was, and I couldn't believe he had been able to hide it from me all these years.

How is this ever going to fit inside me?

I went back down and sucked him hard. He let out a moan and put his hand on the side of my face. His pleasure only fired me up more as I fit as much of his cock in my mouth and down my throat as I could. He grabbed the hair on the back of my neck and pushed down on my head. He wanted me to go deeper, and I obeyed. I went down as far as I could. I realized I couldn't fit all of him in my mouth, so I started squeezing and rubbing the base of him with my hand. His head went back, and he moaned like a lion roaring in the night. A fire lit up inside me as I eagerly sucked him off. After a while, he was moaning louder with every move I made.

"I'm about to come," he said. I sucked him harder, excited that a newbie like me was able to get him to come. *Imagine how good I'll be once I get more practice.* "Are you going to swallow my cum, baby?"

Umm, am I? Was that what I was supposed to do? I really had no idea. "Mhm," I mumbled, letting him know I wanted to taste all of him. His head kicked back again, and I looked up to see a smile on his face.

"Keep going, just like that, just like that," he said. I followed his orders and kept my same rhythm, sucking him hard along his whole length. "Faster," he said. I picked up my speed. "Yes, yes, baby, yes, I'm coming, I'm coming." He said he was coming, but I felt nothing in my mouth. Maybe men only came a little? I thought it would be more. Not like I would know.

I kept sucking him, and then I felt it.

He let out a loud groan and shot his dick deep in my mouth. A rope of cum bursted from his tip. I stopped, thinking my job had ended, and that I needed to swallow his load.

"No, keep going, please!" he begged. I swallowed his first bit of cum and sucked him hard again. Going as far up and down as I could. I was immediately given another rope of his cum. I swallowed it and kept going. He grunted one last time and a little more came out. I kept sucking, not knowing when to stop. "Shhh," he said, while steadying my head. "Too sensitive, now." *Huh, I guess it happens to guys too.*

I slowed down my pace, much to his delight. His dick softened, so I came off of it. *That wasn't so scary after all.* I gave his base one last little squeeze, and I licked the remaining drop of cum from his tip. I looked up at him and smiled. *I guess all those blowjob tips Jessica gave me that I never used actually paid off.*

He was breathing heavily, staring at me. "Thank you. That...that was amazing. Where did you learn how to do that?" Before I could tell him that I had never done that with anyone, that he was the first one to touch me, that his was the first cock I had sucked or even grabbed, he said, "Sorry, that was a dumb question. You don't have to answer." He smiled, and I didn't have the heart to tell him. What if he got scared or thought I was still a kid if he found out how new I was to all of this? I decided I would not tell him for as long as I could. "You're amazing," he said.

Butterflies flew through me. I was so happy I pleased him so well, but I hoped he wasn't just lying about it to make me feel better.

He leaned forward and placed his hands on the sides of my chest and ended up touching my breast. A deep breath came into my lungs as he ignited my passion again. He pulled me up to him and kissed me deeply, and I melted into him. He leaned back again.

"Stand up," he said. I squinted my eyes and looked at him. "Just do it." I got on my feet. I was trembling, both excited and nervous at what he wanted to do next. I didn't know if I was ready to go all the way, if that was what he wanted. "Take off your panties." I caught my breath and hesitated, not knowing where this was going. "Trust me," he said. I did trust him. I reached under my skirt and slid them off my legs. "Now, take your skirt off." I smiled, wondering what he had up his sleeve. I did as he commanded me.

I dropped my skirt to the floor, and his eyes went straight to my shaved pussy. I did it just for him. I saw the hunger in his eyes. I could feel his want for it, and I became wet again.

Jacob lied on his side along his dad's leather couch. "Come here," he motioned me toward him. I got on the couch, and he positioned my body to where my back was along his front, and I was facing away from him. I could feel his soft cock between my butt cheeks. Was it soft because he wasn't really aroused? Or because he just came?

He started tracing his hands along my arms, my sides, and my legs. His touch felt so comforting and warm. I relaxed into him, and we lied like that for a few minutes, his hand exploring my body. No talking.

His hand teased me, getting close to my center, but moving

away at the last minute. I squirmed against his cock. He grabbed the inside of my thigh, and I move myself along him.

The friction of his cock between my cheeks gave it life. *I want to get him hard again.*

Not waiting for him to finally touch my spot again, I ground into him.

"What are you doing?" he asked.

"What I want."

He moaned softly and kissed my neck as I ground into him to make him hard for me once more. His fingers went toward my center again, but this time they didn't trail away. He lightly put his middle finger on my nub at the top, and a moan escaped my lips. Lightly, he applied pressure in small, circular motions. I bit into the pillow. How could I be expected to wait to have him inside me? I wanted all of him *now*. I sensually ground against his cock. It was growing.

He traced his fingertip down my wet slit until he reached my entrance. *Yes. Please.* He applied pressure, and I held my breath, waiting for him to enter. But he traced his finger back up to my top button. I exhaled in frustration, even though it felt good. His moans were quiet and soft as I continued to grind against him.

By now, his cock was as hard as it was earlier. I licked my right hand and put some extra saliva on it before I reached around and spread it along his length. He moaned into my ear. I grabbed his cock and started to give him a hand job. I was able to easily slide up my hand along him with my self-made lube. His body humped into mine on instinct.

"I never knew you were so naughty," he said. I smiled and slid my hand all the way down until I lightly fondled his balls. He moaned and brought his large middle finger to my opening and entered me. I made a high-pitched sound while taking in a breath at his surprise move. His finger felt so big that it was probably the size of two fingers of a normal man. He entered me slowly, inch by inch. I lost concentration on his hand job with how good he was making me feel.

Finally, his whole finger was inside me. I rested into him, never wanting him to take it out. But he did, *and it felt so good.*

He pushed it deep into me again, and I let out a moan. *He's going to make me come again, and I want to do the same to him.* I got back in rhythm with my hand and stroked his long cock. Our movements and moans synced as one.

We both increased in speed and intensity, and my body felt like it was fog floating above his couch. "Yes, Jacob, please, please," I said. I could feel my walls loosening and relaxing around his fingers, ready for anything to fit inside me.

"Please what, you naughty little girl?" he asked as he nibbled my ear.

"Give it to me!" I begged. I would have taken his cock inside me right then and there if he wanted to. He gave off a guttural laugh. I wondered for a split second why, but I immediately knew when I felt another one of his big man fingers inside me. Without warning, I screamed in ecstasy as he slowly pumped me with his fingers. I lost sense of my surroundings. "Jacob, I'm so close."

"Come for me, Abby." Then, his fingers curled inside me toward my upper wall, back and forth, back and forth. They massaged my g-spot, and my legs shook and my body curled. My eyes rolled to the back of my head as I felt my orgasm travel through my whole body. I moaned loud enough for the neighbors to hear as I came on his fingers. But he didn't stop, and it still felt amazing.

"Squeeze me harder, Abby. I'm so close," he moaned in my ear. I squeezed my small hands around his huge cock and pumped him. I could feel his tip in the crack of my ass.

"Do you want to come on my ass?" I hoped I was dirty

talking all right. It sounded so silly in my head, but it seemed to do the trick.

"Yes, Abby, yes!" he called out as he erupted all over my backside. I continued pumping him until I felt him softening. I took my hand off of him, and he took his out of me.

We lay there, panting. Unable to think.

I couldn't believe we had just done that. I couldn't believe *I* had just done that. Little-miss-innocent-who's-never-done-a-thing became a little sexual deviant for a night.

It just felt *so* natural with Jacob. I wasn't timid or afraid. I wasn't questioning whether this was right anymore. It *had* to be right. It was childish to be afraid of what Kyle might think.

But did Jacob feel the same way? Their friendship breaking up was the main reason for us not to do this. Was I being selfish? Did Jacob just want to hook up? Was this just going to be a one-night thing? Should that be enough for me?

No. I wanted more. I wanted to *be* with him.

I wanted to ask him if he felt the same, but I was afraid of what the answer would be. So I just lay here, being his little spoon. I didn't care that we were lying in a mess—though it shouldn't have been too much, since he had just come minutes before. We could clean it up in a little bit. For now, I took his arm and wrapped it around me. He squeezed me tight, kissed my head, and rubbed my skin with his thumb.

This can't be it. This won't be it.

Chapter 14

Jacob

As I cleaned the couch while she got dressed, I couldn't keep my eyes or my thoughts off of her. I couldn't believe Kyle's little sister Abby and I had just done that. She was an animal in the best way possible. I tried not to think about how she'd gotten so good.

I watched her pick her skirt back up, and all I wanted to do was rip it off of her again. An uneasy feeling that this was going to be the only night we did anything like this came over me. She noticed me staring.

"What?" she asked.

"Nothing. I just can't stop looking at you." She blushed. Now that she was dressed, did that mean she was going to leave? I didn't want her to ever go home.

"Are you heading out?" I asked.

"Not if you want me to stay."

"I do." She smiled. "Want to put on a show?" She nodded. I sat on the couch and motioned for her to come near me. I pulled her close, keeping both of my arms around her. She did the same. We sat in silence, staring ahead.

"Oh, shit, sorry. I probably should have gotten the remote before locking you up like this." She squeezed me harder.

"That's okay. This is just perfect," she said. My little Abby. Was she *my* little Abby? I wanted her to be, but it was hard to tell what she wanted. Was this just a one time thing? Just a friends with benefits thing? Something more? We sat there holding each other for a few minutes. Her smell was intoxicating.

"I'm so glad we did that," I said. "I've been wanting to kiss you since I saw your car tackle a trash can." She giggled and squeezed me harder.

"I don't know how much longer I would have lasted if you didn't kiss me," she said. I kissed her on top of her head.

"It ain't much, but it's honest work," I said, channeling my inner meme. She giggled, and we sat there for a minute just holding each other and sneaking in kisses. I started thinking about where this could lead and what our future could hold. *Our* future.

"So, Abby, what do you wanna be when you grow up?"

She laughed. "You know I want to be a teacher." Of course I did.

"Have you applied anywhere yet?"

She sighed, which wasn't the response I was thinking she'd make. "Yeah. I've applied to Washington Elementary, St. Anthony, and Snyder Middle School. They should be calling candidates to set up interviews soon."

She didn't sound excited one bit. "Why do you sound so down? Are those the schools you want to work at?" She took a few moments to answer.

"I mean, not really. But I have no experience, so I feel like I have to apply to lower-performing schools before I apply to a high-performing one. My dream would be to work at Franklin Middle," she said.

"I don't think you need to wait. You could get hired anywhere you want," I said. I couldn't see it, but I could feel her eyes roll.

"You're sweet, but I think you're just trying to get under my skirt again. The *excellent* schools want someone with experience. They even say so on the job listings. They all ask for at least four years of teaching experience."

I shrugged. "Eh. Every job listing says they want experience—even ones that are entry-level positions! I think you should always apply for what you want. Let the human resources person make the decision. Don't limit yourself. You have always been one of the smartest people I've known, and you have the passion, which is what really counts. Any of the top schools would be lucky to have you."

She squeezed me harder and kissed my neck. "Thank you." We sat there in more silence, perfectly content with just one another's presence.

Three hours later, I woke up. We had fallen asleep on the couch. I looked down at her, and she was *out*. I could see a tiny bit of her drool on my shirt. I rubbed her arm to wake her up. She barely opened her eyes.

"Hey, we fell asleep. It's almost midnight." That made her jolt up and almost knock her head into my chin.

"Shit. Midnight?" She looked up at the clock. She checked her phone, and there were a couple of messages from her mom. She sighed. "I should probably get back home," she said. I didn't want her to go. I wanted to tell her we should get an apartment together. Or that we should leave town tonight! Which was stupid, of course.

She looked up at me, and I didn't hesitate. I kissed those soft lips of hers like tonight was the last night I would ever do so. She smiled and then we rested our foreheads together for a bit. Was it normal to feel this close with someone so soon? We both stood up and walked to her car in the garage. I opened the door, and she started to get in, but I took her hand and stopped her.

"Hey," I said.

"Hey."

"I'm just going to go ahead and ask now to save me heartache later. If you say no, it's okay, but I think you should say yes. If you're worried about the consequences, I think we can make it work." I stared at her, waiting for a response. She raised her eyebrows.

"Are you going to ask me a question?" she asked.

Motherfucker, how dumb am I? We both laughed.

"Yes," I said. "Do you want to give this thing between us a real shot? We can hide it from everyone until we figure out how to break it to them, but I think—"

She shut me up with a deep kiss and wrapped her arms around my neck. Our tongues parted each other's lips and danced with each other, and just this simple contact was able to start getting me hard again. I pulled her body closer and we made out for a minute before separating.

"Yes," she said. "I would love to." I kissed *her* this time, and after a bit, she pushed me away. "Okay, okay. I have to go. I'll see you tomorrow. I had fun tonight," she said with a smile.

"Me too. Bye, Abby." I gave her one last kiss before shutting her door.

* * *

I woke up around seven in the morning feeling invigorated. I made myself a banana, strawberry, and peanut butter smoothie with pea protein. When I guzzled it down, I felt like I could take on the world.

About an hour after my smoothie, Abby pulled up right on

time. Well, actually, she was a little earlier than normal. I grabbed my usual things, plus the special goodies for my plan later on, and headed to her car. I got in the passenger seat and leaned over to kiss her, but she backed away like my breath was coming from a garbage can. *I brushed my teeth, right?*

"Umm," I said.

"I'm sorry! My windows aren't tinted, and the neighbors are all walking about." I grabbed her hand.

"It's okay, babe." I saw her cheeks get a little rosy as she smiled and put the car in gear. I guessed she liked that nickname.

We pulled up to work and walked through the lobby, and the thing I had been dreading the last few days was staring me in the face. That asshole of a father I had to deal with the other day. I didn't see Matthew.

He pointed to me, and Abby's dad turned around. "Good morning, you two," he said. Abby and I tried to walk past him, but there was no chance of escape. "Jacob, stick around for a second." Abby stopped in her tracks, but he nodded her off, so she headed outside.

"Jacob, this gentleman came to me this morning to complain about an experience he had here the other day, and he said you were giving him parenting advice?"

I was ready to knock this poor excuse of a father to the ground. Unfortunately, the guy I wanted to be my actual father was standing right there. "All I said was that he shouldn't curse in front of his kid," I said, hoping that would make my actions justifiable.

"Is that it?" Mr. Mike asked.

"I think so."

"You didn't also call him an asshole of a father?"

Well, fuck. I forgot about that part. "Well, I didn't directly call him that, but he was yelling at his kid, and I just—"

"Jacob, I can't have you telling guests how to raise their kids. That's not your job."

"Yes, sir," I said. Mr. Mike was giving me a sympathetic look, but my blood was boiling at Matthew's dad.

"Let's not have this happen again, or I'll have to write you up. Please apologize to Mr. Swanson."

I was livid. My face felt beet red. This motherfucker was going to get away scot-free, and I also had to apologize? They could forget it. Fuck him. There was no way I was going to tell that asshole I was sorry.

But then I thought of the consequences. If I didn't apologize, then Mr. Mike might fire me. If he fired me, then there would go all of my time that I got to spend with Abby. And I would hate to disappoint him, especially since he'd been so kind to offer me this job. I turned to look at the guy.

"I'm sorry. I shouldn't have done that. It won't happen again," I said through gritted teeth.

The smug smile on his face was really getting to me. If I didn't know better, I would have said he was trying to get me to lose my temper again.

"Thanks, kid," he said. "Oh, and Mr. Barber, I don't know if this young man was already off of work that day, but he was playing and swimming in the pool for about an hour during work hours. It looked really unprofessional to me and other guests. I just thought you should know."

I had never thought about killing someone until today.

Mr. Mike looked at me and sighed while shaking his head. The disappointment in his eyes was worse than being fired. He was the main father figure in my life, and it killed me to see him upset with me.

"I can take it from here. Thanks, Jeff," Mr. Mike said. They shook hands, and Matthew's dad walked out and back to his car. Mr. Mike turned to me. "Were you screwing around on the clock?"

"I was swimming," I admitted. "But that little kid was so sad that his dad was ignoring him, and I couldn't just let him sit there in the pool by himself."

I knew he could see the shame on my face. The shame of disappointing him and not being able to explain my side. He put his hand on my shoulder. "Look, you and I both know you're capable of doing any job you want. You should really be actively looking for a better line of employment while working this summer job. And I understand why you did what you did, but you can't get involved with the club members' lives, okay? I love you, Jacob, but I need you to do better. Okay?"

"Yes, sir." I wanted to hug him, but I didn't. This conversation would have gone so differently with my dad. I was grateful to have someone understanding in my life.

He patted me on the back. "All right, good talk, good talk. Now, go help Pat prep for the day."

Pat was chopping some strawberries when I walked up, and he told me to start chopping the vegetables. I started with the onions, and I quickly realized I should have waited to do them last because my eyes started burning and watering, and I couldn't see anything. Through painful tears, I also trimmed some asparagus and pinched the stems off of a lot of green beans.

At first I was thinking, 'Why are we prepping so much food?' But that question was answered as the morning went by and we had a ton of guests come in. The bar was packed with parents eating appetizers and ordering drinks. Kids were running around, wet from the pool. The couches were full of people taking a break from the sun. All of which left me no time for anyone, and all I wanted to do was go talk with that beautiful lifeguard outside.

I did my tasks as quickly as I could. I dried up all the water the kids were bringing inside, I helped Pat with some more prepping and serving guests, and then I took out the trash. It seemed like I had bought myself a few minutes, so I headed out to Abby. The previous night had been magical, and I wanted to keep the magic flowing. When I walked up to her ladder seat, she was busy concentrating on everyone in and around the pool.

"Hey, you," I said. She didn't look down at me. I stood there for a few more seconds until she noticed I was there.

"Jeez, how long have you been standing there?" she asked. She only made eye contact for a second before looking back out at all the guests.

"Not too long. I just wanted to come out and say 'hey.' See how you were doing."

Without taking her eyes off the pool, she said, "That's sweet. I wish I could talk, but there are too many people to keep an eye on. I'm sorry." I wanted to put my hand on her as a comfort to let her know that I didn't mind. That I just wanted to hear her voice. But I didn't need to screw up any more with Mr. Mike around.

"Don't be sorry. We'll have fun later," I said. I winked at her, and she smiled.

"Get out of here before I start kissing you in front of everyone," she said, her eyes back on the water. I started toward the big glass doors leading to the inside, and I saw Mr. Mike looking over in the direction of me and Abby. We made eye contact for a second before he continued on to his next task. *Well shit.*

We hit our peak crowd around two o'clock, but everything started to wind down after that. As I was cleaning up right after closing time, Abby's dad walked up to me. Part of me thought he had found out everything and was going to fire me right then and there.

"Jacob."

"Yes, sir?"

"Now that you've been working here a good bit, I don't think I need to stay to close anymore. Do you think you can handle taking over my extra work from here on out?"

"I sure can, Mr. Mike," I said, relieved this wasn't a more serious conversation.

"Good. Well, I'll see you tomorrow. Oh, almost forgot. Here are the keys. Just hand them to Abby each day when you two leave, so she can give them to me when she gets home."

He handed me the keys and headed out. *Perfect.*

I did my work extra fast over the next hour to make sure I had enough time. I also helped Pat with his stuff, so he could leave early. More than anything, I wanted to go hang out with Abby, but sometimes you had to work hard and reap the rewards later.

A little while later, Pat's closing duties were done, so he left out the front. I locked the door behind him and then went to the main seating area with the televisions to set things up.

When I was finished, I opened the doors to the pool area and called out to Abby, "Hey! Are you done?"

"Almost! I'm about to go change into some regular clothes and then I'll be ready to go," she said.

"Cool, well come inside when you're ready!" I closed the door and waited patiently.

A few minutes later, she walked inside. She'd changed into a regular old t-shirt and some short athletic shorts that showed off those sexy legs of hers. A hunger awakened inside of me to rip them off of her and kiss the inside of her thighs.

"Okay, I'm ready when you are," she said. All I did was stand and smile for a few seconds to see if she would catch on;

it didn't take her long. She looked at the TV screen showing the title menu to watch *Pride and Prejudice,* and she finally realized I was holding a bowl of freshly popped popcorn. A curious smile came across her face. "Well, hello. What's all this?"

I held the bowl in one hand and jiggled the keys to the club with the other. "I figured we could hang out here for a bit and have a date. If you wanted to, of course."

Abby's smile got bigger and bigger. She walked up to me and gave me a soft kiss. "I never knew you were such a romantic. I would love to," she said. We sat down and started the movie with the bowl of popcorn on my lap.

Not too long after sitting down, we finished the last of the popcorn. I noticed there were only kernels left, so I took the bowl off my lap and placed it on the coffee table.

Abby was so entranced by the movie, though, that she must not have noticed I moved the bowl. She reached for a handful of popcorn as if it was still there, but she ended up with a handful of *me*. It made both of us jump and then laugh. Much to my delight, she didn't move her hand away.

"Sorry," she said.

"Don't be. I'm not," I said as my cock hardened under her touch. I leaned toward her and kissed her. She melted into me and started rubbing me with her hand.

"Mmm, you're naughty. We're in a public place," I told her. She squeezed my cock.

"Only for you." Then we ripped each other's clothes off like they were on fire. I pulled her shirt off of her, and she straddled me. Her sports bra underneath was red with a floral pattern, and that color somehow made me even hornier. She ripped my shirt off in turn. We made out, our tongues colliding and tasting each other.

It occurred to me that I hadn't seen her completely naked yet. I loved her red sports bra, but I would have liked it more if it was on the ground. I grabbed it and lifted it up above her head and threw it to the side. I was left speechless by the sight of her breasts. They were perfect. Her nipples were hard, and I couldn't help myself. I went in and started kissing her chest. Her arm was around my neck and her hand on my head. While I kissed and licked and sucked her skin, she ground into my cock.

My lips passed near her nipple for the first time, and I licked it. She moaned softly, "Oh my God." I lightly sucked her nipple and moved my tongue in slow circles around it. She wasn't moaning loudly, but I could tell she liked it with what she was doing with her body. Not wanting to show favoritism, I switched over to her other nipple and lightly sucked it as well. She took in a deep breath. As I sucked her left nipple, I took my fingers and lightly pinched the right. She moaned. "Yes, yes."

She started undoing my belt, but I stopped her. "No, no, no, not yet, you dirty girl," I said. I kissed her lips, and then I flipped her on her back on the couch. She gasped. I bent down and pulled her shorts off of her. The sight of her in just her underwear had my cock dripping. She was perfect. I noticed this last bit of clothing on her was also red.

"Red bra *and* red panties? Was some little devil planning on getting lucky later today?"

She smiled. "Well, I *thought* it would be at your place, but this is a pleasant surprise." I bent down and thread my fingers around the strings of her panties and pulled them down her silky-smooth legs, revealing her perfect pussy. She sat up and finished undoing my shorts. She pulled them and my boxers down in one go. My cock flung up like a rocket, ready to attack. Her eyes went wide. She grabbed my length, pulled it toward her mouth, and started sucking. This wasn't part of my plan, but it felt so good. She eagerly sucked me up and down my length for a minute before I pulled away.

I pushed her onto her back and knelt down in front of the couch. I grabbed the inside of both of her thighs and positioned her where her legs were bent up and facing me. I stuck my head in between her legs and kissed the area around her pussy.

"Oh, Jacob," she said, squirming on the couch. She threaded her fingers through my hair. Once I had teased her enough with a dozen kisses, I put my tongue at her entrance and licked upwards. She gasped. I continued moving my tongue up and down the entire length of her lips, and she moaned every time I reached the top.

After a few minutes, I changed direction and moved my tongue around in large clockwise motions. After a few complete circles, she moaned, "Oh, oh wow, oh, Jacob, yes. Just like that. Oh my God." I did as she commanded, reading her body to see how she wanted me to lick her.

When I felt she was almost ready to peak, I put my whole mouth around her lips and sucked hard. I sucked *all of her* into my mouth. She moaned louder than any time she had last night. I took my tongue and moved it back and forth along her clit as I continued to suck her. "Jacob, Jacob, yes, I'm coming, I'm coming," she said. I continued to flick her clit with my tongue but picked up speed. Within fifteen seconds, the sound of her orgasm filled up the club. Her legs quivered, and she pushed my head away to tell me she was too sensitive for me to continue. I kissed the insides of her legs, wanting to taste more of her.

I picked her legs up to lay her body along the couch, and I got on top of her. My hard cock rested on top of her pussy. I kissed her, but she was unable to do anything but grind into me.

"Jacob," she said.

"Yes?" I kissed her breasts and her neck. She grabbed my ass with both hands and pulled me into her.

"I want you inside me," she said. My heart stopped. I didn't think it would happen this quickly, but I wasn't going to object.

"Are you sure? We can wait as long as you want."

"Yes. I want you now," she said, biting her lip.

"Hang on," I said, fumbling in the pocket of my discarded shorts for a condom. She arched an eyebrow at me, and I grinned sheepishly. "Remember when I had you stop at the drug store this morning so I could get an energy drink?" She gasped "I wanted to be prepared."

My cock was rock hard, already about to explode as I looked down at this naked goddess in front of me.

I tore into the condom, and my heartbeat quickened. *This is it. You're about to have sex with the hottest girl you know. Don't fuck things up.*

I rolled the condom on. Abby was on her back and spread her legs. Her pussy was wet and ready for me. I climbed on top of her, and we both took a deep breath. I grabbed my cock and positioned myself at her opening. I guided myself into it. When I made contact with her entrance, she gasped. Slowly, I pushed my tip inside.

It didn't go in easily. She was really tight, despite the lube on the condom and how wet she was for me. When my whole tip finally slid in, her nails dug into me, and I could see a sign of pain on her face, so I stopped pushing.

"Are you okay? Do you need me to stop?" I asked. She shook her head.

"No, keep going, just keep being gentle. You're just really big." She laughed. That made me even *harder*, if that was possible. I continued to slowly push myself in. Once I was halfway, I could feel her walls relaxing around my cock, and the last half of me slid in easily. We both moaned and made eye contact. I stayed there as her body got used to me and kissed her chest. I pulled myself out, and she breathed in. I pushed myself back in, and she moaned out.

She looked and felt like an angel. I kissed her, and our tongues sword-fought as I slowly pumped my cock into her. Her moans started out soft but got louder with each thrust as the tip of my cock pressed against her as far as it could go.

"You feel so fucking good, Abby. My cock has never felt this good," I said. I maintained my rhythm and fucked her slowly, but deep. She couldn't concentrate on kissing me anymore and instead filled the club with her moans. Her voice and her volume had me ready to explode.

"Abby, I'm going to come."

"Do it, I'm already coming," she moaned in between breaths. The animal in me woke up, and I fucked her harder and faster; and she *loved* it. I thrust my cock as deep as it could go, and I came. Fireworks exploded in my brain with each pump. Her moans turned into whimpers, and then I collapsed on her. We both held each other as all of my feelings poured into her. It was better than anything I had ever felt in the world. I moaned and grunted one last time into her ear, kissing and nibbling it.

Everything felt too good to move, and I stayed inside her for a minute. We didn't speak, but we were hugging, kissing, and our hands were moving all over. She eventually looked up at me. "That was amazing, Jacob."

"You're amazing," I said. We kissed, and then we finally separated. She had a pained look on her face as I pulled out. "Are you okay?"

She nodded. "Yes. I'm just a little sore with how big you are." I felt bad for bringing her any pain, but I couldn't help but smile. There wasn't much else a woman could tell a man to make him feel like he's a king than letting him know how big he is.

I threw the condom away, and we put our clothes back on. It pained me to see her tits disappear. "So, should we finish watching the movie?"

She laughed. "I'm good, unless you really want to."

Now it was my turn to laugh. "No, I'm good."

"I loved the popcorn, but I think I've worked up an appetite," she said.

"Me too. Want to go get something to eat?" She put her hands together and swung her hips from side to side.

"Sure!" she said with enthusiasm. "Do we need to get dressed in nice clothes?"

"No, not where I want to take you."

"Oh," she said. She looked a tad bit disappointed, but that would change once she took a bite.

We locked up the club, got in her car, and I directed her to the restaurant I had in mind. We rolled down the windows as we drove to enjoy the pleasant air. I looked over at her, and she looked so pretty with the way the wind whipped her hair back. I put my hand on the inside of her upper thigh, staking my claim on her. Letting her know that she was mine. We both smiled.

"Take a right here, and then it'll be in this strip up there. Just pull into the parking lot when you can," I said.

"Okay. So which restaurant did you have in mind?" I pointed to the place, and she pulled into a parking spot in front of it.

"Jacob Duncan. Are you taking me to a cheap burger joint for our first date?" she asked.

Huh, I guess this would be our first date. Unless one counted the movie and popcorn with some amazing sex sprinkled on top from earlier.

"Well, we don't have—"

"Because I love it." She put her hand on my leg, and the

thought of her moving it a few inches over to my cock had me getting hard pretty quickly. "Oh my goodness," she said, noticing my shorts rising. "Down, doggy!"

"What can I say? He seems to like you," I said. We smiled and kissed and headed into the restaurant. Though, calling it a restaurant was a stretch. It was just a long counter with barstools. No tables. The only food on the menu was breakfast and burgers. The inside had always looked pretty questionable, but the food was amazing, and they cooked everything right in front of you.

I ordered a burger with caramelized onions, cheddar, and barbecue sauce. Abby ordered a burger with blue cheese, caramelized onions, and sautéed mushrooms. We watched the cook prepare our burgers, then the server put our plates in front of us.

"Here it goes," she said. It was amazing how she could be so cute even eating a burger. She took a bite, and you would have thought I was eating her out again with how much she moaned. "Wow," she said with a full mouth. "This is orgasmic."

"I know." I smiled and took a bite of mine. Perfectly cooked, as always. We didn't talk much while we ate, but we didn't need to. Abby was the woman I wanted to eat burgers with for the rest of my life.

Chapter 15

Abby

It had been a few weeks since I lost my virginity to Jacob, and they had been some of the best weeks of my life. It hadn't been easy to find alone time behind everyone's backs, but when we did, it was magical. Our bodies lost themselves in passion, and we'd been getting *very* efficient at stripping each other down quickly.

I knew I was late to the game with having sex, but I was so glad it happened that way. Jacob was exactly the kind of guy I had been saving myself for. With each day that went by with him, I believed more and more that he would be the one and only guy to have me. Which was exactly how I wanted it. I didn't judge other girls for wanting more than one partner. But this felt right for me.

I still hadn't broken it to him that he was my first...It was silly to keep it from him, but what if he thought I was immature. I planned on telling him, eventually. For now, we were having so much fun, and no big revelation like that needed to mess anything up.

The day was winding to an end at the club. Jacob was

cleaning up around the pool, and I felt tingles in my center when I saw him. I constantly craved him. I loved his sensual touch and the way he respected my body. He cared about pleasing me instead of just making sure *he* got off.

But I equally appreciated the times he was rough and fucked me like an animal.

He must have had been sensing that I was staring at him. He turned around and waved. I wiggled my fingers at him. *Damn, he's fine.* I wished he would come over here, rip off my bathing suit, and put his head between my legs. *The things he can do with his tongue...*

As if my fantasy was playing out, he walked over to me.

"Hey, you," he said.

"Hi there."

"I have an idea."

"Oh, yeah?" *Does your idea have anything to do with us getting naked? Because I'm in.*

"Instead of driving home today, what if we walked? It's so beautiful of a day. We could walk through the park. Maybe stroll past the spot we had our first kiss," he said.

A fire erupted in my belly at the romance of it. But I was hesitant. "That's a bit of a far walk, don't you think?" His dad was out of town again, and I wanted to get back to his house fast so we could undress each other before I had to be back at my house for dinner.

He shrugged. "It'll probably take an hour instead of five minutes to get back to my place. But I think it'll be worth it."

"So we would leave my car here? What will we do in the morning?"

He smiled. "Well, my dad left his BMW, so maybe I could pick *you* up for once. You could tell your parents Jessica picked you up from work and you're spending the night." The fire in me got hotter.

"Sure. That sounds like fun," I said.

We finished cleaning and locking up the club and headed out toward the park. The country club was situated at the edge of a development surrounded by a golf course, which was in turn surrounded by beautiful homes. To the west of us was the park, which was really just a big naturally-wooded area with some walk paths through it.

It took us about fifteen minutes to walk through the golf course before we reached the tree line. We both breathed in the smell of the pines surrounding us and stepped inside. The farther we walked into the park, the darker it got under the trees' shade. For such a beautiful day, there weren't that many people walking around. Jacob put his arm around me, and I felt safe and warm. I snuggled into him, and we slowed our pace, enjoying the moment. There weren't many moments where we could be this close out in public.

We eventually saw the pond in the center of the park. "We must be close to our special spot," he said. The excitement in his voice got me excited, too. What a magical moment that had been. Kissing each other on a dare like we were teenagers.

We looked around, trying to get our bearings. We walked away from the path into the trees but kept the pond in view.

After a while, we saw the area where we had run from the ducks, which helped us remember where we had set up our picnic. Jacob led me by the hand to the clearing.

"I'm pretty sure we were sitting right here," he said. He plopped down and pulled me down with him. It took me by surprise as his weight brought me to the ground like a meteor. My butt hit the earth, and I fell to the side laughing. When we were sitting up again, he looked into my eyes, and I got lost in his. He stretched his hand out over the ground beneath us and twisted it quickly.

"What are you doing, goofball?" I asked. His head was going in circles, looking at the spot his hand had been.

"Oh, I'm just playing spin the bottle. I'm hoping it lands on this hottie next to me."

I felt the warmth in my cheeks spread downward to my center. *The things this boy does to me.* His face finally slowed down and stopped in my direction. He looked up at me and said, "Well why don't you look at that? Hit the target on my first try." I couldn't help but smile at how cheesy he was being. I loved it. He leaned forward and planted a soft kiss on my lips. He started to pull away, but I grabbed the back of his neck and kept it in place. He stuck his tongue in my mouth, and we made out like it was the first time.

The longer I kissed him, the more certain I felt that he was the one. He was the one and only to ever be inside me, and I wanted him to be both the first and the last. I wanted him to be my husband and the father of my children. My insides tingled at the thought.

We stopped kissing and put our foreheads against each other, our fingers laced together. "We should probably keep moving," he said. I nodded, unable to say aloud that I wanted to stay here all night; that I wanted to have him and couldn't wait. But I said nothing.

We stood up and started walking out of our private clearing, our hands clasped tight. I let go of his hand and leaned my back against a tree. He turned to face me.

"What are you doing?" he asked.

"Kiss me more." He smiled and came in, squeezing my hips, and our lips crashed against each other. We separated, and he looked down at me.

"Abby, there's something I've got to tell you." *No, don't ruin this moment, dummy. Keep whatever you have to say to yourself.*

"And I hope it doesn't scare you away." I put my hands on his butt and smiled at him.

"There isn't much that will scare me away from you, Jacob. Or this butt." I gave it a squeeze and he laughed. "All you have to do is stay away from other girls. What is it?"

He looked down at the ground. *Fuck.* Was he going to ruin our romantic outing—or worse, the relationship we had been building?

"I've lived most of my life trying not to get hurt. I hadn't really ever gotten close to people, because I always expected them to be shitty. I had accepted that I would never get close to anyone. Ever. But you, you changed all of that. When I wake up, I want to see your face, and when I get in bed, I fall asleep thinking of you. You're the best thing that's ever happened to me and I...It seems stupid, and way too quick, but with you it's different because we've known each other for so long. I feel like it makes it easier."

He paused, and my mind was racing, thinking of too many things to figure out what he was about to say.

"Abby, I love you. I'm in love with you."

He looked at me, trying to judge whether I thought he was sweet or crazy.

It was the former.

I gave him a deep kiss. "I love you, too, Jacob." He grabbed my face and kissed me back, and we forgot we weren't alone in his house.

Passion and desire filled the trees around us like birds in spring. He leaned his hips into me, and I could feel him hard against my center. I slid my hand down his shorts and under his boxers, wrapping my fingers around him. He grunted with pleasure. He reached his hands down my ass under my panties and found my slit. It was wet, just for him, and he started rubbing me. I got lost in his touch and gasped in his neck as he stroked me over and over again. "I want you," I said.

I pushed him off of me and made my lower half bare in one fell swoop. He dropped his shorts to his ankles, his cock shooting straight up. He started to unwrap a condom and looked around to make sure there were no people who could see us.

Suddenly, I had a crazy thought. "That first night, you said you were safe, right" I said, looking down at him. He nodded in confirmation. "Then no condom. No barrier. I want to feel the *real* you." The words came out on their own, but I didn't disagree with it or regret it. Jacob was *the one*. I knew what I was getting myself into.

He had the look of a wild animal in his eyes, ready to *take* his mate. I bent down and drew him into my mouth, running my tongue over his tip. He moaned and put his hands behind my head. I went down as far as I could, but it was too big to go all the way. I stood back up, and he picked me up by the underside of my thighs, leaning my back against the tree. I was wet and ready for him, and when his tip hit its mark, it slid right in. He didn't stop until he was all the way to the hilt. I gasped, feeling his large tip brush against my G-spot. *Holy crap.* It all felt *so* much better than with a condom. I could feel the grooves, and the bumps, and the ridge of his head. It was amazing how much better it felt than just a smooth silicon surface. *I don't think I ever want to have sex with a condom again.*

He thrust into me, hard, and I couldn't stifle my loud moan.

"Shh, the whole park is going to know," he teased.

"I...can't," I tried to say, but he was going so deep and so hard that I could barely think. I kept moaning loud enough for the ducks at the pond to hear. I felt the bark of the tree against my lower back with every thrust, but the slight pain only made my orgasm more intense. I squeezed him with my thighs as I came, moaning into his ear.

"Abby, I'm going to come."

"Don't pull out. Come inside me, Jacob," I said, only half believing that I was saying it.

He groaned and fucked me harder, making me moan with each thrust.

"Yes, yes, give it to me," I told him. He thrust his dick as far as it could go inside me and quivered as he exploded. His fingers dug into my thighs, and I dug mine into his back. He softly thrust into me a few more times until it was all out of him. We stayed like that for a few moments, unable to move from the ecstasy of it all.

"I love you," I told him.

He kissed me. "I love you too, Abby. More than anything." We kissed and hugged and breathed as one and I could swear that no one else in the history of histories had ever felt as good as I felt at that moment. We were inseparable.

Kind of literally with him still inside me...

All good things must come to an end, though. He slid himself out and set me down.

We put our clothes back on and walked out of the clearing, hand in hand. When we stepped onto the sidewalk, I tried to pull my hand away out of habit of hiding our relationship from everyone. But he squeezed harder and didn't let go.

I felt warm and fuzzy, still feeling him inside me, and I was ready for round two.

I'm all his, and he's mine.

Chapter 16

Jacob

Fred's was a dive bar in town that served multiple purposes: having a guys' night and trying to pick up girls. Kyle was intent on doing both. He—rightly—thought that I wasn't spending much time with him this summer, and he also wanted to see if there was a girl who could help him get over Melanie.

Jay, Kyle, and I walked in, and it looked like we were only going to accomplish one of his goals. The place was practically empty except for the old-timers sitting at the bar. The pool table in the back corner called our name. After few rounds of pool, and a few rounds of beer, we did what every group of guys does. We talked about girls.

"So there I was, in the restaurant parking lot, fucking the waitress who served our table that night, seconds away from finishing, when some guy came up to the car and smashed my window in," Jay said. He liked to talk with his hands, waving them about in order to keep our attention.

"Holy shit," Kyle said.

"Yeah, you're telling me. So he starts screaming at us through the broken window. Apparently he's the manager of the place, *and* her ex-boyfriend."

"Oh fuck," I said.

Jay nodded. "Oh fuck, indeed. So here he is, yelling at her that she's a whore and whatnot. And here I was, pissed that he broke my window. So I just kept fucking her while he screamed and finished what I started. She didn't seem to mind."

"Jesus, dude. You are fucking nuts," Kyle said.

Jay shrugged. "Yeah, but that's nothing new. I tell you what, though, I think I've gone through most of the chicks in this town."

"Maybe you should move on to the next town, partner," I joked.

"I don't know. There's still some hotties left. Like your sister's friend Jessica."

"Hey, back off. If any of us is going to get with Jessica, it's going to be me," Kyle said, taking a big swig of beer. "But I know that would make things weird with Abby if it ever happened, so I've refrained from ever trying. I've definitely thought about it, though." Kyle squatted down at the pool table to see if there was a good shot he could make.

"Speaking of Abby, I don't mean to be weird, but I was at the pool club the other day and got to see her," Jay said. He wiggled his eyebrows up and down. "Your little sister's all grown up, Kyle." My body tensed. I wanted to give him a hard push in his chest. She was *mine*. I was becoming territorial.

"Yes, that is weird as fuck, Jay. Fuck off," Kyle said.

Jay put his hands in the air. "Hey, man, no disrespect intended. I was just stating the obvious. I think she is stunning, don't you think, Jacob?"

Of course I agreed. I thought she was the most beautiful girl in the world. I gritted my teeth, ready to tell him I didn't want to hear him say another word about her. Luckily, Kyle cut me off.

"Can it about my sister, man. Not something I want either of you to talk or think about." But Jay didn't know when to shut up.

"Well, the reason I bring it up is, I was wondering if you would be okay with me asking her out on a date. Proper. She's the kind of girl I could see myself settling down with." It was a good thing the bar was dimly lit because my face felt as a red as a boiled lobster. As Jay said this, Kyle took his shot, and the pool stick bounced off the cue ball. He stood up and looked at Jay like he was the dumbest person in the room, which very well may have been accurate.

"Jay, if you try to date my sister, then you and I are both going to lose a friend. I don't want to know that one of my buddies is fucking my sister. Especially one who has already fucked half the town. Jesus Christ, what's wrong with you?"

Jay held his hands up again. "All right, all right, I was just asking. Thought it would be best to get your blessing first before I tried." *Shit*, I thought. Maybe Jay was both smarter *and* a better friend than I was. "I'll go get us the next round as a peace offering," he said.

Kyle shook his head as Jay walked to the bar. "Can you believe him? Trying to date Abby? There are a million girls out there, but he wants to date my sister? We would never be able to have any guy talk again." I felt sweat trickle down my back.

"Yeah, that's messed up," I said. I felt ashamed of myself. A *coward*. How were Abby and I going to work out long-term? Kyle was my best friend in the world, but I was head over heels for her. If I had to choose, who would I pick? Hopefully I never had to pick, because this last month had given me my answer.

"Yo, while Jay is out of earshot, since I don't want to offer him the same thing, why don't you come work with me? We could be partners and flip houses twice as fast and make a bunch of money. I don't understand why the fuck you're working as a pool boy. I could use the help with that property I bought, and you would definitely make more money than whatever my dad is paying you. I just don't understand your logic."

The logic? The logic is that I like seeing your sister in a bathing suit and spending all my time with her, I thought. I scratched my head. "I told you before. I'm not too keen on manual labor. Plus, I don't know if working together would be good for our friendship. Some people say to keep your personal lives and professional lives separate, right?" *But fucking his sister will work out just fine for your friendship*, the voice in the back of my mind whispered in torment.

Kyle shrugged. "Whatever. I guess that makes sense. But you gotta find something better than a pool job that is meant for someone in high school. Just know that the offer's always on the table, if you ever change your mind."

I wanted to tell Kyle that I didn't need money, but it was a secret I kept so close to my chest that I couldn't even tell my best friend.

* * *

"You what?" she asked me right as I was taking a bite of fried chicken.

"You heard me. I hate Brussels sprouts. They're disgusting."

Abby shook her head. "You foolish, foolish man. You're missing out. Have you ever had them roasted in the oven until they're nice and crispy?"

"Nope, and I never will. Disgusting, I tell you. Like eating baby cabbages that have been marinating in a Tupperware of farts." She cracked up at the last part. God, I loved seeing her laugh.

"That'll change. I'll change you," she said with a wink. She was getting better at winking now that she was trying it all the time with me. Every time she did it, I just wanted to grab her face and kiss it.

"Sorry, dear, but there are some things you'll just never change about me. Don't worry, though. That just means more stinky mini fart cabbages for you."

I wasn't particularly a skilled cook, but I wanted to have her over for dinner. So, earlier, we got some great fried chicken from Willie Mae's, a popular restaurant in town, and I ordered all the sides. Mashed potatoes, honey biscuits, coleslaw, and French fries.

We talked about other foods we liked or disliked until we finished eating our dinner. Then we moved to the couch to watch a show, but I just wanted to keep talking to her.

"So," I said.

"So." She turned to me. Her hair whipped around, and she had the cutest smile on her face.

"So, how is the job hunt going? Which of your dream schools have you applied to?" She rolled her eyes.

"I told you, I'm not even going to try. My dream schools, like Franklin Middle, are dreams for a reason. They only accept the best teachers."

"Exactly. I'm looking at one of them right now," I told her.

She kissed me. "Jacob, I love you, and I love how supportive you are, but how can I be one of the best teachers if I don't have any experience teaching?"

"I just know you'll be great at it." It killed me to think she didn't believe it herself. "Do you have your computer in your car?"

"Yes..." She raised her eyebrow at me.

"Go get it. You're going to apply to every school on your wish list. Tonight."

"Jacob..."

"I'm serious. Where are your keys?"

She laughed. "In my purse by the kitchen table." I headed for the kitchen, causing her to turn around on the couch. "Jacob, come back and sit with me. Stop being silly."

"Nope. Not until you reach for the stars like you should," I told her. I grabbed her keys and walked out the door. She shouted something at me as I walked out, but it was inaudible as the door shut behind me.

She shouldn't settle for anything less than what she's really capable of. I wasn't going to let her waste her summer when she should have been hustling some principals.

I grabbed her computer and walked inside. I was greeted with Abby's bare shoulders, and it made my blood hot with lust. She heard me and turned around. She had gotten naked while I was away. Her nipples were hard and calling to me.

"What are you doing?" I asked.

"I want you." She motioned me to join her on the couch. I walked toward her and placed my hand on her cheek.

"You're so beautiful." My thumb caressed her skin. "But this won't work. We've got jobs to apply to." I picked her shirt off the ground and tossed it in her face. She feigned shock.

"You're *denying* me?"

"Somehow, yes. I guess it just means I care more about your future than my present."

She put her shirt back on. "Well, when you put it that way..."

Over the next hour and a half, we visited the websites of five schools she would love to teach at and applied to each of them. When we started, I told her to choose them as if she had been teaching for twenty years, especially since most of them asked for at least five. It was so much fun watching her get excited, picking out which ones were her top choices. It seemed like it was the first time she really saw herself teaching at a place of her choice instead of whichever one would hire a new grad.

I closed the laptop. "I think five is enough to apply to in one night."

She hugged and snuggled me. "Thank you," she said, breathing me in and letting out a loud exhale. "I'm so happy I have someone who believes in me when I don't believe in myself." I kissed her because the moment was perfect. She grabbed my cock, but I moved her hand away gently. I needed to focus. Something had been on my mind the last week, and for some reason it was only coming up now.

"What's wrong?" she asked.

The words had a hard time coming out. It was one of those questions you wanted to know the answer to, but then again, you might not. I sighed. "Abby, I care about you so much. I want to make sure I'm doing everything I can to make you happy. One of the things that I think the most about is...how I've been...performing."

She squinted her eyes like she didn't understand what I was saying. So I looked downward.

"Oh, Jacob—"

"I just want to be better than any guy you've been with, so I want you to tell me what I'm doing wrong, and what I'm doing right. It won't hurt my feelings. I want to be the best you've ever had."

She smiled and squeezed my hand. "Jacob, I can say

without a doubt that you are the best I've ever had, and you're the worst I've ever had."

I never knew my heart could leap as high as the Empire State building and then jump to its death within five seconds.

"Uhhh," I said.

"Because you're the *only* one I've ever had. I've...never had sex before you. I've never even touched a penis before yours."

Excuse me?

She looked down at our hands, not meeting my eyes. "I haven't told you yet, because I didn't want you to think I'm some little innocent thing and get scared off. I know some guys like taking a girl's virginity, and others are terrified about the girl getting too attached. I didn't know how you would react."

My pulse was in my throat. *Abby is a virgin? Was a virgin? I* took Abby Barber's *virginity? The first thing I thought was Great. Now Kyle is really going to kill me.* But that only lasted a second when I realized that...she was *really* mine. She had *only* been mine. She had never been anyone else's. The thought that she had been so naturally intimate and sexy with me, without having any prior experience, set my heart ablaze.

Our minds connected, and we both lunged for each other's clothes. Down to just our underwear, she climbed on top of me. My hands removed her sports bra like it was a threat to her well-being. Her nipple was inside my mouth before I knew it was there. She squeezed me with her arms and ground into me, making my cock hard with lightning speed. I pulled my boxers down and tugged her panties aside. Her eyes were *begging* for me.

She lifted her body to put my tip at her entrance, and she slid all the way down. A moan escaped both of our lips at the same time. Abby took control and rode me all the way up and down. She found her rhythm and fucked me hard, like it was the last night we would ever make love. Every time she came all the way down, she moaned in a higher and higher pitch.

"Yes, Jacob, yes."

Words couldn't describe how amazing I felt right now. "Fuck me, Abby." She fucked me harder and faster, and I could tell she would reach her climax soon.

"I'm about to come," I said.

"Come in me," she whispered in my ear. I slapped her ass and squeezed it hard. She continued to pound onto me, and I grunted, releasing into her. She kept fucking me, milking me dry. My eyes rolled into the back of my head—I had never felt anything so good.

"I'm coming, I'm coming," she said. She increased speed and then filled the house with her scream as she orgasmed. She collapsed into me, and I held her like she was the dearest thing in my life.

Because she was.

I kissed her throat and moved up until our lips connected with a sweet, tender kiss. She relaxed down into me again, exhausted. My cock was still inside her, and I was happy to keep it there as long as she wanted.

"So," she said.

I smiled. "So."

"First, that was amazing, and I love you."

"Agreed," I said while giving her butt cheek a good, hard squeeze.

"Second, I just realized you keep getting on me to apply to my dream schools, but what about you? What does your future look like? Surely you won't be a pool boy your whole life."

"Don't worry about me. I've got everything figured out," I lied.

"Oh really? So, what do you have figured out?"

"You'll see one day," I lied again.

She rolled her eyes. "Well, if you're going to get on me about my future, I'm going to get on you about yours. It's my job as your girlfriend."

I smiled and squeezed both of her butt cheeks this time. "I love hearing you call yourself my girlfriend."

She smiled. "And I love calling you my boyfriend." We squeezed each other tight, our love for one another transferring throughout the whole of our naked bodies as I held her close, caressing her back and softly kissing her shoulder.

My thoughts went back to what she'd asked. What *was* I going to do with my life? I wasn't desperate for money. I had plenty. But I did need a sense of direction. I needed something to take up my life other than her. I hadn't really been thinking about it, because I had been content with being a pool boy that gets to work with the love of his life.

But what would happen when she became a teacher? There wouldn't be any reason for me to stay. It would quickly turn into a boring, menial job when I didn't have her in a bathing suit to look at.

Did I want to be a lawyer, like my father?

Hell no.

Did I want to go to trade school and become a plumber or an electrician?

Nope.

I couldn't help but think of my mother. When I was growing up, she'd always told me, "Jake, you can be anything you want to be when you grow up. You're so talented. Follow your passion."

I loved her for saying that, but was that the best advice to give a kid? It was important to support your child, but by telling them they could do anything, you weren't helping them in their path to choose anything specific. I felt like because of that advice, I had become a jack of all trades, but a master of none. I had gone through life thinking I would surely find a job I was passionate about sooner or later. But I never had.

What if I never would? Day trading stocks was great for money, but it was passionless. It didn't excite me. I would have to make a conscious effort to figure out what excited me from now on and see if I could make a career out of it.

Chapter 17

Abby

Y̲ou know what's lovely? When you wake up to your man kissing you between your legs until you scream.

Know what's even sexier? Watching him cook you scrambled eggs in nothing but an apron.

Yum.

Um, chef? Yeah, I'll take a side of them butt cheeks while you're at it.

I'd told him like three weeks ago that I loved scrambled eggs with ham, onions, and peppers, and this amazing man had gone to the grocery store sometime this week and bought all the ingredients to cook for me. When I walked into the kitchen with the coffee already brewed and the butter at room temperature just waiting to be spread on some toast, I thought for the millionth time that I'd found the right guy.

The past few weeks had been amazing. We hadn't had to worry too much about getting caught by anyone, because his dad had been traveling for work a lot. Something about corporate depositions, Jacob had told me. Apparently, we were going to have to figure something out soon, though, because he was coming home and wouldn't need to travel for a while. But I also needed to be careful about how often I was "spending the night at Jessica's" before my mom got suspicious. Sometimes I wondered if she knew where I was really going. I mean, she was my *mom*, after all. They basically always knew when you lied to them. But enough of worrying. I needed to learn how to live more in the present and enjoy all the great things I had going for me.

My insides tingled at the thought of making love as much as we could while we had the house to ourselves. We were so limited on when and where it could happen. Doing it at work was risky, but hot. My house was an obvious no. Where else could we go? We probably used up all of our luck doing it in the park. Were we going to have to start getting a motel room? That just seemed weird and dirty...

The smell of onions and ham sautéing together brought me back to the present, and my eyes got a present of their own when I looked up to see his firm butt. The black apron covered his whole front, but behind him, there was only the string tied in a bow to keep it all together at the small of his back. I wasn't much more clothed, wearing just the shirt he'd worn yesterday. His scent on it was intoxicating.

Jacob lifted the pan and scraped the eggs onto two plates. At the perfect time, our toast popped up with a nice golden-brown color and he put them next to the eggs. He walked over and placed my food in front of me.

"Bon appetite," he said and kissed me on the cheek.

"Looks delicious, Chef Jacob."

My knife slid into the soft butter with ease, and I spread it on my toast. I finished it off with some strawberry preserves and took a bite.

"Mmm," I mumbled. I took a bite of the eggs. "Mmm, oh my God, those are good."

"Thanks. The key is to brown the ham, then add the onions and bell peppers and cook them until they are soft. You get a lot more flavor with a little patience. I've been watching YouTube videos so I could cook for you."

Some silence passed as we enjoyed our food. Thoughts of how amazing everything had been floated through my head. The way he respected me, held me, loved me. It felt too good to be true sometimes. Which led me to think: could it be?

I tried to imagine ways this could all come tumbling down. The teacher in me wanted to lesson plan for every scenario— even in life. I didn't think he had another girl he had been seeing. When would he have had time to? He was either at work, with me, or with Kyle. Well, he wasn't even with Kyle much nowadays, since I was stealing all of his time. Jacob had gotten a text from him that morning asking what he was up to. I wasn't sure if he'd even responded.

I guessed it was possible for him to find time to see someone else if I wasn't with him twenty-four-seven, but I didn't think he was that kind of guy, and I hadn't had any evidence to suggest it. This was just my destructive nature trying to find flaws in everything, believing that I didn't deserve anything good in my life.

One thing that bugged me was how secretive he could be. Like when it came to his future plans, he wasn't very...open. We had both graduated college. Shouldn't he have had things more figured out? I didn't care what he did, but I really wanted to call bullshit on him when he said he had a plan. No plan would be better than a plan he wouldn't tell me because what did that even mean? If I was the love of his life, why would he keep his future plans secret from me, unless he had no plan?

The only other explanation would be that I was *not* part of his plan. That we had no future. That he was going to move to a different city once summer ended. Or move to another country and I was just something for him to do to pass the time. I mean, it would make sense. Why else would a smart guy like Jacob choose to be a pool boy? Why else live with his asshole father instead of getting his own place? Was it possible he'd pretended to fall in love with a girl he had only been dating for a month so that she'd give up her virginity to him and he could claim his prize?

Was this really possible? Could that last month have meant nothing after all? Could all my daydreams about our future together be nothing but dreams? The vacations we were going to take, the house we were going to live in, the children we would have...My body shuddered in terror when I looked at him.

But I saw him smile at me, and it all melted away.

What the fuck are you thinking, Abby? Why was I trying to sabotage my own happiness? Why would I make things up like that?

It was like having a nightmare where someone you knew was really mean, or hurt you, and you wake up thinking it had happened in real life. That was what this felt like. What was wrong with me?

He saw the look on my face. "What's wrong?"

I looked into his piercing eyes, and all those negative thoughts were washed away. "Nothing. Just thinking of how perfect you are," I said. He grinned and took a big bite of toast.

"I fink yer perfet too," he said with a full mouth.

I giggled. But even though I felt like I could trust him with anything, my mind tried to go back to that negative space. *He was perfect now, but boys are boys. They cheat and think it's okay. He can't be trusted. Protect yourself. Don't let it happen to you again.*

Shut up, stupid! It was dumb of me to have these thoughts. I knew it deep down. But I couldn't keep the paranoia at bay. I had been hurt before. It couldn't hurt to ask him about it, right?

"Hey, can I ask you something stupid?"

He lifted his eyebrow. "I can't tell if you meant to put a comma after 'something,' or if you want to ask me something that's stupid," he said. But I knew he was messing with me. So I gave him what he deserved and rolled my eyes. He laughed. "What is it, dearest?"

I trembled with nerves. "I know this is dumb, but I just have to ask...Are we...exclusive? Like, have you been seeing any other girls while we've been together? I'm not suggesting you have, I just...wanted to make sure what we were?"

He was looking at me like I was an idiot. *Thank God.*

"Abby, are you crazy? You're the only girl in the world I want to look at or talk to. Trust me, there are absolutely no other girls. Never have been. Not in person, no texting. Nada. Zip. What would make you ask something so crazy?"

"I told you it was stupid! But sometimes I have random, silly thoughts."

"Mhm. What about you?"

"What about me?"

He raised his eyebrow. "Are there any guys I need to worry about?"

If only I were drinking orange juice, I would have sprayed it out through my nose. "You're funny, Jacob."

"You asked me. I can ask you."

"Jacob, no guys talk to me. Ever."

"It's because they're intimidated by your beauty."

I snorted. Again, where was the orange juice when I needed it? "Uh-huh. Then why do guys have no problem walking up to Jessica? Even *you* can't resist staring at her."

He tilted his head. "What?"

"Oh, come on," I said. "That night at the bowling alley. I

saw you looking down her shirt." The confusion cleared, and Jacob laughed.

"Abby, I looked away from *your ass*, and my eyes landed on her. She was the last thing on my mind that night or any night."

I stared at him. "Are you serious?"

"A hundred percent," he said. "I was struggling that whole night to hide my hard-on every time I looked at you. You were making me insane with that outfit and your perfume. Shit, your whole family was there! I didn't want to get caught staring at you. Jessica is a lot of guys' type, but *you* are mine. You're the only one I want. Part of me still thinks landing you was too good to be true."

I blushed hard, looking away. Searching for a safety net, I decided to answer his original question. "No, Jacob. You're the only one for me...at the moment."

His mouth dropped open in mock outrage. "At the moment? Someone is going to have to pay for that comment with some tickle torture." He got out of his chair. I took flight and ran out of the kitchen while he chased after me. I poorly chose to run to the front of the house, where the only other place to escape was out the front door. It would have been an option if I had *anything* else besides his shirt on. His hands surrounded me and found all of my vulnerable spots.

"Jacob, no!" I squealed and giggled as he tickled me. It was no use to resist, though I still tried. He eventually stopped and just held me. I felt so safe and relaxed wrapped up in his big arms.

Our bodies stiffened to stone at a loud knock coming from the front door. We stood still as if there was a T-Rex staring at us.

"Who is that?" I whispered.

"No idea. Just ignore it. Probably some salesman." The windows were opaque, so whoever it was couldn't see us well, but they would be able to see us if we walked away. We stood our ground.

More loud knocks resonated throughout the house.

"Is it your dad?"

Jacob shook his head. "No way. Why would he knock?"

Dumb question, Abby.

We ignored the visitor, but whoever it was hadn't left yet. Jacob's phone went off in his pocket. He carefully took it out.

Kyle: Hey man, I'm at your front door. Come let me in.

"Fuck," we both whispered in unison.

"What do we do?" I asked.

Jacob looked around. He pointed to the small guest bathroom a few feet away. "One second!" Jacob yelled back to Kyle. *What the fuck was he doing?*

He shuffled our bodies as one to the bathroom. He took off his apron, grabbed a towel and wrapped it around his waist, then nudged me inside. I closed the door and put my ear up against it, hoping to hear their conversation. Jacob opened the door.

"Look! He's alive! Not like I would know with how little I've seen or heard from you recently," Kyle said.

"Sorry, man. I've been busy."

"And he's...answering the door in a towel?"

"I was, uh, just about to hop in the shower."

"Gotcha." Then silence for a few seconds. Kyle started again. "So, uh, are you gonna let me in?"

"No."

"No?"

"Yes."

"Yes I can come in?"

"No."

I couldn't see anything, but I imagined Kyle was scratching his head in confusion.

"So, that's it? Do I at least get an explanation why we can't hang out? I was hoping you and I would be chilling this summer, but ever since I got dumped, it's like you've gotten even more distant. Is there something I should know about? Did I do something wrong?"

Kyle didn't sound happy.

"No, of course not," Jacob said.

"Then why does it feel like you don't want to hang out with me anymore?"

Silence again. *Come on, Jacob! Tell him something. You're creative enough to make up some excuse. Say you've been working, or depressed, or I don't know, anything!*

"You know what, man? Fine. Don't tell me what you've been up to. Just continue to be a giant pussy." The end of his sentence trailed off, making it sound like he was turning to walk back to his car.

"Kyle! I'm seeing someone!" Jacob shouted.

"What?" Kyle said.

"*What?*" I whispered. Are we doing this *now?* Was he going to tell Kyle about us without talking to me about it first? *Without making sure we both put some clothes on?*

"You're seeing someone?" Kyle repeated. He sounded close to the door again.

"Yes. She's actually hiding inside right now, which is why I can't let you in," Jacob said in a lowered voice.

"Why would she be hiding from me? Do I know her?"

Talk about my heart pumping like it's running a four-hundred-meter race. *Why yes, you have known her a while... since she was born.*

"She's hiding because if I'm dressed in just a towel, do you think she has any clothes on either?"

"Well, holy shit. You dog! Why didn't you tell me? Is this why you've been MIA the last few weeks?"

"Yeah...I don't know. It's kind of fun keeping things secret. And you just got dumped, so I didn't know how you'd react."

"How I'd react? Dude! I'm fucking ecstatic for you!"

"Thanks, man."

Kyle lowered his voice. "So, how hot is she?"

Barf.

"Uh, she's pretty hot. But I don't know if you would think so."

This is weird.

"Well, you'll have to show me a picture of her later."

Please don't.

"We'll see."

"Man, I'm so glad you're avoiding me for sex and not because you were upset with me. Well, I'll leave you guys to it. Give it to her good, bro!"

And barf again.

"Later, man," Jacob said. The door shut, and I opened mine. Jacob and I just looked at each other, communicating through brain waves alone. I dashed to the kitchen pantry.

Jacob followed. I reached for a box of chocolate chip cookies and started eating. He laughed.

"How can you eat cookies at a time like this?"

I spun my head to look straight at him. "Jacob, that was a really stressful moment. This is the perfect time to eat cookies." He smiled and shook his head. "So, are you going to give it to me good?" I asked sarcastically while making a disgusted face.

He seductively walked over to me, his lips an inch from mine. He dropped his towel, and I started thinking about him pounding me against the pantry shelves. His hand was slowly moving toward my chest, and I caught my breath.

"Eh, I think we need to focus on what's really important. Cookies," he said. He reached into the box I was holding and popped one into his mouth.

Chapter 18

Jacob

That whole morning, the only thing I could think about was how I was the one to take Abby's virginity. I would be head-over-heels for her regardless, but finding out that I was the first one inside her just felt like an enormous source of pride. And if it was under my control at all, I hoped I could stay her one-and-only for the rest of our lives.

I was brought back to reality after a small kick from Matthew splashed water on my face. He swam right by me and headed for the wall.

"Good job, dude!" I said to Matthew as he finished his first lap of swimming by himself. He lifted his tiny arms to the edge and clung to the red brick.

"Wow! I can't believe it!" Matthew exclaimed. Seeing a kid be so excited was one of the best feelings in the world. Especially when it came to this little guy with his absent father. *I feel you, my dude.* Who knew if he had any real friends, either? I had never seen one come to join him at the pool.

I looked up at Abby sitting in her lifeguard chair, and she was beaming. With the sun shining bright, I first thought she was beaming at Matthew for his successful lap, but as my gaze stayed trapped by her beautiful face, I saw she was looking at me.

When I thought about my future, and if I wanted kids, the only thing that stayed in my mind was the idea of having them with Abby. No one else. I didn't want to have them for at least a couple of years after we got married, but when I thought about the next ten years of my life, it definitely involved both me and Abby teaching our children how to swim in our own pool. Then, once the kids were away, we could go skinny dipping at night and play with each other under the water.

Okay. Making a mental note that our future mansion needs a heated swimming pool and a hot tub. I looked back at Abby and smiled. I couldn't wait to live with her one day.

Abby broke our shared gaze and turned her vision to someone behind me. I saw her mouth, *oh my God.* I turned around to look at some guy smiling as he walked straight for her. He looked very familiar, and unfortunately, he was not ugly. I didn't know what to do. I felt the need to go protect her from another guy trespassing on my claim. Or should I have just let her be?

As he got closer to her, she started playing with her hair. *What the fuck! Don't girls only do that when they're nervous or being flirtatious? Why would she be either?*

This *trespasser* got directly under her and leaned on the ladder of her chair. A little too close for my taste. She was still playing with her hair, and she was smiling as they talked. I had seen other guys try to hit on her, but never anyone who could ever have a chance with her. None of them made her look like she did at that moment.

"Mr. Jacob! Wanna see me swim another lap?" Matthew asked. I regretfully couldn't keep watching over Abby and this stranger with Matthew calling. If the lifeguard was distracted by some asshole, who was going to save Matthew if he started to drown?

"Okay, buddy, this time I'm going to time you. On your mark, get set, go!" I said, as he pushed against the side of the pool.

After a couple of laps, Matthew's mom called him away. As Matthew exited the pool, I saw Abby's admirer writing on a piece of paper, which he then handed over to her before walking for the exit. We made eye contact as he passed me, still standing in the pool. He gave me a smirk and a nod, like he knew she was my girl, but he was going to take her anyway. *God, why does he look so familiar?* I stared him down with cold eyes until he passed me. When I saw him walk through the doors, I headed over to Abby.

"Hey, you," she said. *Damn, she's cute, but she's not going to get away with flirting with another man that easily.*

"So, who was that?" I asked. The accusation in my tone was obvious. She rolled her eyes and smiled.

"No one for you to worry about."

"Well, actually, I think I do need to worry just a little. The only times I've seen you act so flirtatious the last few weeks were when you were talking with me."

"Oh my God. I was not flirting."

I mimicked playing with my imaginary long hair and laughing. She snorted and shook her head. "Well, he obviously was flirting with you. How do you know him?"

She sighed. "That was Tony Catalano. From school? Don't you remember? He just came by to visit is all."

Holy fuck. Tony Catalano. He was every girl's crush in high school. I *knew* I had recognized him.

"How did he know you were here?" I didn't want to sound like I was interrogating her, but I felt like I had a right to find out some info about a guy who was trying to get *my* girl.

"Babe, it's not a secret my dad owns this place. I used to work here in high school, and we've both seen people we know over the last month. Either he heard from one of them, or Jessica messaged him where I was...Actually, yes, I'm pretty sure we can just blame this on Jessica."

I looked at her hands and saw she was still clutching onto the piece of paper he gave her and felt the rage pushing blood to my reddening face. "So, are you gonna call him?" I nodded toward her closed hand.

She looked down at it and laughed. "Jacob, no, of course I'm not going to call him." She crumpled up the slip of paper and threw it in the pool. "Now make sure you skim that up, pool boy," she said with a smile on her face. I knew she was trying to lighten the mood, but it wasn't working.

"I'm just still trying to figure out why you blushed and played with your hair when he started talking to you."

"Jacob! Enough! I wasn't *flirting*. I was flustered because Jessica sent him a message pretending to be me, and it was uncomfortable to see him here, so I was fidgeting. You're reading too much into this. You are the only one I want. You. And if you don't believe me, then you need to grow the fuck up and trust me a little bit."

"Jacob!" Pat called out. "Can you come in and help me with the drink machine?"

"Sure thing!" I called. I looked back at Abby, who smiled and gave me the slightest air kiss so as not to raise suspicion. I smiled back, but it felt forced. Fake. I hated seeing her smile and laugh with a guy like that.

I walked toward the club door like a dog with its tail between its legs.

Chapter 19

Abby

This morning, I made it my goal to have all my ducks in a row.

Huh, how cool would it be to have some baby ducks as pets? Following me everywhere, swimming in the pool with me, at my feet and ready to eat my pizza crust. Mmm, pizza.

Focus, Abby!

Right. Anyway. I had my first interview with a school that morning. It wasn't one of my dream schools, but a girl takes what she can get. It was in the town next to us, which I had never really driven through before, as I was pretty sure my mom had always avoided it. But I had to start somewhere, and they had a job opening online.

Step one was complete: I arrived early for my interview. I may have actually arrived too early...The receptionist showed me the chair I was sitting on about forty-five minutes ago, and I still had fifteen minutes until the meeting was scheduled. I was getting kind of hungry, and I had to pee. But I didn't want to get up and have the principal see an empty chair if she came to get me a few minutes early.

I didn't think there was any more prepping to do. I'd printed three copies of my resume and cover letter, both of which I had basically memorized. I'd written down a bunch of interview questions and gone over them a hundred times, like I was studying for an exam. If I kept thinking about this interview, I was going to get the nervous sweats and be gross.

So, what could be a fun distraction while I waited?

Jacob. So sexy. So sweet. Sometimes when I thought of us being together, I worried it was all going to come crashing down any second. Surely something was wrong, or he was faking it, right? Why did I deserve such a perfect guy who turned girls' heads any time we went out in public? But I needed to be nicer to myself. I *did* deserve him.

I laughed inwardly. It had been kind of cute how jealous he'd gotten the other day when Tony came to visit me. Which would have had me over the moon a few months ago, but now, I couldn't have cared less. I was beyond happy with Jacob, and there was nothing Tony could have said that would have made me want him in any way.

I used to daydream about maybe becoming Mrs. Catalano one day. Now, he could have handed me a million dollars and a diamond ring, and I wouldn't even hesitate to turn him down and run into my Jacob's arms. When I dreamed of my future these days, I always pictured myself walking toward Jacob on that altar. I didn't care if he was a pool boy for the next ten years. He was my soulmate, and I was perfectly content.

Still, him getting jealous had been pretty cute. I mean, I'd probably get jealous too if a hot girl came walking up to him and gave him her number.

More like I'd slap a bitch. Okay, not really because I'm not that confrontational.

But I'd be thinking it.

I hoped Jacob knew he had nothing to worry about. He had my heart, and his number was the only one I needed.

The principal's office door opened. "Abby? I'm ready for you."

I stood up, brushed off my skirt, held my head high, and walked toward the door. I was ready to make good eye contact and give a firm handshake, but she was looking at her phone and turned back into her office without meeting my eyes...I followed behind her. She sat at her desk with her eyes still glued to her phone.

"Should I close this?" I asked as I gestured to the door. She looked up, and I finally got a hint of eye contact.

"Sure. It doesn't matter," she said. I closed the door because I figured that was how an interview was supposed to go. Before I sat down, I decided one of us had to introduce herself.

"Hi, Ms. Occhipinti. My name is Abby Barber. It's a pleasure to meet you." I held out my hand, never expecting it would hang in front of her for so long. She lowered her phone, and I saw she had been Facebook messaging.

She reached for my hand without even looking up, and I grabbed what felt like a dead sea slug. Limp. It was like shaking the hand of a cadaver.

"You, too," she said. I opened my folder with my printed resume and cover letters, handing her a copy of each.

"I know you have the digital version of these, but I thought I'd print them out for you as well."

She looked up at my papers and smirked. "No thanks, darlin'. There's no need. Our filing cabinets are too stuffed already." She reluctantly pushed her phone aside. "So, you want to work at Harding Middle, do you?"

Do I? I mean, it is not my number one choice, and judging by the interaction I've had with you, I want to stay ten miles from this school at all times. Plus, it's dirty as shit and looks like y'all use the hallway as a pigsty. But I need a job.

"Yes, Ms. Occhipinti. It's my dream to work at Harding Middle. The reasons being—"

"Hold up right there, honey," she said as she pointed a finger in the air. "No need to waste both our time with a big speech. If you want the job, it's yours."

Excuse me, what?

"Oh, I—are you not going to ask me any interview questions or ask me about my degree? Or—"

"Listen. I'm a busy woman. You seem like a smart-enough lady. We need teachers, and you need a job. We haven't received as many applicants as we need. So, if you want the job, it's yours. I could have Courtney up front get you started on the paperwork today. You can come back in about a month and start decorating your room. Does that sound good?"

My mind was racing. I was imagining talking with this woman for at least twenty minutes. My dad had told me that some interviews could last hours. I couldn't believe she was offering the job to me this quickly.

"Well?" Ms. Occhipinti said.

"Um, thank you so, so much for the offer. Is it all right if I go home and talk it over with my family?"

Ms. Occhipinti shrugged. "Sure. Take your time," she said as she picked her phone back up. She looked up at me like she was surprised I was still sitting there. "Have a good evening, kid. You can let yourself out."

"Thank you so much for your time," I said as I stood up. I didn't feel like shaking a raw meat patty hand again, so I went for a wave instead. I thought I heard her mumble, "Mhm" as I walked out the door.

I got in my car and checked my phone. I had a few texts from Jacob.

. . .

Jacob: Good luck, babe! You got this!

Jacob: Do you like cookie dough or mint chocolate more?

Jacob: Let me know how it went when you're done!

Jacob: Did she offer you an amazing teacher salary of $300 million because you're so amazing?!?!

I smiled as I read each of his messages. God, I felt like a lucky girl. I texted him back.

Me: I'll tell you in person in a bit.

As I drove to Jacob's house, I tried to come up with a decision on my own about whether or not I should accept the position. It was definitely not the ideal school to work in, but would any of my dream schools even want to hire someone with no experience? Weren't they "good" schools *because* they hired people who had at least *some* experience? More than zero? I just felt like I would be an impostor teaching at an advanced academy for my first year.

Pulling into Jacob's garage, I still hadn't come up with an answer. Thinking about my future was making me pretty anxious, but it all melted away when Jacob wrapped his arms around me as soon as I stepped out of the car. He followed up with a kiss on my forehead.

"Hey, you," he said.

"Hey," I sighed with exasperation. "Jacob, I just don't know—"

"Nope. Stop talking. Follow me," he said as he took my hand and pulled me inside.

We made our way to the kitchen and stopped at the island. He turned around, put his hands on my butt, and lifted me up and onto one of the stools. There were two spoons in front of me. Jacob walked to the freezer and turned around with two pints of ice cream. Cookie dough and mint chocolate chip.

"I figured you were busy and couldn't answer me, so I just got both. Which one do you want?"

He was such a sweetheart.

"Mint chocolate please," I said.

"Oh thank God, because I hate the stuff," he said.

"You what?" I couldn't believe anyone didn't like mint chocolate. I was pretty sure it was a sin.

"Yep. It's repulsive. Why would anyone put those two flavors together? It's an abomination."

"Jacob, if you don't like mint chocolate, I'm not sure this is going to work between us," I joked.

He shrugged and took a bite. "Fine by me. I wouldn't want our kids to inherit a taste for it," he said with a full mouth.

Our *what?*

I felt my face flush, and my belly felt warm at the thought of a little Jacob running around a tiny house because we didn't want to wait until we had money to have kids.

Jacob started coughing, and cookie dough ice cream shot out of his mouth and down his shirt. His face turned red, and his eyes darted around the room. I started to worry, but it finally cleared. Whether his face was turning red because of choking or mentioning kids, I wasn't sure.

"Chocolate chip," he wheezed.

"Never knew cookie dough could be so perilous," I mused. "I don't remember ever choking on mint chocolate. Must be the better of the two."

"Life's no fun without a little danger," he said, still wheezing. "Now, unfortunately, I'm a child and need to go put my shirt in the wash. You want to come see me take my shirt off?"

I could tell his mind was on more than just me watching him take his shirt off. "Tempting, but I'm really enjoying my mint chocolate ice cream," I said as I put another spoonful in my mouth.

As soon as I took the spoon away from my lips, he kissed me, and I melted faster than the ice cream in my mouth. But the kiss didn't last long—Jacob quickly pulled away, gagging.

"Disgusting," he said. "Kissing you is off limits until you brush your teeth and get that nasty taste off your lips." I almost spit out my ice cream in laughter, but I caught myself. He smiled and walked to the laundry room.

I took another bite of ice cream, and I saw Jacob's phone light up right next to me. I didn't mean to pry, but his phone was face up and I couldn't help but read the text after I saw it was from "Katie."

Katie: Hey Jacob, I just wanted to let you know I'm in your hometown. Would you want to go get coffee sometime? Dinner would be even better ;) Let me know!

Who knew a few lines of text could have such an impact on me? My stomach felt hollow. My cheeks burned. And the ice cream in my mouth tasted bitter. I put my spoon down and held on to the edge of the island for balance.

Who was Katie? And why was she texting my man for dinner plans? Before I could process it any further, Jacob came back, only wearing his boxers. But his sexy body wasn't doing anything for me right now.

He walked over to me and pressed his body against mine. "I know we just ate ice cream, but I'm ready for dessert round two," he said. His hands traced the edges of my body down to my legs and spread them wide. He started to kneel down, but I stopped him.

"I'm actually not interested at the moment. Too much ice cream," I lied.

"Oh, well, that's okay. We can take a rain check."

"Yeah. By the way, I think your phone went off while you were gone," I said. He checked his messages, and his eyes slightly widened before he put his phone back in his pocket. "Who was it?"

"Oh, nobody important. You want to watch a movie or something?"

Now he's changing the subject... "Sure," I said.

"Cool. Why don't you go pick something out, and I'll put all this up before it melts. Is the trash can a good place for your mint chocolate?"

"Hardy har har," I said. Normally, I would have genuinely laughed at his joke, but I had too many thoughts going through my mind. Mainly, who was this girl? Second, why did he say she was "nobody"? Third, *who was this girl?*

I turned on the television, but before I could start scrolling through a few movies, I realized how parched my mouth was. I got to the entrance of the kitchen, and the ice cream was still out. Jacob was typing on his phone. I felt the color drain from my face.

He's probably texting Katie back. I felt even more hollow than I had before. He'd obviously lied about wanting to make sure the ice cream didn't melt.

I decided I could stay parched. If I put anything in my mouth, I might puke. *Do I surprise him and ask what he's doing? Do I storm out?* I wondered how many girls he was talking to. I'd thought we were exclusive. And just like that, memories of boys leaving me for other girls washed over me.

I couldn't figure out how, in the span of a few minutes, we had gone from him mentioning our *kids* and me daydreaming about us getting married, to feeling such distrust.

Had it been a mistake to trust him?

Instead of confronting him, I chickened out and went back to the television. Instead of doing the one task I was given and picking a movie, I just scrolled. Countless options, but there was nothing to watch.

Chapter 20

Jacob

Standing in line, all I could do was keep daydreaming about Abby. I just wanted to spend every minute with her. Hold her hand. Kiss her. Make love. I couldn't believe I was lucky enough to be her first. *And hopefully only.*

"Kathryn?" the barista called out. My heart skipped a beat at the name. I looked around the cafe, worrying that the universe was playing some cruel trick. But the girl who grabbed the cup was a stranger. I turned the music up, and my headphones drowned out most of the cafe noise. I took a step forward in line.

Last night had been a bit weird. Abby had seemed to be in a great mood when she came over despite her strange interview, but then her demeanor had completely changed. She hadn't seemed interested in the movie that I ended up picking out. I had tried getting her to choose one, but she couldn't make up her mind.

And then she hadn't wanted to touch me. Usually we couldn't keep our hands off of each other. I asked her if something was wrong, but she said everything was fine. I planned on trying to get her to spill the beans the next time I saw her. I was too crazy about her for there to be anything wrong between us.

My phone vibrated. A text from Kyle.

Kyle: Yo yo yo, Derek is having a party tonight. You could be my wingman, since you have a mystery woman.

I was about to text him 'no thanks,' since I was going to try to hang with Abby tonight, but I could have sworn someone just called out my name.

"Jacob?"

My heart froze in my chest. It was someone in the back of the line, but it was hard to make out their voice because of the music in my ears, other than that it was a woman. She sounded familiar. What if the universe *did* play a trick on me and send Katie here at the same time...Maybe if I just ignored it, she would go away...

"Umm, Jacob, there's no way you didn't hear me. Hello?" The more she talked, the better I recognized the voice. I smiled, paused my music, and turned to face her.

"Ha, hey, Jess!" I waved. "Sorry, had my music too loud. *And* I can't really function before I have my coffee."

She stepped out of her spot in line and came up to hug me.

"Oh, me neither." I gave her a puzzling glance, since she was currently as chipper and bright-eyed as a squirrel in a field of peanuts. "This will be my second cup of coffee of the morning." She turned to the girl behind me. "Mind if I cut in next to my friend?"

The girl had a scowl on her face and looked like she was in more need of coffee than I was. But I didn't blame her.

"Yes, actually. I do mind. I've been in line for ten minutes," the girl replied.

Jessica squinted her eyes at her like a tiger ready to pounce. "Well, either I cut in and order my coffee, or I'll stand to the side and my friend here is going to order it for me anyway. So, it doesn't really matter..."

The girl rolled her eyes. "Fine. Whatever." I felt bad for her, but I couldn't really argue with Jessica's logic.

We walked up to the counter. "Good morning. What can I get you two?" the barista asked.

I nodded to Jessica, and she playfully nudged me in the ribs. "What a gentleman. I would like a caramel Frappuccino with whipped cream, please," Jessica said before turning to me. "I'm going to go grab a table. I'll Venmo you."

"And for you, sir?" the barista asked.

"Just a medium black coffee for me, thanks. Oh, and whatever the girl behind me is getting, put her order on my card as well," I said. It was the least I could do to try to make her day better after Jessica kind of shat all over it. The barista smiled at me.

"That's nice of you," she said. I gave her my name, paid, and then went to join Jessica.

She was studying me with a smirk on her face as I sat down. "What?"

She leaned forward. "I've heard through the grapevine that there has been quite a bit of kissing between you and my best friend."

If I had been drinking my coffee, I would have spit it out just like the ice cream last night. *I need to get that under control. I can't keep staining my clothes.*

"So she told you." I wasn't sure whether to be upset or not. I guessed it was to be expected, since best friends tell each other everything. But we had been trying to keep this under wraps as much as possible.

"Of course she told me. We tell each other everything." Unless I was mistaken, her eyes took a quick glance toward my crotch.

"I'm the one who's lucky," I said. "But you can't bring this up to anyone else. I feel weird even talking about it out loud in public like this. Kyle doesn't know yet. We don't know how to tell him."

She zipped her lips. "Secret is safe with me. And sorry for sending Tony over her way...I sent him a message before you two were a thing. He was her high school crush, so I was just trying to help a sister out." The memory of some other guy flirting with my girl made my blood boil. But I couldn't blame Jessica, since she hadn't known.

"You're off the hook. But if you send any other guys her way, I'm sending Kyle your way."

"Gross!" Jessica said with a smile and a wink. "I'd like to wash my clothes on his abs, but he's too aggravating for me to spend more than two days together without going crazy. How many days could you see yourself spending with Abby?"

"All of them," I said simply.

"Well, isn't that the cutest thing I've ever heard! I didn't know it was so serious."

It was more than serious. "Jessica, if I tell you something, will you promise not to tell Abby? Or anyone, for that matter?"

"Lips will be sealed." I held out my hand, and we shook on it.

"I know it's soon, and I feel like a crazy person for thinking about it so early...but I just love her so much that I started looking at engagement rings on my phone last night while she was on the couch looking for a show to watch. Is that not crazy?"

She slapped my arm. "Jacob! That's amazing! Who cares if it's crazy! Aw, are you two in love?"

I beamed. I just wanted to pour everything out. It was isolating not being able to talk with anyone about any of this yet. So it felt nice not having to hold it all in, and even better to have encouragement. "Yes. Do you think it's too early?"

She hesitated. "I mean, it's pretty early compared to people our age these days. But when you know, you know, I guess. Plus, you two have known each other forever."

"Right. And just because I'm looking at rings doesn't mean I'm planning to propose anytime soon. But it never hurts to look, right?"

Jessica smiled widely. "Of course not!"

"No rush, but do you think you could find out her ring size for me? I don't know how to get the info from her without it being obvious."

"I don't need to ask! She's a four and a half."

I noted it in my phone in my Abby note. "But, Jessica, you really can't tell anyone. You can't tell her or *any* of your friends. No matter what. I don't want to scare her off."

"You got it," she said.

"Jacob!" the barista called out.

"You paid. I'll go grab them. Plus, I'm so excited that I can't sit still much longer." The barista and I made eye contact when I looked to see if Jessica needed any help. She was still smiling at me. Apparently she really liked my gesture to the girl behind me.

As soon as Jessica sat down, she started sucking on her straw like she only had a minute to drink the whole thing.

"Whoa, Jess. Calm down. You're going to get a brain freeze," I said. She shook her head.

"One, thanks to you, I'm too excited to calm down. Two, people have told me my whole life that I will get brain freezes, but it has never happened. I love *everything* cold. Give me a box of snow for my birthday. Leave me stranded on a mountaintop in the middle of a snowstorm for weeks with no contact with the outside world for all I care. Cold is life."

"Wow. Well, I guess you've found your passion."

"Yeah. I can't wait to move away from here and live in a state where there is actually winter. Not in the cards yet, but it's all part of my plan. But speaking of *passion*, how is it being naked with Abby?"

I raised my eyebrow at her. "A gentleman never tells."

"Ugh, Abby never tells me what happens behind closed doors either. Nothing about you and nothing about that guy in college, whereas I'm an open book."

I felt a ton of bricks crash down on me. That *guy in college?*

"Why do you look like you just found out Santa Claus isn't real?"

"It's nothing. I just—I thought she was a virgin."

"Oh, I'm so sorry! I figured you two had already talked about it. Please don't tell her I told you. Shit. I feel like a terrible friend," she said.

We *had* talked about our pasts, but it seemed Abby had lied straight to my face. I wouldn't have cared if she'd hooked up with anyone before me. It made me queasy thinking of her being with anyone else now that I was with her, but it wasn't like I had any claim to her before this summer. It would not have been a deal breaker. But lying about it was always worse.

"Oh, wow, I just noticed your cup," Jessica said.

"Hmm?" I said. All sounds in the coffee shop were just kind of going in one ear and out the other. And it seemed like Jessica was just trying to change the subject.

"Look at your cup. Looks like somebody likes you."

I turned the cup in my hand and saw ten digits near where my name was written. I looked up toward the counter and made eye contact with the barista again. She waved this time. I shook my head and waved my hand near my throat to let her know I wasn't interested. She looked embarrassed and went back to her work. Poor thing. At the same moment, the girl behind us in line came up to our table.

"Hey, I just wanted to say I'm sorry if I was a bit cranky earlier. Thank you for buying my coffee. That was really sweet," she said.

"No problem," I said. She walked out of the restaurant.

"I didn't know you bought her coffee. No wonder Abby has been so crazy about you. You're cute *and* nice. That's a rare combo when it comes to men," Jessica said.

All of a sudden, my mind was back to Abby. And all I could feel was the hurt from her lie. Why did she keep this from me? Did she hook up with someone she had feelings for? Was it Tony, and that was why she didn't want to tell Jessica about it? Ugh. I could taste vomit in the back of my throat.

I was suddenly not so keen about hanging out with Abby that night. So I pulled out my phone and replied to Kyle's text.

Me: Sure. A party sounds fun.

"You texting Ms. Sexy Barista over there? Because then we're going to have to fight." Jessica asked jokingly.

"Not a chance. Just texting with Kyle," I said.

"What does that sexy, aggravating man want?"

"Trying to figure out what to do tonight. Our friend is having a party."

"Oh, boys' night, is it? Makes sense, since we're having a girls' night."

"Yeah, you have fun with that." I wasn't really listening to her. My mind was in another space. "Okay, Jessica. I think I'm going to head out. I'll see you later."

"Maybe tonight after our dinner? The girls can come meet up with the boys?"

"Yeah, maybe," I said. Though I wasn't sure what I wanted. Maybe some space from Abby was what I needed.

I was still brushing my teeth when I heard Kyle's horn honking in my driveway. I was only on my next tooth when I heard him honk again. *That little shit.* I finished up and ran outside. The asshole honked again as he saw me locking the front door.

"Really?" I shouted at him.

He stuck his head out the window and had a smile on his face. "Sorry! Couldn't help myself," Kyle said. I walked to the passenger seat, and he honked again while I was near his hood. I jumped, even though I should have expected it. Kyle was cracking up.

"You're *hilarious*, dude," I told him. The sarcasm in my voice was thick.

"One of my many amazing qualities." He backed out of the driveway and sped off. A few minutes went by without us saying anything, which was pretty normal behavior for guys. "So, you ever going to tell me who this girl you're seeing is?"

I would love a friend to vent to and discuss my recent revelations about Abby.

Unfortunately, Kyle was the worst man for that job. "Not yet, man."

He looked over at me, perplexed. "I don't get it. That's what guys do. We talk about the girls we're fucking. How big their tits are, what their favorite positions are. Why is this one different?"

"She's just a special circumstance. I'll tell you soon, I promise. But I don't want to talk about her like she's a piece of meat." I could feel his eyes on me.

"I mean, the only reason I could see you keeping your love life so secret is if you were dating somebody we know. Is it Jessica? She's pretty hot, but I already called her." He laughed.

I shook my head. "No, and even if it was Jessica, I would still tell you no." There was another pause.

"Is it Abby?" My face felt hot. *Do I lie? Do I tell him the truth now?* I was upset at Abby for lying to me, so how could I be okay lying to my best friend?

I decided now was as good a time as any to tell him. Hiding it from him had been fun and risky, but it made our relationship so much harder. Everyone would benefit if he just knew. Before I could say anything, though, Kyle started laughing.

"Oh, man, could you imagine? You and Abby together? What a train wreck that would be." He laughed some more.

"Ha, yeah, man. Hilarious," I said.

In the silence that followed, all I wanted to do was text her where I was going. I knew she was probably already on her main course at the restaurant with her friends, but I just wanted to let her know I was thinking of her. I put my hand in my pocket to find my phone, but it wasn't there.

"Shit," I said. "Can you call my phone?"

Kyle called it, but there was no sound and no vibration. I felt all along the floor and around the car seat.

"Fuck. I must have left it at home."

"Don't sweat it, man. Everyone could use a break from their phones every now and then. It'll make the party more fun. Speaking of which, here we are," he said as we pulled up to a house. It was a single story with some simple bushes in the front garden. Derek said the rent was a great deal for the location.

We walked inside and went straight to the keg. Once our cups were full, Kyle said, "Let's chug!" Before I could think about objecting, he started draining his glass, so I had to join him. *Might as well, since I've felt like shit all day.*

Once our cups were emptied, we filled them again. I didn't see anyone I knew, so I followed Kyle into the living room. The house seemed typical for a guy just graduating college. A worn couch, carpet that was a little dirty, no paintings or anything hanging on the walls.

I scanned the room, thinking I might see at least one person I knew, since I was from this damn town and all, but they were all unfamiliar faces. Then the crowd shifted, revealing a blond woman who I recognized immediately.

Katie. What the *fuck* was she doing here? She caught my eye, smiled, and waved.

I turned to Kyle. "Is this your doing?"

He smiled a big, toothy grin. "Of course! She said she was in town for work and that she texted you but didn't get a response. So I responded for you. Told her to meet us here. Hence why I was honking at you to come downstairs."

Fuck my life. "Not cool, man. You know I'm seeing some-one," I said.

"Uh, I beg to differ. I think it was *very* cool of me, actually. You've said literally zilch to me about this mystery girl. I don't know what her status is. She could be a fuck buddy for all I know. Whereas you and Katie have history. She could be the real deal. Any other guy would be thanking me right now. She is hot as fuck." Kyle looked perturbed, but I didn't care. How dare he invite the girl who took my virginity without telling me?

"Well, I'm not thanking you. I'm out of here, man," I said.

"Whoa!" Kyle held his arm in my path. "I know you're a gentleman, and a gentleman would not leave that girl all by her lonesome over there at a party where she doesn't know anyone. Go talk to her! You can tell her you're with someone. For fuck's sake, man. Stop being a pussy."

As much as I hated him right now, I couldn't argue. It would be mean to leave her stranded here. Especially if she only had him to talk to.

"Fine." I took a big swig of beer and walked over. She looked the same, but it did nothing for me now. Even though I was hurt by Abby at this moment, she was still all I wanted. "Hey, Katie. Fancy seeing you here." She stood, and we hugged each other hello, her hand brushing my back.

"Hey, Jacob! It's great to see you," she said. "But, judging by your face, it looks like it's not a good surprise?"

"Yes, my best friend decided to leave out the part where he invited you. I guess I would have known if I had ever answered you. Sorry about that."

"Sorry about which time? The time you didn't answer me last night? Or how you ignored my texts after we hooked up way back when?"

"I...um..."

She laughed. "It's okay. I'm just messing with you. I'm not upset. Though I have always wondered. I thought the night went well."

I almost spit out my beer. "You did? I never called you because I was embarrassed about how I...uh...performed." She laughed again.

"Never even crossed my mind, really. I knew it was normal for people hooking up for their first time together."

I didn't know what to say. "Well, I'm sorry. I shouldn't have ignored you," I said.

"It's okay. Water under the bridge. So what are you up to these—"

"Listen, Katie, I just want to be upfront with you and not

lead you on or anything. I'm currently seeing someone. And it's pretty serious. That's why I didn't answer you last night or today. I didn't really see a point."

"Oh." She looked like she heard the puppy she wanted to adopt at the shelter was no longer available. "Well, I guess I can't be mad. Disappointed, for sure. But I hope you are happy." Poor thing looked down in the dumps.

"So, what brings you into town?" I asked. She took a big gulp of beer.

"I live about an hour away working for a marketing firm, and I'm here meeting with one of our clients all week to shoot a couple of commercials. Well, I guess in all honesty I'm just shadowing someone in my firm who actually knows what they're doing, since I've been working with them for about a month."

The idea of working on branding and getting a company's name out in the world excited me. I pepped up for the first time all day. "That's awesome. I would love to do something like that," I said.

"Oh, I remember. And, hey, if you're really interested, we're looking to hire for another entry-level position. I could probably get you an interview."

"Wow. Um...sure. Yeah, that would be amazing." I would need a different job, eventually, once Abby began teaching. There was no point working at the pool if she wasn't there. And an hour-long commute didn't sound too bad.

She nodded. "Sure thing. I'll ask my boss and let you know when I get back. But before I do that, there's something I need to know."

"Go for it."

"Who is this lucky woman and what is she like?"

I was about to say it might be too weird telling her about my new girlfriend, but then I thought how nice it would be to talk to someone out of town who had no idea who Abby was. If Katie was willing to listen, maybe it would be good to get things off my chest since there was no one for her to tell except Kyle.

"If I tell you about her, will you swear yourself to secrecy?" I asked.

She zipped her lips and threw away the key.

"Okay then. It's Kyle's sister," I whispered. "But let's go find somewhere more private."

Chapter 21

Abby

I stared at my phone, willing Jacob to answer me. But it wasn't working. I had texted him a couple of times this evening, but he never responded. I didn't even know what he was up to tonight. And the only thing popping up in my mind was that he was spending it with whoever "Katie" was.

I hated feeling jealous. I knew I didn't have to be jealous of anyone. I knew how Jacob felt about me. But if she was nothing to worry about, why hadn't he told me who it was that texted him when I asked him about it? Why was he smiling at his phone afterwards? I had an uneasy feeling in my stomach, and I hated it.

"Cheers to all of us finally getting back together after all these years," Jessica said. I was still staring blankly at the table when Jessica nudged me with her foot. I came back to life, put on a smile, and picked up my glass.

"Cheers! It seriously has been too long," Tabitha said.

"Cheers!" Mallory said.

"Cheers," I murmured. I really needed to get out of the

funk I was in because the night was supposed to be a joyous occasion. Jessica, Mallory, Tabitha, and I used to be inseparable in high school. But then Jessica and I went out of town for college, and Mallory and Tabitha went to schools much closer to home. We all took a sip of our drinks and put our glasses down.

"So, tell us everything. What have y'all been up to? I have a general idea of your lives, thanks to Instagram. But let's pretend we're all back in high school gossiping in the cafeteria during lunch," Jessica said.

"Shoot," Tabitha said. "It's funny how, back in those days, I couldn't wait to grow up. But now that I've started working, I just want to go back to when we had no responsibilities. It *is* nice to have money, though." Tabitha was always fun to hang out with. She was dirty blonde and had a thick Southern accent. She was originally from Mississippi.

Tabitha was the one you wanted to go to parties with. She was always looking to have a great time. Whenever she and Jessica were out together, you knew the night was going to be memorable. Tonight, she was wearing a shiny light purple dress.

"What are you doing these days?" I asked. I knew she had gone to nursing school, but I wasn't sure what specialty she ended up in.

"I work at a plastic surgery clinic. And I'm loving it. I either assist people in trying to look better, or I'm helping people who are in need of actual medical treatment. It's a great job, and I make great money. The hardest part is not stripping down the doctor whenever we're in the office alone together." We all laughed.

"So you've got a hottie for a boss?" Jessica asked.

Tabitha nodded aggressively before she took a sip of her cocktail. "Oh, yes. And he's single. And he makes a bunch of money. I might be too young for him, but I definitely flirt whenever I can."

"Makes me worry about my husband's future and dealing with a bunch of hot nurses trying to flirt with him," Mallory said, nudging Tabitha

"Well, your husband isn't single. My boss is."

"How *is* Chad doing?" I asked Mallory.

She sighed. "He is exhausted. He knew med school would be tough, but he didn't really know how draining it would be until he got in the thick of it."

"I bet," I said.

"So, when is the big day?" Jessica asked.

"Oh yeah. Congrats, in person," I said.

Mallory smiled and showed us the back of her left hand. "Thank you, thank you. It still feels weird wearing it. We haven't set an exact date yet, but we are thinking about next May."

"That's less than a year away!" Jessica said.

Mallory's eyes opened wide. "We know. But we just want it to be over with. It's not going to be a big wedding, so it won't be too much to plan. We want to do it before summer gets too hot, and we don't want to wait until the fall. Because we are *ready* to make babies."

"Wow. So soon?" I asked. I had thought about having children earlier rather than later, but I wasn't sure people our age did that anymore. It seemed like everyone was waiting until they were at least thirty. I was suddenly thinking of making babies with Jacob and smiled. A quick glance at my phone showed he hadn't answered yet.

"Yeah. I know most people these days get married and wait a few years to have a baby, but we are ready. We've been dating since we were fourteen. That's eight years! We want to have kids young so we still have the energy to deal with them. I don't know. I don't know how to explain it. But enough about me. My settled life isn't as exciting as y'all's, I'm sure. Do y'all have any *tea* to spill?"

"The only man in my life right now is my boss," Tabitha said. "I'll let you know if anything develops."

"I think I've practically made out with every guy we went to high school with, so my options are mostly dried up in this town," Jessica said. "But I've got plans to find a man in another town. I don't think there are any here that I want to pursue. No lifelong prospects at least."

I looked over at her questioningly. Her leaving town was news to me. She saw my stare. "I don't have any definitive plans yet," she reassured me, "but I'm ready to get out of here. Going to college and meeting new people left me with a taste for adventure. I don't want to stay here. I think it's a great place to live, so I don't blame anyone for wanting to stay. But I want to live around mountains. Around snow. I don't know where I'm going to go. Maybe Colorado? Montana?"

"You can't leave me," I said, pouting. "I won't allow it."

"I'm sorry, bestie. But this chick is ready to fly away from the nest." I reached out and grabbed Jessica's hand. If she left, I would lose *another* one of my closest friends. I didn't have Rebecca with me anymore, or Kelly, or Tonya. I thought I could count on Jessica staying, but it looked like I was going to be left all alone. Of course I had Mallory and Tabitha, but all that time apart had made us seem a little like strangers.

Maybe I should go with Jessica when she goes. Or go meet up with the other girls in Dallas. I was sure Jacob would follow me.

"What about you, Abby?" Tabitha asked me.

"I don't have any plans to move away just yet. The only thing on my mind is to find a job teaching."

Tabitha shook her head. "That's very interesting, and we'll

get into that, but I wasn't asking about your work life. Is there any *man* in Abby Barber's life?"

Jessica looked over at me with a grin. She didn't hide it from the table very well.

"Oh, I know that look! There is definitely somebody," Mallory said.

I blushed.

"Confirmed," Tabitha said. "Tell us everything."

"There's nothing to tell." I took a sip of my drink.

"Wow. You guys smell that?" Tabitha started sniffing the air. "Oh yeah, I know what that smell is. It's bullshit!"

Everyone laughed, even me. "Yeah, I smell it, too," Jessica said. I shot her a look. *Betrayal!* "I'm sorry!" she said. "But this is what we do. What we *did.* Don't you remember how fun it was talking about our crushes in high school?"

"I remember *you* always having a crush on Abby's brother and talking to us about it whenever she got up from the table," Tabitha said, sipping on her straw.

"Oh, whatever," Jessica said, rolling her eyes, but she smiled. "Who didn't have a crush on Kyle? He never needed to work out and just looked amazing all the time. Each of you all had a crush on him at different times in high school, too. Don't even lie."

"Admitted, your Honor," Tabatha said.

"Y'all are gross," I said.

"Why do you think I wanted to go to the pool so much?" Jessica asked me.

"You're ruining the water for me," I said.

"I was with Chad the whole time, of course. But I may have had a couple 'why choose' fantasies involving him and Kyle if I'm being honest," Mallory said.

"I'm legit going to vomit," I said.

They all laughed, and I shook my head.

"But back to my question," Tabitha said. She opened her palms toward me. I was hoping our food would get to our table so I could just stuff my face with it and not have to answer questions. "We know there's somebody. It's been a long time since we've hung out like this, but I still know you, Abby Barber."

"Spill it!" Mallory yelled. A few of the restaurant's patrons looked over at us hooligans.

I sighed. "Fine. I guess there's no hiding it from y'all. Yes, I am seeing someone. But I can't get into it." And that was all I said.

Tabitha and Mallory shared looks with each other and then with me and Jessica. "There's no way that's the only thing we're getting out of you. Who is he? Where is he from? What does he do? If he is my boss, I'll kill you," Tabitha said.

"He's definitely not your boss," I laughed. "I can at least tell you that."

"Why can't you tell us? Is it someone we know?" Mallory asked, her interest really piqued now.

I shrugged, trying to play innocent. But my face was terrible at giving me away. It felt beet red.

"Oh yes, it *is* someone we know," Tabitha said, leaning forward.

"You guys, I don't think you're going to get a name out of her," Jessica said.

"Ugh, fine. At least give us something. Is he gorgeous? Rich? Both? Older?" Mallory said.

"He's a little older, but not by much. Yes, I think he's gorgeous. But he is definitely not rich."

"Well, are y'all exclusive? Is this just a fling? Are y'all in love?" Mallory said.

I thought about all the things I loved about Jacob. How he

constantly thought about me. The way he held me. The way he loved me. I smiled.

"Aw, I think she's in love," Tabitha said. "Cheers to love!" Everyone put their drinks in the middle of the table, and we clinked our glasses. A big smile spread across my face, and I was all giddy inside.

* * *

The giddiness had faded as dinner went on and I still hadn't heard from Jacob. I thought maybe the only reason he hadn't answered me was because he was taking a nap, but now it had just been too long.

"So, what's after this?" Tabitha asked.

"Yeah, let's go out or do something. We don't have to sneak into bars anymore," Mallory said.

"Though I do miss convincing bouncers to let us in," Jessica said, shaking her chest.

"Woo!" Tabitha shrieked, causing people in the restaurant to give us strange looks again. We each had had a few drinks.

"I don't know. I'm kind of tired. I might just go home," I said. My real plan was to go drive by Jacob's house and make sure he was okay. Maybe I was getting upset for no reason. What if something had happened to him? Now I was worrying about him.

"Boooo!" Jessica said. "Why don't we go join your brother and Jacob?"

What?

Jessica saw the confusion on my face. "Yeah, I ran into your brother's friend Jacob this morning at PJ's Coffee. He said he and Kyle were going to some house party tonight."

Jacob went to a party and didn't tell me about it? My paranoia seeped in again.

"Oh man, speaking of Jacob. Hubba hubba," Tabitha said. "I saw him at the grocery store the other day and couldn't believe my eyes. He's like a whole new person. He's so hot now. I might even give up on my boss and go after him." I clenched my fists under the table and forced myself to breathe.

I took out my phone and texted him again.

Me: *Are you at a party?*

"But yeah, a party could be fun. Do we have the address?" Mallory asked.

"I didn't get an address. But we could probably get in touch with Kyle and ask him?" Jess looked over at me. She was silently saying that I should text Jacob and ask him for the address, but she didn't know that he was ignoring me.

"Yeah, I'll text him."

Me: *Hey, Jessica said there's a party tonight? Mind sending me the address?*

"Your brother is still single, though, right?" Tabitha asked me, moving her eyebrows up and down.

"Come on, Tabitha. I just ate." Should I have even been entertaining the idea of going to a party? I had my interview at one of my dream schools the next morning, and I still needed to pack for our beach trip. "Girls, I think I'm just going to call it a—"

I felt my phone vibrate.

· · ·

*Kyle: How did y'all hear? And idk. Not sure if I want my little
sister messing up boys' night.*

I took in a deep breath. So Jacob *was* there.

Me: I have three girls I can bring.

Kyle: 641 Atlantic Ave.

* * *

The Uber turned from the main street into a neighborhood.

"Is anyone having déjà vu right now?" Tabitha said. "This
feels like when we went to Kristen Finney's parties way back
when."

"Yeah, except we don't have to sneak out or lie about where
we are going," Mallory said.

I never had to lie to my parents about high-school parties.
They knew I was a good kid. But I knew that not everyone was
so lucky. Some people had helicopter parents. Rebecca's stories
of her high school years came to mind. She had told me that
they chilled out much more once she got to college though.

The car pulled up to the address. It was a modest-looking
one-story house.

"Is this the right place?" Jessica said. We all looked out the
window at the house. It was nothing like high school. There
was no one hanging in the front yard. The music wasn't blaring
enough to shake the car windows. People were moving around
inside, though.

"I think this is it, y'all," I said. We all got out of the car, and
music was coming from the backyard. I took a deep breath and
shivered with nerves. Who knew what I was going to find in

there? The girls walked forward, but I was frozen in place. Jessica turned around and saw me standing still. She came back and threaded her arm through mine. "Let's get in there, girl," she said.

Tabitha opened the door, and we could finally hear the regular noises of a party. Tons of people talking, others playing drinking games in the kitchen, and music playing through the house's surround sound. We had barely closed the door before some random guy walked up to Jessica.

"Welcome, welcome," he said.

"Hi there," Jessica said.

"Can I get you a drink?"

"You can *show* us where the drinks are," Jessica said.

"Sure thing. Right this way. By the way, my name is Derek. Welcome to my place." He held out his hand and Jessica took it. He led us over to the keg. Jessica did not look excited. On our way over to it, I looked for Jacob, but I didn't see him.

"Do you have anything else?" Jessica asked.

"You don't even know what's in it," he said.

"It doesn't matter. If I see a keg at a house party, it can really only be a couple of things, in my experience."

Derek shook his head. "I'm a civilized person. I don't have any nasty light beer in there. I got a keg of Abita Strawberry. That way, the guys *and* the gals could enjoy it."

"Oh my God!" Tabitha squealed. "I love that stuff." Tabitha leaned forward and got a cup. Derek took it from her and started pouring her a beer. He looked at Jessica again. "You could learn a thing or two from your friend there. It's a whole new world these days. They've got great tasting beer now."

"Doubtful," Jessica said. Derek handed the cup to Tabitha, and she took a sip.

"Mmm, that's so good," Tabitha said. "Jessica, you've got to at least try it." During this whole conversation, I kept looking around the party, but there was no trace of Jacob or my brother. Jessica took a sip of the beer. Before she tasted it, she had a scowl on her face. But after she took a gulp, she looked surprised.

"Oh, wow. That's fucking delicious," Jessica said. "Yeah, I'll definitely take some of that," she said.

Derek smiled and nodded, grabbing another cup and filling it up. "Does everybody want some?" We all told him we did.

"Well, hello there, ladies, and Abby." I turned around, and Kyle was standing there, drinking his beer and looking at the girls I'd brought.

"Hey, loser," I said.

Kyle looked at me like he regretted giving me the address. "I would be wondering why I let you come to this, but then I wouldn't have had the pleasure of being introduced to your friends. Hi, I'm Kyle," he said, brushing past me and reaching his hand out to Tabitha.

She looked at him like he was an idiot. She took his hand and shook it. "I know, Kyle. I've been to your house many times."

He looked at her, confused. Tabitha waved her hands in the air. "It's me, Tabitha. One of your sister's best friends from high school? And this is Mallory? Ring a bell?"

"Holy shit," he said. "I didn't recognize y'all. It's, uh, dark in here."

"Uh-huh," Tabitha said.

"You look great," he stammered.

Tabitha took a sip of her drink and then turned to Mallory. "Do you need to use the restroom?" she asked. We had all used the restroom at the restaurant before we left, so the girls knew she was leaving for a different reason.

"Sure! It was so good seeing you again, Kyle," Mallory said before she and Tabitha walked away.

"Yeah, you too, uh…" He looked at me.

I shook my head. "Mallory," I enunciated. "Tabitha literally just said it."

He swatted at the air like it didn't matter. "Whatever. I'm drunk. It's dark. And they have changed a lot in the past four years." I saw his eyes go straight to Jessica's chest. Instead of being aggravated, Jessica looked like she was popping her chest out even more. She enjoyed toying with him. "Jessica. Looking good," he slurred and smirked.

"So, who did you come here with?" I asked him. I came here for a reason.

He looked at me like I was stupid. "Who do you think?"

My heart started thumping in my chest. It was torture trying to get information out of him while having to pretend that I didn't really care that much. "Oh really? He's here? I haven't seen him."

Kyle shrugged. "I think I saw him walk outside with his little lady friend," he said.

I could see Jessica looking at me out of the corner of my eye. She probably noticed my face fall, but she also had to pretend like nothing was abnormal about Jacob being with a girl.

"Oh. I didn't know he had a lady friend. What does she look like?" I asked.

Kyle smiled. "Let's go see," he slurred again. He led the way, pushing through people dancing, and past the beer pong game. He opened the sliding door and took us outside. There was another table set up on the patio out here, and there were a bunch of people in groups throughout the yard. The fence was lit up by string lights. Kyle, Jessica, and I looked around for Jacob.

"There he is!" Kyle said, pointing to the gazebo.

I looked over, and he was sitting under a gazebo on a love seat with some blond girl I didn't recognize. I was really hoping for the best. That she was somebody from high school or some-body he used to know. But our town was not that big, and I had never seen her in my life. My heart felt like it was beating outside of my chest. "Who is that?" I asked.

Kyle took a big sip of beer, and some of it dribbled down his chin. He wiped it away. "That's this girl he hooked up with in college. Her name's Katie. She's hot as fuck." He held out his beer as if to salute Jacob for landing her.

It wasn't the description I would've given her, but she was beautiful. Jacob had a smile on his face and seemed so excited to talk with her. She had her chin in her hand with her elbow resting on her knee, looking like he was spilling the secrets of the universe. She looked entranced.

Then she reached out her hand and grabbed his, caressing him with her thumb. I felt like my heart had been ripped out of my chest and was being stomped on the ground. I wanted to stomp over there and tell her to back off, that he was mine. But I was not a confrontational person.

Kyle finished his drink. "I'm going to go get another beer," he said and then burped. He walked back inside. I put my arm out and steadied myself on Jessica.

I was still staring at Jacob. I didn't want to cause a scene. Not around all these people who knew me and Kyle. And I would've had to deal with Kyle's bullshit too. "Jessica, can you call an Uber?"

"I'm already on it. We should be able to get one here in less than five minutes."

I turned around and hung my head low. My knees were wobbly, and I was afraid I was going to fall.

"Abby, I'm so sorry," Jessica said. "Should we go talk to him? Want me to slap him?"

It was impossible to hold back the tears, and they started

streaming down my face. I shook my head. "Let's get out of here."

Just as we had entered the party, Jessica put her arm through mine and led me inside. I kept my face toward the ground to hide from everyone. I was crying. No, bawling. A few people noticed, but most were drunk or too entrenched in their own conversations. I still felt so embarrassed.

We walked by the keg, and Kyle was pouring himself a drink while talking to Tabitha and Mallory. Mallory noticed us and registered my expression.

"Oh my goodness, girl! What happened?" Mallory said.

I turned my face away from Kyle. I didn't want him seeing me cry. But it was impossible for him not to notice.

"We're leaving. I just called the Uber. Let's go wait for it out front," Jessica said. Tabitha and Mallory put their drinks down and came to my side.

"Whoa, what happened?" my brother asked.

"I don't want him to know that I'm crying," I sobbed quietly to the girls.

"Where are y'all going?"

"I forgot I need to get home and let my dog out," Mallory said. "It was good seeing you! We'll see you later!" And with that, we walked out of the house and waited in the front yard.

As soon as we got out the door. I started sobbing uncontrollably. I couldn't believe I'd thought Jacob and I shared a special connection. Clearly, I'd been dead wrong. Once again, I fell for an asshole. The girls were rubbing my back and consoling me while we were waiting by the curb.

"The Uber is almost here," Jessica said. I heard the front door close. Headlights were coming down the road.

"Hey! Wait up!" Kyle ran up to us as our ride pulled up. He touched my shoulder, and I tried to hide my face, but then he put his other hand on my other shoulder and turned me to face him. "Hey, hey. What's wrong? What happened?"

Jessica tried to get between us. "Kyle, it's nothing. Let us get her in the—"

"I wasn't asking you. Baby sis, what's wrong? Did someone say something to you? Did someone do something to you? Tell me." His voice was angry.

More tears were coming out of my eyes as I shook my head.

"Abby, talk to me!"

I wriggled out of his grip.

"She doesn't want to talk about it! Let us get her in the car. We're leaving." Kyle reached out for me again, but Jessica pushed him with force. He lost his footing and fell on the grass.

"What the fuck!" I heard him shout. But then I was in the backseat of the car. The doors shut, and we were on our way home.

Chapter 22

Jacob

"So, yeah. Long story short, I'm crazy about her."

Katie smiled and reached out. She grabbed my hand and rubbed it with her thumb. I let her hold it for a few seconds before gently pulling it back.

"That's so great, Jacob. I'm so happy for you. I really am. I'm a little let down, because I came all this way thinking you and I might reconnect." She laughed. "But I can see you're in love. And I wish you and Abby nothing but the best."

"Thanks. I can't tell you how much of a relief it is to be able to get all of that off my chest. I don't really have anyone to talk to about it."

Her face looked like she wanted to roll her eyes. "Is it really that big of a deal? Would your best friend not be excited that his best buddy is dating his sister?"

I shook my head. "I know Kyle, and he's going to be pissed. But hey, maybe it's not that big of a deal. I mean, we're *eventually* going to have to tell everybody. But right now, it's new and exciting. We just don't want to bring any drama into it by telling her brother or her parents yet. And we think it would be better to tell everybody once we're past the beginning of our relationship. You know, they may cast doubt on whether we're going to work out as a couple or not, and if we should really be doing this and risking it not working out, which might mess up my relationship with Kyle and his parents. I mean, they've basically been my family for most of my life."

Katie shook her head. "If you say so." She looked like she was going to add something, but then she looked toward the house. "Did you hear that?"

I didn't hear anything over the music. I shook my head, but then I heard what she was talking about.

"Jacob!"

It was Kyle's voice. He pushed his way through a group of people. His face was angry, and he was walking right toward me.

"Maybe that Band-Aid is going to be ripped off earlier than you and Abby were planning," Katie said.

I stood up to meet Kyle. *Fuck. Did he really find out some-how?* "What's up, man?"

He was out of breath, and grass clung to his sleeve. "I'm sorry to disturb you guys. But do you know what happened to Abby?"

Fear shot through my body. What did he mean, what happened to Abby? Was she okay?

"What do you mean? No, I don't know anything. What happened?"

Kyle was shaking his head and looking suspiciously at people in the backyard. "Fuck if I know, man. I left her for like thirty seconds to go inside and get more beer, and before I knew it, she was walking out and crying."

Wait. Abby was here?

"I chased after her, but she wouldn't tell me what was wrong. I was wondering if you saw anybody go up, and, I don't know, grab her inappropriately or anything? I'm ready to beat somebody the fuck up right now."

If anybody touched my baby, I'm also ready to beat somebody the fuck up, I thought. I reached into my pocket to grab my phone and text her, but I remembered it was still on my bed. *Fuck. I need to get my phone.*

"Should we go? I mean, so you can go check on her?"

Kyle put his hands on his hips. "Um, I'll go. I'll call a ride. But you stay. I didn't mean to interrupt whatever y'all got going on."

Katie stood up and put her purse on her shoulder. "No, it's actually fine. I was about to head out, anyway." I gave her a small grateful smile.

"Aw, well, that's a bummer," Kyle said looking from her to me.

"No worries. I'm sure we'll see each other soon enough. I'm only an hour away now." They hugged, and Kyle walked off.

"It was great seeing you," I said. I leaned in and gave her a hug.

"It was great seeing you, too. Oh, before I forget." She pulled out her wallet and handed a business card to me. "Check out the website and see if you like the place. I'm serious. Reach out to me and I'll let you know if you can get an interview."

"Thank you so much. You'll definitely be hearing from me."

A few minutes later, Kyle and I were in the car and on our way back home. The ride was torturous and felt like it took forever. I needed to know if Abby was okay. But my line of communication to the whole world was in my fucking room.

The car stopped in front of my house, and I fist-bumped Kyle. "Let me know if you find out anything about Abby. If somebody at that party hurt her, I'll gladly go back and teach them a lesson with you."

"Thanks, man. Will do. I'll see you tomorrow when we pick you up for the beach. We're going to leave our house whenever Abby is done with her interview and gets back."

I ran up to my room. There it was. Just lying on my bed. I picked it up and saw that I had more than a few missed texts from Abby. *Shit.* I had a missed call from her as well.

I called her. I needed to hear her voice and know that she was okay.

But it went to voicemail, so I sent her a text.

Me: Hey, I left my phone at my house. Please call me when you can. I need to know you're okay. Kyle said you came to the party we were at and that you left crying. Please let me know what happened.

I sent the message and waited. And waited. And after thirty minutes of waiting, I didn't know if she was ignoring me or asleep already. It would make sense that she was already in bed because she had her big interview the next morning.

I got under the covers and tried falling asleep, but I stayed up for hours worrying about her.

* * *

My phone dinged. I awoke from my dreams and shot up in bed. I had woken up countless times throughout the night and checked my phone to see if she had texted me back, but she never had. I finally saw her name on the screen. The clock showed it was four in the morning...

. . .

Abby: Jacob, I didn't want to do this over text, but I think it needs to be done before we leave for the beach trip. I don't think you and I are going to work out. I think we should end things. It probably wasn't a good idea for me to fall in love with my brother's best friend, anyway. You hurt me, and my heart is broken. I'm sure time will cure this like it always does, but I'm going to need a lot of time.

What the fuck?

Surely, this was still a dream. Surely the girl of my dreams was not breaking up with me over a text message, and not even explaining why.

And how was she the one who was mad at *me*, when I was the one that should be mad at *her* for lying about me being her first?

I called her. I was angry. The line rang once. And then it went to her voicemail. *She fucking ended the call.* I went to text her.

Me: You can't do this. You can't break up with me over text message and not even tell me what I did wrong.

Abby: If you don't know why I would be angry, then it seems like I should be glad that I dodged a bullet.

Me: ???

. . .

Abby: I can't do this right now. I need to try to get some sleep before my interview. Please stop trying to contact me.

Fuck that, I thought. I called her. It went to voicemail. I called her again. I got her voicemail even quicker that time. I called her again, and then I heard a different type of message. "This customer is unavailable. Goodbye."

Holy fuck. She blocked me?

Chapter 23

Abby

Knock knock knock. I shot up in bed and looked at my clock.

"Honey? You need to leave soon. Were you planning on eating breakfast in the car?" my mom asked from behind the door.

"Shit! Shit!" I screamed at the top of my lungs. I pulled the covers off and stood up at the same time that my mom opened the door with a worried look on her face. Realization came to her.

"Oh, honey. Are you just waking up?"

I never sleep late. Being professional was my life mantra. After the events of last night, and now this, I just stood in place, in shock. My eyes watered. My mom rushed over and hugged me.

"Shush, baby. No time to cry. You need to brush your teeth and get dressed and head out as soon as possible. Where are your keys? I'll go start your car and put a bottle of water and a protein bar in it for you." I pointed to my keys on the dresser.

She grabbed them and then squeezed my arm, and hurried out of the room.

I took a deep breath and ran to the bathroom. My reflection in the mirror made me want to crawl back into bed and just not show up. My eyes were red and puffy from crying all night, and my hair was a mess. I didn't have time to fix anything. My interview was in ten minutes, and it took fifteen minutes to drive there.

I brushed my teeth, put on my navy pantsuit, and ran out the door. My mom was holding the driver's door open and shut it behind me. "Go get 'em, sweetie!" she said. I backed out of the driveway and raced toward my future.

* * *

Jogging to the front door was not in any of my daydreams about this interview, but here I was. The person who liked to be forty-five minutes early to things was now ten minutes late. Just the thought of me ruining this opportunity by oversleeping threatened to bring on the tears. But thankfully, I kept them at bay.

I pulled on the main entrance doors to the school, and they wouldn't budge. I looked around. There were cars in the parking lot, so I knew there were people inside. There was an intercom to the right of the door, so I pressed the button.

No response. I pressed it again and waited thirty seconds. Still no response. Nervous sweat, made even worse by standing outside in a suit in the heat of Texas summer, started pooling in my lower back. *Great, now I'll smell even worse.*

I pressed the button a third time.

"Good morning. How may I help you?"

"Yes, hi, I'm Abby Barber. I'm here for an interview with Ms. Stefanski."

"Oh, Ms. Barber. Ms. Barber for an interview at nine o'clock?"

"Yes, that's me."

"All right. Ms. Stefanski assumed you were a no-show. You can open the door when you hear the buzz."

A loud buzzer went off, and I walked inside. The cool air conditioning washed over me. Five random faces turned to me. They were all sitting in chairs around the lobby, holding folders in their laps. They were all dressed professionally, either in pantsuits or pencil skirts, and their makeup and hair looked pristine.

Holy shit, I thought. So many people interviewing for the same position. And they all looked older than me, like all of them had been teaching for at least a decade. I was by far the youngest person in the room. Why was I even there, competing against so many people who had experience when I had none? *I should just walk out the door.*

"Hi, Ms. Barber." The front office secretary waved me over. "Ms. Stefanski is interviewing someone else in your time slot, but I'll let her know that you're here whenever she's done. You can have a seat anywhere," she said with a smile.

"Thank you," I muttered. I sat down and felt everyone's eyes on me. *Great. Everyone knows I was late for my scheduled time.* I thought about how I likely ruined my chance for this position, and tears started welling up in my eyes. *Not again.* Three deep breaths later, and I calmed down.

Why? Why, of all nights for this to happen, why did it have to be the night before this interview?

Maybe twenty minutes later, footsteps sounded from around the corner. A man who looked like he was in his forties walked through the lobby and out the door with a folder in his hand and a smile on his face. A tall blond woman appeared in the entrance to the hallway. "Ms. Becky, I'm ready for the next one."

"Your nine o'clock showed up about ten minutes late. Would you like to see her now or later?" Ms. Becky asked the principal while nodding over my way. Ms. Stefanski looked at me and thought for a moment.

"No. Send me whoever we had scheduled next." And so Ms. Becky sent a candidate back to their interview. And then the next one about thirty minutes later. Then another one. *Shit.* I was going to make my family leave so much later for our trip than they had planned.

After a while, the secretary stood up. "Ms. Barber? Ms. Stefanski will see you now."

I awoke from my daze, jumped from my seat, and hurriedly walked over to her. In the middle of us shaking hands, she started walking. "Ms. Stefanski, it's a pleasure to meet you." We only walked past two doors before she was motioning me into her office.

"It's nice to meet you, too, Abby. I'm glad you decided to show. Please have a seat." She shut the door and sat in her chair at her desk. She looked like she wanted the interview to be over already.

"Yes, I'm so sorry I was late."

"It's not the best start. Why were you late? Any good reason?"

I got in a wreck? My imaginary dog died? Aliens abducted me for a few hours?

"I overslept," I said.

The principal did not hide her disappointment. "Well, I can tell you that here at Franklin Middle we expect our teachers to be where they say they'll be at the required time."

"Yes, and once again, I'm so sorry. I am never late to

appointments, but I was dealing with some personal issues last night."

"Got it," Ms. Stefanski said. She didn't look convinced. "Okay, well, now that we've gotten that out of the way, we can start the interview."

"Sounds great."

"Could you pass over a copy of your resume?" I smiled. Going over my resume was my favorite part of any kind of interview, because I always knocked it out of the park. It showed that I always had fantastic grades and had been involved in numerous clubs and volunteer organizations ever since high school. I looked down at my purse, where a manila folder with three copies of my resume should have been, but it was nowhere to be seen.

A wave of panic came over me. "Oh no," I said.

"What is it?"

I closed my eyes and shook my head. "I forgot my resumes at home."

"I see." For the thousandth time this morning, I felt like crying. "Well, I can pull up your application and print a copy. Would you like me to print one for you as well?"

I wanted to sink through the floor. "I would really appreciate that." This had to be the worst interview she had conducted in her career.

After what seemed like an eternity, we both had a copy of my resume in our hands. "Yes, Abby Barber. Now I remember. Your outstanding application is the reason you have this interview, since you have no experience. Not only is it your resume filled with community involvement, but you've put it together clearly and presented it well. You would be surprised how many adults submit resumes that look like they were put together in five minutes. Different fonts, nothing aligned. So, your terrible start just got a lot better." She smiled at me. It looked like she was trying to make me comfortable.

It worked. I smiled back. "Thank you."

"So let's see, I have here a list of questions on these two pages that I normally ask potential teachers interviewing for a spot at my school. But they are all meant to be directed toward someone with teaching experience."

I should have just kept sleeping. That would have been better than being kicked while I was already lying on the ground. Then the principal threw the papers up in the air, and they floated down to the floor.

"So, since I can't ask you those questions. Let's just talk. What's your story?" Her smile was warm, and I immediately felt so much better. And I started rambling about my life.

I told her I was born and raised here, that I went to college and studied French before landing on education. I told her I worked all my summers at my dad's pool club and loved teaching swimming lessons. That I wanted nothing more than to be a teacher. That I moved back home right after college and immediately began applying for jobs. That Franklin was my top choice.

She smiled. "That makes me feel good. But why Franklin? For all I know, people are telling that to the principals at every school. So give me some specific reasons why you want to work here."

I smiled. I was going to knock this answer out of the park. I could answer this question in my sleep. "Well, first of all—" My phone started ringing on high volume. "Fuck," I said, unintentionally, as I reached inside my purse. I looked up in horror at what I had said out loud. My body froze, and I was unable to silence my phone. The principal's eyes were wide. She looked down at my phone, which I finally managed to silence. I saw her sigh, and I lost it. From being late, to not having my resume, to not having my phone on silent, to dropping the F-bomb during an interview, all on top of me and Jacob breaking up less than six hours ago, I started crying. And this time I couldn't stop. Ms. Stefanski stood up.

She handed me a box of tissues. "I think that's a good stopping point," she said. That just made me want to cry more.

I shook my head. "No, no. I can finish. I've just had the worst twenty-four hours."

"It seems like it," she said. She reached out her hand toward me. "Thank you for coming, Abby. It was very nice meeting you. I have some more candidates to interview before making a decision. I hope your next twenty-four hours go better than your last." She walked around her desk and opened the door. I felt like a dog getting kicked to the curb.

"If you need to gather yourself before you leave, there's a bathroom down the hall."

I shook my head. "I'll be fine. Thank you for the opportunity to interview with you." I walked down the hallway, through the lobby, and out the front doors. I was anything but fine.

I slammed the door behind me with a force that made the foyer shake and strode through the living room. My mom saw me from the kitchen. It looked like she was packing some food in a small ice chest for the car ride. "How did it go?" she asked, though by her tone and the look on her face, I could tell she already knew the answer.

"I don't want to talk about it."

"I'm sorry, honey. It's only one school. Chin up." She smiled at me, trying to give me some emotional support. But I didn't want any at the moment. "I think I already know the answer, but are you packed yet?" she asked.

I shook my head. "No. Not yet." *Fucking hell.* I hadn't packed at all. I was supposed to last night after dinner with the girls, but then we went to that stupid party and everything went to shit.

She nodded. "Okay, well, why don't you go do that and then we can leave as soon as you're ready. Everyone else is packed and ready to go." Great, because I was late to my interview, my slot time was pushed back, and now I was delaying my family's vacation.

"Okay," I said. I headed upstairs. I just wanted to get back in bed and sleep for another day or seven. *Maybe I should just skip this trip*, I thought. I was already miserable, and it was going to be *more* miserable because Jacob was going to be there with us, and I wasn't ready to face that. I was moments away from telling my mom that I was just going to skip the beach this year when I heard her greeting Jessica downstairs. *Shit.* I'd forgotten Jessica was joining us. I didn't want to deprive her of going. I opened up my suitcase and started throwing things in it.

"Abby! Jessica is here! Are you packed yet?" my dad called from down below.

"No, I'm not ready yet!" I called back irritably. I was going to blow up if anyone else asked if I was packed.

"Okay, well hurry if you can! We have a dinner reservation we need to make!" I wished he knew what I had been through last night and this morning. Maybe then he would have given me a break. But that would be opening another can of worms. I just shook my head and kept packing things.

"What's up, bootylicious?" Jessica asked as she walked in. "I'm ready to get my beach on." She pumped her fists in the air like she was at a rave and gyrated her hips. I looked over at her and her face dropped. "I'm sorry, sweetie. I was just trying to get some good vibes going." She came over and wrapped me in a hug.

"I appreciate it."

"So what's the update? Have you and Jacob talked?"

I took a deep breath and tried to respond, but I couldn't think of anything to say, so I just hung my head low and was on the verge of crying hysterically. "I'm a mess, Jess. I couldn't sleep because of what happened last night, and then I broke up with Jacob via text this morning." She gasped.

"Oh, Abby, I'm so sorry."

I started crying. "And then because I was up all night, I slept past my alarm, or snoozed it, I don't know. But I was late to my interview. I looked like a wreck. I didn't have my resume. My phone rang during it; it was the worst interview I could have imagined at the school that was top of my list. I'm just so sad right now."

Jessica rubbed my back.

"It's going to be okay. Everything happens for a reason. I'm here for you." I hugged her back tightly. "Jacob's not still coming, is he?"

"As far as I know, he is.

Jessica shook her head. "No way. I'm texting him right now. What's his number?" She grabbed my phone off my bed and started scrolling through my contacts. I didn't have the energy to stop her. And maybe I didn't want to. I didn't want him there.

"Come on, slacker. We should have been on the road an hour ago," Kyle said in a snarky tone. I looked over to see him standing in the doorway, leaning against the frame with a smile on his face.

"Get out!" I screamed. I picked up a pen on my nightstand and threw it at him. He ducked out of the way.

"Jesus. I was just joking. Are you still upset from last night? I wish you would tell me what—"

"Beat it, Kyle." Jessica walked over and slammed the door in his face. She turned around and let out a deep breath before coming over to hug me again. "Fuck boys. Let's get you packed."

* * *

It was moments like these that I was happy to have a friend like Jessica. She helped me get packed much quicker than I would have been able to by myself. It seemed like in no time at all we were in the car and backing out of the driveway. She was also a saving grace, because Jacob had texted back, *Fine, I won't come.*

Hopefully being at the beach would allow me to forget about everything that had happened in the last twelve hours. Or maybe the seclusion would make me focus on my problems even more. Either way, I was going to need a lot of mac and cheese.

It was hard to get over the sadness that permeated through me. I had been looking forward to a fun weekend at the beach with Jacob. And I had kind of thought this weekend would have been perfect to tell my family about us. But that plan was now dead.

"Hey, Abby, can you pass me a bag of chips?" Jessica said from the back. I reached down into the bag of snacks my mom had packed and handed her one. Because she was the smallest, Jess was crammed in the last row of the car with the luggage that wouldn't fit in the trunk. Looking back at her, I didn't think I would have fit.

My body noticed the car make a turn it shouldn't have. We were now on Jacob's street, and it was not a shortcut to get out of the neighborhood.

"Where are we going?" I asked, feeling a lump in my throat grow as I predicted the answer.

My dad made eye contact with me in the rear-view mirror. "Picking up Jacob, of course." He chuckled at the thought that I would ask such a silly question, because the plan had always been for Jacob to come on the trip with us. I turned around to look at Jessica and she shrugged.

"I thought he wasn't coming anymore for some reason," I said.

Kyle looked over at me. "Where did you get that idea from?" He looked at me knowingly, as if he knew I was trying to hide something.

"I don't know. I guess I just imagined it." *Fuck*. I was not ready for this. I had already mentally prepared myself that I would not have to deal with him for at least a week until we got back in town. My heart quickened its pace as my dad pulled the car in front of my ex-boyfriend's house and honked the horn. I looked at the door and thought to myself, *Stay inside. Stay inside!* But then it opened, and he came out with a duffel bag. One that would likely drown Jessica. I took a deep breath and let it out before unbuckling my seatbelt. I started to shift over into the center seat.

"No, that's fine, Abby. I'll sit in the bitch seat this time," Kyle said.

My first reaction was to crane my neck out the window to see if pigs were flying, because Kyle had *never* offered to sit in the center seat our whole lives. What was happening?

Does he know?

Chapter 24

Jacob

I hated being in awkward situations, and the car ride was *extremely* awkward. Mr. Mike even commented on how quiet we all were in the back. Then we got to the condo and unpacked, and that was awkward. By the time everything was put away and situated, it was getting dark, so we went to our dinner reservation at a seafood restaurant. And that was *awkward* as fuck, too.

Maybe I should have listened to Jess and stayed home.

But fuck that. Abby was going to break up with me over text message and then tell me I couldn't go on the vacation that her brother invited me on? Screw that. Plus, I needed a way to talk to her, since she blocked my number. I was going to make it my duty to find a moment alone with her this week so we could talk. We would be trapped in close quarters for the next five days, so I figured it was my best shot at seeing what went wrong.

So far, however, it had not been easy. When we were unpacking the car, she made sure to always have Jess at her side. Then one time when she went to the bathroom last night, I got up from the table to wait for her, but then Kyle needed to use the bathroom too and was in the hallway behind me. When we got up this morning, she came down to the beach with her parents and Jessica and had not left them.

I caught the football that Kyle sent flying toward me and threw it back at him. I was going to break a finger if he kept throwing it this hard.

I looked over at Abby sunbathing, and I just wanted to be lying next to her. I wanted everybody to know about us. That we loved each other. But was she worth it if she was going to act like a child by not talking to me?

Kyle asked her how her interview had gone yesterday, and she said she didn't want to talk about it. I just wanted to hold her. And give her a kiss on the temple and tell her it was all going to be all right. That things happen for a reason.

The football came at lightning speed and hit me in the neck. I had been looking at Abby and not paying attention. Now I was bent over, holding my throat and coughing. Kyle jogged over with a smile on his face. He picked up the football and then patted me on the back.

"What the fuck, man?" I said, my voice hoarse.

"I'm sorry, bro. Maybe you would have caught it if you weren't staring at my sister."

Shit.

He saw the unexpected look of horror on my face. "Yeah, man. I figured it out. I'm just surprised it took me this long to catch you off guard."

"I was just looking at—"

"No more bullshit, dude. I know y'all have been hanging out together. It all makes sense now. All those times I tried to hang out with you, knowing that you weren't hanging out with any of our other friends from around here, and you would always say that you were busy doing something else, even though you weren't at work. You were just fucking my sister."

"Kyle—"

"No, Jacob. Shut the fuck up and listen. I mean, what is this? Are y'all just fucking? Is it something more?"

I was finally able to fully stand up. My throat was killing me. "We're nothing anymore, man. We're over."

Kyle squinted at me. "Ha. Yeah, that makes sense now why she's been so crazy lately." Then he smiled. "Well, then, good! Better it ended now than later." He took a big breath and smiled some more, like he'd accomplished some grand mission without having to lift a finger. *Asshole.* "All right, you want to play more football?"

"No thanks. I think I'm ready to lie down for a bit," I was able to mumble through the gravel inside my throat.

He slapped me on the back, and we made our way back to our chairs. As we came over, Abby noticed us. She stood up from her towel, said something to her mom and Jess, and walked back toward the condo.

"You all right there, Jacob?" Mr. Mike asked.

"Yes, sir. I've always wanted a *second* Adam's apple," I croaked. I sat down in one of the chairs and took in the sun. My heart was still racing after that confrontation with Kyle. It hadn't been pleasant, but it was like a Band-Aid being ripped off. I wondered how it would have gone if I'd told him that his sister and I were in love with each other at one point in time.

After half an hour of absorbing some rays, I was sweaty, smoldering, and sad. *Why did I put myself through all this torture of coming on this trip?*

"Oof, I'm thirsty," Jessica said, sitting up.

"Would you like a water? Gatorade? Capri Sun?" Mrs. Kathy asked her.

"No, thank you. I'm more in the mood for a daiquiri or a margarita or a Piña Colada. Or a Capri Sun with vodka."

"All out of those, unfortunately," Mrs. Kathy laughed.

"I saw a bar on the beach on my walk this morning. Would anybody want to go?" Jessica asked. No one answered. "Okay, so looks like I'm the only alcoholic in the group, huh? I guess I'll just go by myself."

"Well, we can't have that happening," Kyle said. "I'll come with you. You coming, Jacob?"

Hope lifted inside me. Two obstacles were about to be down the beach and out of my way to go talk to Abby. "No thanks. I don't think I can drink anything after that football moved my esophagus around." Kyle looked at me skeptically. "If I drink now, I'm not going to be able to go out with you later. I'm going to save it." That seemed to satisfy him. He nodded, and then he and Jessica walked down the beach together in search of the bar.

I knew I couldn't leave right away in case Kyle looked back and saw me go up to the condo to be with Abby. So I waited a few minutes.

"Jacob, what's new these days?" Mrs. Kathy asked me once Kyle and Jess were gone. I opened my eyes to look at her. Her face differed from the happy, carefree expression she usually had when talking to me. She was still smiling, but it seemed like she was asking for something else.

"Oh, nothing much, other than working at the pool. Though I guess I might be interviewing for an entry-level marketing position soon."

"Oh, wow," she said. But it still seemed like that wasn't the answer she was looking for.

Mr. Mike, however, leaned forward in his chair to join the conversation. "What's this I hear?"

"Yeah, sorry, boss," I said with a smile. "An...old acquaintance from college works in marketing and told me I might be able to get the same kind of position that she got. It doesn't pay much to start off, but there is a ladder I can climb."

"That's exciting!" Mr. Mike said. "Whatever it is, I'm sure it's more than that stickler at the club is paying you." He winked. "But no, really. I hope it works out for you. This pool boy thing was just something to keep you busy and out of the house while you found something. So I hope your acquaintance pulls through." We talked for a few minutes about how I was interested in advertising and marketing but didn't really have any experience. Then I told them I had to use the restroom.

I walked into the condo and saw Abby reading her book on the balcony. I took a deep breath and slid the door open. The look of disgust on her face when she saw me made me a combination of depressed and angry at the same time.

"Jacob, please leave me alone."

I stepped onto the balcony and closed the door behind me. "No. I'm not going to leave you alone. Because we're adults. Adults talk things out. You can't ignore things like a child."

"I am not a child!" she said.

"Well, you're acting like one!" I snapped. I felt bad. But her lack of communication was killing me. I hadn't slept well in forty-eight hours. I just wanted to talk, but she was so defensive, and I wasn't the one who'd lied. She stood up from her chair and tried to walk past me, but I stepped in her way. Her eyes were focused on the floor. She was doing everything she could to avoid my gaze.

"Jacob, let me through."

"No. Not until you talk to me. Not until you tell me why you broke up with me. How am I supposed to defend myself if you don't even tell me what horrible thing I did?"

"Because I don't need to give the courtesy of talking anything out to a liar and a cheater!" she said. She pushed me aside, slid the door open, and went inside. She tried slamming it shut on me, but I put my arm through it and held it open. She turned to walk away from me. I was scared and didn't know when I would be able to get her alone and talk things out with her again, so I grabbed her arm to keep her near me.

"You need to tell me what the hell you're talking about. I'm too crazy about you to just let you end things between us."

"Let go of me," she said.

"Tell me. Tell me the real reason you're breaking up with me. Because I don't know what lie I could have told that would cause you to end this. Especially when I found out *you* lied to *me* about something pretty big, and my only plan was to talk to you about it. I know this is all new for us, Abby, but fuck! It's like none of it meant anything to you."

"No!" she said, trying to pull away. But I held her close. I couldn't let her go. I needed to know.

"Then talk to me! Tell me!"

We heard the key card enter the lock in the front door and beep. I let go of her, and she hurried away from me. Her dad opened the door, and she pushed past him, crying. He looked back at her and then at me. "Honey, are you okay?" he called out to her.

"I'm fine!" she screamed. I could hear the elevator dinging in the distance. Mr. Mike turned back to me. "What was that all about?" he asked. I didn't know how to respond. Why tell him about my relationship with her if there was no longer anything to tell?

I shrugged. "I'm not sure. She's a closed book."

Mr. Mike put his hands on his hips and hung his head low. "She's been off ever since she woke up late for her interview yesterday. Apparently, it didn't go well. She is probably still upset with that."

"Yeah. Maybe." My soul was aching to be with her again.

To comfort her. To fix whatever I had done wrong. To fix us. But maybe our last chapter had already been written.

Chapter 25

Abby

The elevator doors opened, and I strolled out through the lobby. Goosebumps immediately covered my whole body. Why did condominiums at the beach always make the lobby so cold? Didn't they know that people were wet and basically only wearing underwear? *We don't need it to be this cold!*

My eyes felt red and puffy from my brief cry upstairs. I had put my sunglasses on while still in the elevator so no one would notice. But now I was the only crazy person wearing their sunglasses inside.

I walked through the glass automatic double doors and took a big relaxing breath as soon as the warm air and sunshine covered my body. I needed to be away from Jacob, and I really just wanted some space from everyone. I couldn't believe he'd held me there like some kind of barbarian.

The pool area looked enticing, since I knew no one around it. But all the chairs were taken. Soon enough, my feet were stepping through the hot sand toward our spot. Thankfully, Kyle and Jess weren't there anymore. It was just my mom.

My butt sank into the chair, and I opened my book. I didn't need to see my mom glance over at me. I felt her concerned look.

"Everything okay, honey?" she asked.

"Everything's just dandy, Mom."

There was a short silence before she stood up and got in front of me. "I'm going to go on a walk. Want to join me?"

I turned a page in my book, though I hadn't registered the last two paragraphs my eyes had skimmed. "I don't really feel like walking. Thanks, though."

She nudged my leg with her foot. "Please? I need a buddy."

I looked up at her, and she was giving me a pouty face. "Fine." I placed my bookmark on the page I was on and closed my book.

She hugged me as I stood up, and I hated to admit that it made me feel better. "I love spending one-on-one time with my girl."

We walked in silence down the beach in the opposite direction of the bar that Jess and Kyle had gone to. It was a busy weekend. Most of the crowd looked like families; but there were a few groups of what seemed to be bachelor and bachelorette parties. We passed some jellyfish in the sand and some dead fish. Then we saw a couple that was lying on towels in the sand, holding hands. I let out a sigh, thinking how nice it would have been to be holding Jacob's hand if he wasn't such a pig.

My mom looked over at me. "What's wrong, Abby?"

I shook my head. "Nothing's wrong, Mom."

She gave me a knowing look. "You know it's no use lying to your mother, right? You're a part of me. I know you. So tell me."

"I guess I'm upset...because I ruined my interview." I was still too chickenshit to tell her about me and Jacob. Maybe I never would now. It was embarrassing. A failed attempt.

She nodded. "That's it?"

"That's it," I lied.

"Hmm. Well, honey, there's more fish in the sea."

I scrunched my face at her.

"You know, if fish were jobs," she said.

"Yeah, I guess so. I just really wanted *this* fish to work out. But maybe it was for the best because I actually found out that this fish wasn't all it seemed to be."

"Oh. Is that so?" A cool wave came up and washed the sand off our feet.

"Yeah. This fish, I mean school, seemed like it was a perfect fit for me in every way. It seemed like I was meant to be with, I mean *at,* this school for the rest of my career. But I was doing some research, and it seems like this school has been cheating."

"What? Cheating? What do you mean?"

Oh jeez. What kind of lie was I digging myself into now? Hadn't I learned that even white lies have consequences? "On its test scores. Apparently, Franklin Middle was reporting high scores, but they were lying. Pretending."

"Oh, wow. I haven't seen that yet. You'd think that I would have gotten a notification on my phone from one of the local news stations." A small snippet of silence followed. "Are you sure the source is reliable? Have there been more reports or news articles on it? Where did you read this?"

My eyes misted. "It's a reliable source, Mom. Just trust me," I said with a lump in my throat. My mom stopped walking and grabbed my wrist. I turned away so she wouldn't see my face.

"We're not really talking about the school, are we, Abby?"

I shook my head. She knew. She'd known the whole time.

For the hundredth time since the party, I started crying. And it was an ugly, full cry. I felt more comfortable with her than anyone in the world, and I just let everything out. She pulled me into a strong embrace and rubbed my back.

"Shhh," she said. "It's okay. It's okay. You're going to be okay."

"It's not okay! I met a guy and went from feeling like I was on top of the world, and now I feel like I have been continuously falling and haven't even reached the bottom yet. I thought I had found the one, Mom. And then I caught him in a lie about another girl. He broke my heart."

"Oh, honey. Why didn't you tell me? We could have made some excuse for him not to come on the trip, if we had known that he hurt you like this."

I pulled back to look at her.

She gave me half of a smile and put her hand on the side of my face. "Sweetie, you think your dad and I didn't know about you and Jacob? Your father saw Jacob looking at you differently when we went bowling at the beginning of the summer. Why do you think he offered for Jacob to work at the pool? We were on to y'all before you two even knew it yourselves."

I knew that the earth was constantly spinning around on itself at about a thousand miles per hour, but suddenly I *felt* that spinning in real time and almost lost my footing. But she caught me.

"Abby, I told you. I *know* you. Kids always think they're so good at hiding things from their parents. They think they're sneaky enough to not get noticed. But they forget that parents were kids once, too. We know all the tricks in the playbook." I hugged her again.

"I'm sorry we hid it from you."

"Don't be sorry. Your father and I understand why. But come on. Let's keep walking and you can tell me as much or as little as you want. Who knows, maybe this former kid who fell in love once or twice might have some good advice."

So we walked down the beach and I told her everything. Well, not *everything*, of course. But I told her how we both felt an immediate attraction toward each other when we first saw each other this summer that had never really been there before. That we became inseparable and wanted to spend all of our free time together. How I thought he was going to be the one. And then how all of that came crashing down when I saw him with Katie. She listened the whole time, never interrupting.

"I just...Never in a million years would I ever expect Jacob to do something like that," she said when I was done. I clenched my hands into fists.

"I know. I thought he was one of the good ones."

Her eyes studied me. "Are you *sure* there's something to worry about? You didn't actually see them kiss or do anything else, right?"

"Mom, he didn't tell me she had texted him, and he didn't tell me that he was going to a party, when he basically tells me everything else that he does. And then when I get to the party, he's sitting outside, smiling and talking. I saw her take his hand." What more did she need to know?

She had the audacity to shrug. "Have y'all talked about it?"

"No. I can't stand to speak with him. Or to even look at him. Just the thought of him sneaking around with *her* while he and I were together makes me sick."

She looked at me like she wasn't convinced. "I don't know, Abby. It just doesn't add up. He has always been a sweetheart. And your father and I have seen how he looks at you. He adores you. I really think you two need to talk before it's too late. Let him explain. He deserves that much." I shook my head. "Abby, all you saw was a girl touch his hand. You didn't see them kiss. You didn't catch them in bed together. You didn't catch them sexting."

"Mom!"

"Oh, calm yourself. I know what sexting is."

"I know what I saw," I said stubbornly. "She was looking at him all starry-eyed."

"And maybe she does have feelings, but it doesn't mean *he* does. Abby, when you date someone, you're going to need to get used to the fact that other people are going to be attracted to them too. And yes, some people might try to break up your relationship. But all of that doesn't matter if you found a good, loving partner who respects you and doesn't give in. I love you, baby. And you have my full support always. But I love Jacob too, and I'm just not convinced this is what you think it is. Talk to each other tonight. And if he did cheat on you, let me know, and I'll squeeze a bottle of eye drops in his drink and make him be stuck on the toilet for the rest of the trip," she said. I shook my head but couldn't help but laughing. She laughed too, and the seagulls above echoed us.

She'd made some good points, but I wasn't convinced. "Fine. I'll talk to him tonight."

She wrapped her arm around my shoulder pulled me in for a side hug. "Good. You talk to him, and I'll go to the drugstore and buy some eye drops just in case."

* * *

My mom and I strolled down the beach much further than we ever had. By the time we got back to our chairs, they were mostly empty except for our belongings.

We walked into the condo to the smell of pizza. Muse's Pizza. It was our favorite place to order from when we came to the beach. Everyone was sitting at the dinner table.

"There they are!" Jessica yelled. She sounded drunk, or at least tipsy. She grabbed two big Styrofoam cups and handed one to me and one to my mom. "Kyle and I got large Piña Coladas for everybody with two extra shots in each one."

"Come get some delicious pizza, my beautiful ladies!" my dad said. He was *definitely* feeling his two extra shots. Jacob still hadn't turned around to look at me. How was I going to get him on his own and talk to him? Maybe I could wait until Kyle went to shower.

My mom and I made our way to the table and sat down. I tried making eye contact with Jacob, but he was avoiding my gaze. One sip of my Piña Colada later, I felt like my tongue was soaked in rum. It tasted fine, but I just wasn't in the mood to drink. I pushed the cup away from me. "I think it's too strong for me," I said. Within a second, Jacob snatched it up.

"I'll take it," he said. His eyes still looked anywhere but at mine. Jess, Kyle, and Jacob were all dressed up while I was still in my bathing suit.

"Are y'all going somewhere tonight?" I asked. I felt out of the loop.

"All *four* of us are going out on the town tonight," Jessica said while motioning her finger in a circle. "So you need to eat your pizza and go get dressed."

Going out was the *last* thing I wanted to do. I wanted to talk to Jacob. And I did not want to do that at a bar, especially if either of us was drinking. "I don't know. I think I may just stay in tonight," I said, still trying to catch Jacob's eye.

"Fine by me," Kyle said.

I shot him a mean glare. He stuck his tongue out at me. I looked over at Jacob, trying to give him hints that I wanted him to stay, too. If we could get Kyle and Jessica to leave, I would be able to get some privacy with him. But he was still interested in looking at anything but my face. It was making me upset.

"Come on, girl!" Jessica said enthusiastically. "We're on vacation. Let's make the most of it."

I was shutting down. "I'm going to stay in," I repeated, forcing all of my mental energy upon Jacob to see if I could make some kind of telepathic connection to tell him that I needed to speak with him.

"Aw, don't be a party pooper. Let's go on an adventure. I like adventure. I want to do things. Go places. Climb mountains," Jessica said.

"Then go!" It came out louder and more aggressive than I wanted it to, and I immediately regretted it. She was obviously on a different level after drinking for the last couple of hours while I was stone cold sober.

There I was. The crazy girl ruining everyone's vacation again. Kyle shook his head, and Jessica became silent. Jacob acted like I was Medusa. Another awkward dinner in the books.

I hated myself.

Chapter 26

Jacob

The bar was crowded, and I couldn't hear any distinct voices. It was all white noise, and the cold beer in my hand was static as it went down my throat. After the incident in the condo with Abby today, the only thing I could think about was to drink my pain away. I had tried everything else.

It wasn't my idea to start drinking. I had walked back down to the beach a few minutes after Abby left crying. I sat for a bit, and then Kyle handed me a drink. It was pretty strong, and the numbness it gave me felt good. And then Abby's drink made me feel even better.

I was almost to my inebriation limit. Or maybe I was already past it. Deep down I knew that I had had enough tonight already, but stopping was easier said than done. Especially when I was feeling like shit the last two days.

Jessica came back from the bathroom and sat on her barstool next to me. She noticed Kyle on the other side of the room talking to a couple of cute girls. She snorted.

"Do you think I'm attractive?" Jessica asked me.

What the fuck is this shit? "Jesus. Is this some sort of trap?" I hiccupped and looked at her, half expecting Abby to be dressed in camouflage a few paces behind her. Her eyes were still transfixed on Kyle.

"No. I was just curious if boys like you, or Kyle, found me to be attractive."

I rolled my eyes. Surely she knew the answer to that question...She was a cheerleader. She'd had guys—and girls, I was sure—pining for her her whole life. *Why don't pretty people know they're pretty?* "I would never say this unless I was completely drunk, and since I currently fit that requirement, I can say without a doubt that you are indeed attractive, and everybody knows it." I clinked my beer with her mostly empty cocktail glass. "Cheers!" The rest of my beer went down my gullet.

Her eyes were still far off. "Cheers. I'm glad *you* at least think so," she said. The bartender noticed our empty drinks and came over.

"Another round for the both of us!" I screamed over the music. The bar was getting more crowded as the night went on. The bartender set to work, and Jess looked over at me.

"Are you sure you need another one? Should we get some water in us first?"

"Psh. Water shmater," I said.

She rolled her eyes. "Hey. Now that Kyle isn't hovering, what the fuck is wrong with you?" She slapped my shoulder.

That had come out of nowhere. "What the hell?"

"You and Abby. She was head over heels for you, and you betrayed her?"

I couldn't help but laugh and shake my head. "I didn't betray her. I don't know what she thinks she knows, because she won't even talk to me about it, but I didn't fucking do anything. It's like she's still in goddamn high school. I tried to get her to be an adult and talk to me about it, but she blocked my number. So I've tried to speak with her in person multiple times this trip, but she has made an effort to never be alone. The one time we had privacy today, she didn't want anything to do with me. So I've given up."

"Wait, so you're saying that you didn't—" She was cut off by Kyle walking up with two blond girls.

"*This* is my best friend Jacob!" he slurred at them. He had his arm around the waist of one in a short black dress. The other one, wearing a yellow top and short jeans shorts, held out her hand. I quickly shook it and let go as she introduced herself, but her voice was swallowed up by the roar of the crowd as some radio hit came on. No matter. I didn't care what her name was.

Jessica grabbed her newly made drink and walked out onto the dance floor, mumbling something. She didn't look too happy. Kyle looked back at her as she brushed past him and then turned to me. He scrunched his face at me. "What was that about?" he shouted. I shrugged and took a big gulp of my new, crisp beer.

"I want to dance!" the girl Kyle had attached to his side yelled.

"Let's do it!" he said. "Come on Jacob! Let's go dance."

I just shook my head. No fucking way did I want to dance right now. "No thank you. Y'all have a lovely time." The girl in the yellow top looked disappointed.

Kyle leaned in to my ear. "These girls are a package deal, man. Be a good wing man and help me out. You owe me," he said.

Well, fuck me. I hated being guilted into things. But maybe if I went out there and shuffled my feet a bit, he would be closer to forgiving me for going after his little sister. His little sister, who I wanted to be holding at that very moment.

Breathing in her hair. Kissing her soft lips. Caressing her body.

Kyle yanked on my arm and pulled me out of my daydream. I spilled my beer on the bar and my shirt. "Shit. Sorry," I said, though I wasn't sure if I was saying it to the bartender, the girls, or to myself.

We walked out onto the dance floor, maneuvering between bodies moving side to side and jumping up and down. We finally found our own spot and danced as a group. The yellow-top girl—staring up at me and standing way too close—kept asking me questions, but I continued to ignore her. I couldn't have cared less what she wanted.

After a couple of songs, I went to get another beer. The wait had gotten much longer, so I didn't get back to our spot on the dance floor until three or four songs later. Kyle was nowhere to be seen. His girl was gone, too. But yellow top was still there. She smiled when she saw me. She was pretty, but she wasn't the girl that had been on my mind. "Where did they go?" I asked.

She shrugged. "I don't know. Who cares!" I turned to walk away and go find Kyle, but she grabbed my hand and pulled me closer.

"No thanks," I said. I tried to walk away for the second time that night, but she looped her fingers through my belt loops and pulled me toward her. "I said fucking no," I snapped and pushed her away. I hadn't thought it was a hard shove, but she stumbled and hit the ground hard.

Within a second, there was a circle of people staring at her, and then at me. Angry faces. People were pointing their fingers at me.

"He just knocked that girl down!" someone shouted.

Suddenly someone pushed me hard in the back. I lurched forward and spilled my beer all over some random guy in front of me. He shoved me, and I dropped my glass on the floor, sending beer and shards of glass all over everyone's shoes. Some guy a few inches taller than me came up and pressed his forehead into mine and yelled into my face. I pushed him, but I was so drunk that it didn't do much.

So he punched me in the face. I stumbled back. My eye was searing in pain. I took a swing at him, but my drunken state had me moving in slow motion. He caught my wrist and then punched me hard in the stomach, knocking the wind out of me.

A moment later, big strong hands were dragging me by the shirt. I saw people clapping and flipping me off at the same time. The bouncer took me to the door and lifted me into the air by my shirt. "Don't fucking come back," he said. Then he gave me a hard shove, and I tripped onto the asphalt, scraping my hands and my knees. I couldn't see it, but I knew I was bleeding.

"What the fuck?" a familiar voice said in the distance. I looked up to see Kyle and Jess running toward me. *Were they hanging out here without me? Were they leaving?* They knelt down beside me as I sat up with my head in my hands.

"Dude, are you okay? What happened?" He stood up and yelled at the bouncer, "Yo! What the fuck?"

"Your friend pushed a girl down on the dance floor and then started a fight!"

"Jesus." Kyle squatted beside me again. "Is that true?"

I looked into his six eyes. "Yes? And no." I didn't know whether the spinning was worse when I kept my eyes open or closed. *Why did I drink so much?*

Jessica was looking at my scrapes. "Kyle, go inside and get some water and napkins. And close our tabs. I'll wait to call a ride until you come back outside." Her lipstick looked smeared, but that may have just been my blurry vision.

We sat there for what felt like an hour. But it was probably only a few minutes. I was starting to spin less.

"Was it worth it? Getting so drunk?" Jessica asked me.

"Whatever," I said. "I just needed to do something to get me to stop thinking about Abby."

"And? Did it work?"

My body sagged. "No."

"Look, I'm going to get to the point before Kyle comes back. I know earlier you said that this is all a big misunderstanding on her end. And I know she hasn't been easy to talk to. But if you really love her, then you can't give up. You can't try a couple of times, call it quits, and then drink your problems away. Maybe she's not acting like an adult, but you can be twice the adult for her."

I didn't know how to get it through Jessica's head. "I told you, I've tried. She doesn't want anything to do with me. And anyways, I also found out she lied to me about something big. So you tell her I need an apology, too."

"First of all, I'm not telling her shit. You can do that yourself. Second of all, what do you mean?"

"She told me she'd never slept with anyone else, and then the other day *you* told me she had. I wouldn't have cared either way. But the fact that she lied to me about it, and kept up the lie, that's fucked up. So she's not the only one dealing with trust issues."

Jessica was silent for a minute. "Well, look, I don't know how to answer that. You'll have to get into it with her. I know she seems sad and distant now, but I've never seen her as happy as she was when you two were dating. I think if y'all just talk and work things out, you'll both end up happier. Maybe it was a misunderstanding. Or maybe you both need to learn to forgive each other."

I wanted to give her the same answer that I had already

given her a few times, but Kyle walked up with the water and napkins. I gulped down one of the cups, and Jessica dipped the napkins into the other cup and rinsed my wounds.

I wanted to make things better, but would Abby give me the chance?

Chapter 27

Abby

The sand was cool on my feet as I stepped off the boardwalk. The sun still hadn't risen yet, but it was close. I took a deep breath and looked around me as the empty beach came alive with the beginning twilight of a new day. There were dolphins surfacing in the distance, and seagulls were walking in the sand, pecking down at any left-overs from the day before.

The beach was clear and pristine. No people, no chairs, no toys. It was just how I liked it. I zipped up my phone in my pocket, and I started running.

It had been a while since I had taken a good run, so I didn't know how long it would last. But it was something I always liked to do at the beach. Especially that morning.

Going to sleep last night was difficult. After they all left to go out, I went on the balcony to read my book, but I was too distracted to even get through a single page. So then I scrolled on my phone for a couple of hours before going to bed and lying there awake for far too long. I eventually fell asleep, but then I woke up when Jessica came into the room.

Poor thing was trying to be as quiet as she could, but I opened my eyes as soon as she opened our door. After that, I drifted in and out of sleep. I kept thinking about what bar they'd gone to, and if Jacob had hooked up with some random beach girl while I was in the condo thinking of him. So I thought if I woke up early and went for a run, it might clear my mind and make me tired enough to actually get some sleep tonight.

I ran for thirty minutes, and then I turned around. Running long distance to me was like riding a bike. I had a small cramp, but I just pushed through it, and it wasn't too bad. The whole clearing-my-mind thing didn't really work, though. With every stride I took, I just thought of Jacob. And that damned interview.

I was still kicking myself over everything that had gone wrong that morning. Would I ever not feel like shit about it? I may have had an actual shot at the job of my dreams, and I blew it. I knew it was all on me. I hated that I hadn't shown Ms. Stefanski who I really was.

And I felt bad about how I handled things with Jacob. Maybe my mom was right. Why *hadn't* I let him talk? Why hadn't I let him explain? I didn't know. Was I scared that the answer spoken out loud would confirm everything? Was I afraid that he would tell me a convincing lie, and I would just accept it because I was desperate for his love? Or was I just afraid of letting myself have something real?

I stopped and took a breather, clasping my hands behind my head. Beach attendants were out setting up chairs now that the sun was up, and other runners and casual beach strollers were trickling out. A cute couple was holding hands as they passed me by.

I wanted *that* again. And I was ready to grow up. Ready to talk things out with Jacob and find out the truth, good or bad.

Find out why he lied to me about that girl texting him, and why he didn't tell me he was going to a party with her.

And I was going to finish that damn interview, too.

I pulled out my phone and dialed the number for Franklin Middle. The voicemail was expected, since it was still early. The recorded message played and then the beep sounded. My heart was racing. "Ms. Stefanski, hi, this is Abby Barber." *Why did I call while I was still out of breath?* "I just wanted to call and say that I hated how my interview went. I'm so grateful that you gave someone with no experience a chance of even interviewing with you, because you are my role model and the school you have built would be a dream to work at. But you did not see the real Abby Barber that day. You asked me why it was my dream to work at Franklin Middle, and I never got to answer. And I don't care that you've probably already picked someone else for the job; I just need to get it off my chest. Working for you at Franklin would be a dream come true because of the way you let teachers teach, and because of the way you allow for varied methods of instruction. Your school's test scores are so high because you don't make all your teachers follow the same methods, or the newest fad that the Department of Education is putting out there. If a teacher is a good lecturer, then you allow them to lecture if you see the students are learning. If the teacher wants to teach outside among the trees, you let it happen. If the teacher wants to play music to get the students to learn, you allow it if it works, while so many other principals out there can be so narrow-minded. I would be a great hire because teaching is my passion, and I love our town. And even with all the trials and tribulations that teachers face these days, I'm in it for the long haul. So, I just wanted you to hear that. It's mainly for my benefit, I think, because the person you interviewed is not an accurate representation of who I usually am—"

"Thank you for your message. Goodbye."

My rambling had reached the time limit. *Whatever*, I thought. I'd probably made myself seem like even a bigger fool, but I needed to do that.

Suddenly, I felt reinvigorated and was ready to fix everything in my life. I looked toward our condo building and ran.

* * *

JACOB

Loud laughter from somewhere in the condo woke me up. The room was still dark with the shades drawn, but the sunlight coming through the door told me it was already late morning. I sat up and rubbed my eyes, which immediately made me flinch. My left eye was painful to the touch.

Kyle's bed was empty. My throat felt like a dry sponge, and I quickly emptied the glass of water on my nightstand into my mouth. My head was pounding with an excruciating headache. I felt hungover as shit.

The door opened and Kyle walked in with a towel wrapped around his waist. "Ah, the beauty queen is awake, I see." He flipped the light switch on, practically blinding me. He grimaced when he saw my face. "Actually, I think you may need to sit out this pageant."

"Shut the fuck up." On top of everything else, I felt sick to my stomach, not knowing whether eating some food would make me feel better or worse. Kyle dropped his towel and put some boxers on.

"The shower is open. I wanted to let you sleep is much as possible, but you need to go wash up and get dressed pretty quickly. We need to leave for brunch in about twenty minutes."

"Fuck," was all I could muster. Skipping brunch sounded very appealing at this moment. I didn't want anyone to see me, and I *definitely* didn't want to rush to get ready. I felt like utter shit. But I didn't want to seem ungrateful to Mr. and Mrs. Barber. They'd invited me on this trip and not asked me to pay a dime.

A few minutes later, the hot, steamy water felt good on my face. It made the cut near my eye, and the scrapes on my knees and hands, sting; but it made everything feel clean. It was also slowly getting rid of my hangover. I started slowly remembering the events from last night. And the one that I was currently fixated on was Jessica talking about forgiveness. I was ready to forgive Abby for anything and everything to get the chance to be with her again. And I hoped she was willing to forgive me for whatever it was I had done. Life was—and would be—so miserable without her. My lips ached to kiss her again.

I finished showering, wrapped a towel around myself, and closed the door to my room behind me so I could change. I stepped over my suitcase and heard a soft knock at the door.

"Yes?"

"Hey, it's Abby. Can you talk?" That *voice*. That sweet angelic voice wanted to speak to me again? I practically ran over to the door and cracked it open.

"Hey. What's up?"

"Can I come in, so we can talk alone?"

"Of course." I had been thinking about this moment for days, but I hadn't imagined I would be practically naked while doing so. She came in and shut the door. She looked gorgeous in her blue dress. Her eyes went down to my towel and then to my face.

"Oh my God! Jacob! What happened to you?"

"It's nothing. I'm fine. Long story short, I got kicked out of the bar last night for being a drunk idiot. But what did you want to talk about? I don't know how much time we have before we need to leave. And I don't think this is up to the dress code," I said, looking down at my towel.

She gave a soft laugh, and it was the best thing I had heard in days. It made me smile.

"Right. I wanted us to talk. First, I want to say I'm sorry for being so non-confrontational and avoiding this. I guess I was scared. But I'm upset about this girl Katie."

"Katie? Why?" What the hell was she talking about?

"Well, I know she was the one who had texted you while we were at your place, and you hid it from me. So that was the first red flag. And then I had to find out that you were at a party from Jessica, which I found weird, because I thought we told each other everything; so it seemed like you were hiding that from me too. And what did I find when I got there? You on the loveseat with some girl you used to fuck, and she was caressing you like she was going to climb you right then and there."

I saw how upset she was getting, and instinct made me put both of my hands on her arms in a soft, loving way to try to calm her down.

And my towel dropped to the floor.

"Goddammit," I said. I bent down to pick it back up, and she laughed, covering her eyes. I stood up, moved her hands away, and looked deep into them. "Abby, I'm so sorry—"

She backed up a step. "So it's true? You were hiding her from me?"

I shook my head. "No, let me finish, please. I'm sorry I didn't tell you that it was her texting me. It was really no big deal. It didn't even occur to me to tell you because it was nothing We had a one-night stand in college, but that was it. I never called her again or responded to her messages."

She didn't look convinced. "So how did she end up at the same party as you?"

I nodded toward the door. "Your stupid brother. She contacted him because she couldn't get in touch with me. She told him she was in town for work for a couple days, and he invited her to the party. He didn't tell me until I was already there."

"Okay. So what was your plan that night? Why did you two need to be off all alone talking?"

It was kind of cute how she was jealous, but this was a bit much. "You know what, in all honesty, yes. I think she was trying to get in touch with me so that we could hook up again." Abby's face looked like all of her fears came true. "*But* I told her that I was madly in love. With you. And she was happy for me. Abby, I haven't been able to talk about you to anyone. I can't talk to my best friend about it, or anyone else we know. My mom is dead, and my dad avoids me. But she lives out of town and doesn't know anyone, and she swore not to tell Kyle. So after weeks of keeping you a secret from literally everyone in my life, I practically gushed out everything I had been thinking for all that time like a dam had broken."

She looked relieved, like a huge weight had been lifted off her. "Oh. God, I feel like such an idiot," she said. "But why didn't you tell me you were going to a party?"

I looked down at my feet for a second. "Because I was kind of upset with you that day."

She looked shocked, which made sense. "Why?"

"I ran into Jessica at the coffee shop that morning, and I found out that you being a virgin was a lie." She covered her face. *So I guess it's true*, I thought. She looked embarrassed. "But look, I don't care. I never would have cared. You could have slept with anyone you wanted before we got together, and it wouldn't have mattered. And I know you probably lied about being a virgin to protect my ego, but I don't care anymore. I just needed a day to cool off about it. I know how much I please you, and that's all that matters."

Her hand was still covering her face, and she started laughing. "This is what I get for lying," she said. Suddenly I was wondering what her body count was and if I was truly the best she had ever had, like she'd told me. She finally uncovered her face. "Yes, I lied about my virginity. But not to you."

Now I was the one to be confused.

"I told Jessica a while ago that I had had sex because I knew she was having plenty of it while I was stuck in a book. She was the hot college cheerleader with a different boy on her arm every year. I didn't want her to think of me as her dorky virgin roommate. It was a stupid lie, I know..."

"Oh, well, I—"

The door handle turned, and Kyle almost swung it into Abby. "Yo, dude, are you dressed yet?" he said. He saw her behind the door, inches away from me, still in just a towel. He glared at me. "Get dressed, dude. Come on, Abby." He nodded for her to leave.

"Can we have another minute?" she asked.

"No. Y'all are already making us late as it is," he said.

"Come on, man," I said. Abby and I were so close to working everything out.

Mr. Barber yelled to us from the other side of the hallway. "Everyone ready? They'll give up our table if we miss the reservation!" Abby gave me a quick smile and then left the room, brushing past Kyle.

He stared at me for a second, then shook his head and slammed the door.

Chapter 28

Jacob

Everyone placed their order, and then we sat in silence as the jazz band played. Abby's dad looked back and forth between everyone at the table.

"Why is everyone so quiet? Usually, the four of you can't keep your mouths shut, but now I don't even know if I could pay any of you to say something."

"Michael," Mrs. Kathy scolded him.

"What? We're on vacation. Everyone is supposed to be happy, but it seems like everybody hates the beach."

Abby stood up. "I'm going to run to the restroom," she said. I stared at her as she walked off. We needed to finish our conversation. I tried to stand up, but Kyle grabbed my shirt and pulled me back into my chair. He leaned over into my ear. "What are you doing, man? What's your problem?"

I shook my head. "You're being ridiculous, dude." I stayed in my chair, not wanting to make a scene. I would find some time to talk to her after brunch. The band finished their song, and I saw Abby in the distance walking back to our table.

"All right, ladies and gentlemen. This is the time where we

invite any of the guests out there to come up and make a request. I have this glass jar in front of me and some pieces of paper and pencils. Just write down your song suggestion and put it in the bowl. Or, the first one who comes up to the stage can just whisper it in my ear. There's also a tip jar next to that bowl, if you want to let us know how much you enjoyed our music."

A crazy idea came over me. I was tired of the games. Tired of the secrecy. I quickly stood up and walked to the stage. I needed to get there before anyone else.

"Well, looks like this guy is in dire need of a song. Slow down, young buck. Safety first," he joked, drawing laughs from the crowd. He crouched down on the stage to reach my level. "What will it be? A love song to a beautiful lady?"

"Actually, I was going to see if I could borrow your mic," I told him.

He laughed. "Sorry. We're kind of a one-singer band."

I pulled out my wallet and put five one-hundred-dollar bills in his tip jar. His eyes grew big. "I don't want to sing. I just need to say something to some people here. And yes, one of them happens to be a beautiful lady."

"Well, shoot. Why not?" He held out his hand and pulled me up onto the stage. I looked back toward our table. Abby had almost made her way back, but she was standing, frozen in place and staring at me.

"Testing." My voice reverberated around the restaurant. Everyone at our table was looking at me like I was a crazy person. And maybe I was. "Hi, everybody. My name is Jacob. And I don't plan on taking too much of your time. But I just needed to come up here and say some things to this one-of-a-kind girl that I know, named Abby." I looked at Abby, and everyone's eyes followed mine. "She was right in front of me my whole life, but I didn't really see her until recently. We fell in love with each other this summer, and I know deep in my heart that she is the one for me. My soulmate. We recently hit a rough patch, but Abby, I love you. I'm sorry I wasn't mature enough to be open with you, and I need us to get back together."

My poor angel. She was pretty far away, but I could still see how red her face was with everybody in the restaurant staring at her. She turned around and started walking to the door.

"Abby, I am beyond in love with you, and I don't care who knows." She stopped and turned back around to face me. "Our time together this summer has been the most fun I've ever had. And if you want to walk away right now, just know that you're prolonging the inevitable, and that I will keep embarrassing you at brunches and dinners until you give me another shot. I've known you for most of my life, but I've only *really* known you for barely two months. Every time I think of my future, your beautiful face is in it front and center. I think of you in a white dress walking down the aisle toward me, I think of us starting a family, and I can clearly see your face when we're both in our eighties. You have a few wrinkles, but you're as gorgeous as ever. I love you, Abby, and I know you love me. It's time we stopped hiding it from everybody. So what do you say? Can we try this out again?"

Abby laughed out a sob and nodded. I quickly handed the mic back to the singer and jumped off the stage. We ran toward each other and embraced. The whole restaurant started clapping.

"I love you," she said. I kissed her deeply, and everyone in the restaurant clapped even louder. I looked over at our table, and her parents had their arms around each other and kissed. Mrs. Kathy had tears in her eyes. Kyle had his arms folded and was looking at me, but he didn't look as pissed as he had when I first started my speech. He was redder in the face than Abby was when I had started.

I kissed Abby's forehead. "I love you too, baby."

The clapping faded away, but everyone was still looking at us. "Well, wasn't that just the cutest thing you ever did see?" the singer said into the mic. "Okay, are there any other proclamations of love we need to take care of before we start playing music again?" The crowd laughed, with Abby and I joining them.

I took her by the hand and led her back to our table. Everyone had a big smile on their face, except Kyle. But I didn't care. If he couldn't grow up and accept the love his sister and I shared, then maybe he wasn't the friend I thought he was. I looked at Abby, and her face was getting redder as we got closer to everyone. She was the most beautiful thing in the world. She was all I needed.

Chapter 29

Abby

My feet felt light as a feather, even as they sank through the wet sand. I looked up at Jacob, and it felt like my body might have floated away were it not for his hand interlocked with mine. He caught my eye and smiled. We kissed, and a billion butterflies erupted in my stomach and flew out toward the sunset behind us.

We walked to the beach bar to have some privacy. When we passed behind our chairs on the beach, only my mom and dad were there. They didn't see us sneak by.

We finally made it to our destination. It was my first time being here. There was a pool with a walk-up bar in the middle of it, and it was surrounded by palm trees. The water was slightly warm as I walked in deeper, but my body was refreshed after a few sips of a Piña Colada. I was starting to realize why Jessica was so tipsy from one of these. Jacob and I were mostly just staring at each other and people-watching. He leaned in to kiss me, and instinct made me back away, afraid someone we knew might see. The look on his face made me laugh.

"Sorry," I said. "Old habits die hard." I leaned in and kissed him deeply.

"It's definitely going to be an adjustment," he said. "Think of all the energy we'll save not hiding behind people's backs!" He gave my hand a squeeze.

"But hiding it from everyone was half the fun," I said with a wink.

"Whoa! That was a perfect wink! You finally got it down," he said, giving my butt a hard squeeze.

"Get a room, you perverts!" a familiar voice called out. Jess swam up behind us and took a seat. Where had she come from?

"What are *you* doing here? Did you follow us?" I asked.

"Psh. I've been here a hot minute," she said, placing her drink on the bar.

"You don't like public displays of affection?" Jacob asked her.

Jessica shook her head. "Nope. You'll never catch me making out with anyone in public," she winked.

I couldn't have held in my snort if I tried. It was so loud that a few people looked over, likely expecting a pig to be swimming with them.

"Yeah, just kidding. Y'all keep snogging each other for everyone to see." She held her drink out. "Cheers to the public snoggers!" We all clinked glasses and took a sip.

"Uh-oh," I said. Kyle was approaching. So much for privacy. I slid off of my submerged barstool and took my drink with me. "Come on," I told Jess. "Let's let them talk."

"No, you stay," Kyle said as he approached. I had had enough awkward moments on this trip. I didn't need anymore. His face was blank.

"Boo, Kyle, stop ruining the vibe," a tipsy Jess cried out to him. He just looked at her and gave his head a slight shake. Then he turned to me and Jacob.

"Look, guys. I, uh, I just wanted to tell y'all, from the bottom of my heart, that I'm sorry." I could feel how surprised Jacob was. Kyle had barely muttered a word to us after Jacob took the mic hostage earlier today. "I'm sorry I made such a big deal about you being together. I guess I got freaked out that it might affect our friendship," he said to Jacob. Then he turned to me. "And I just wanted what was best for you. But I can tell y'all are more than just a fling. You seem to make each other happy. So, I wanted to give you my blessing."

"Not that they need it," Jess said.

"Not that you need it," Kyle echoed with a smile. He held out his drink.

Jacob clinked his cup. "Sorry we hid it from everybody."

"I would have done the same. Cheers to new beginnings," Kyle said. He clinked Jess's cup before we all met our drinks in the middle.

"Next round is on me," Kyle said, motioning the bartender over when we had finished our drinks a few minutes later.

"Nah, man, I got it," Jacob told him.

"I insist." Kyle handed the bartender his credit card. "Actually, you know what? I'm buying everyone drinks," he yelled to the dozen people in the pool. "But make ours first." He winked at the bartender.

"Whoa!" I said. "Where are you getting that kind of dough?"

Kyle smiled, and he probably only gave in because he was already here drinking before us. "Okay. I'm going to tell all of you a secret that I haven't told anybody." He lowered his voice. "I became a millionaire recently."

We all furrowed our eyebrows.

"Huh?" Jess mumbled. What was he talking about?

Kyle's smile grew wider. "I bought Bitcoin way back when. I should have sold, but I never did before it crashed. So I waited for it to rise again, and I sold it all two weeks ago. So now, I've got two million dollars in the bank."

Jess reached over and slapped his arm. "You've got two million dollars in the bank, and you let your parents buy pizza and pay for brunch?"

"Well, I can't act suspicious! I shouldn't even be telling you three." He pointed his finger at each of us. "And I expect this information to stay among the four of us. I don't want it getting out to anyone. I'll tell Mom and Dad when I'm ready. But nobody needs to know how much money I have."

"Why not?" Jess said.

"Because it's nobody's business. I don't need to be attracting gold diggers. Anyway, I'm going to spend it all."

"On what?" I said. Man, what would *I* do with that much money?

He had a glint in his eye. "I'm going to use it to start a real estate empire. I'm going to use the money to buy houses and renovate them. I'll sell some and rent out others." He looked hopeful for the first time in a while. It was probably good for him to get this off of his chest.

"Wow, Kyle, that's amazing. Can I be your first tenant? I need to get out of Mom and Dad's house," I said.

"I'll see what I can do," he replied with a smile. He looked over at Jacob. "What's wrong with you? You look like you just saw a dead person. Are you not happy with my success?"

I hadn't noticed that Jacob had kind of slumped over and looked...I don't really know. Sad? Regretful?

"What's wrong?" I said, rubbing his back.

Jacob let out a sigh. "Nothing's wrong. And, no, of course I'm very happy about your success. I guess I just...feel bad, because you came clean to the group, and I haven't."

Oh God. Was this something bad?

"I guess if you're telling secrets, I have one of my own. I've never traded Bitcoin, but I have been day trading for the last four years. I've built it up into a pretty large sum. Some days, with a few clicks, I make more money in an hour than I would in two years with my pool job." He looked up at me and mouthed, 'sorry.' I felt like an hour had passed without me saying anything. So many thoughts were going through my mind. But there was only one at the forefront.

"So, you could have afforded a car this whole time?"

Jacob shrugged. "Well, part of the reason I have so much money is I hate spending it." He smiled. "To answer your question, yes. But, if I had had a car, then I wouldn't have had all that extra time with you." He gave me a loving nudge in my side with his elbow. I couldn't believe he had such a big secret that he hadn't told me, but all I could do was smile and kiss him.

Jessica whooped.

"Gross," Kyle said. So I grabbed Jacob's face and kissed him even harder. Kyle groaned out loud.

"Hey, Kyle, you can make out with me, and we can give them a taste of their own medicine," Jessica said.

I immediately released my lips. "Jessica! Don't you dare!" I knew she was joking, but I knew my friend *and* my brother too well. They didn't need an excuse to eat each other's faces.

We all laughed, and Jacob pulled me into his side. He made me feel so good that I could have stayed in that pool forever.

* * *

It had been four weeks since our trip to the beach, and I was still daydreaming about Jacob announcing his love for me at the restaurant. I was especially remembering all the times we were able to sneak away to be intimate. Sitting next to him in the hot tub. Straddling him in the ocean. Sneaking off into the stairwell late at night.

Now, I was back home. Back at work. And my heart felt empty without Jacob. Shortly after we got back, he received a call from Katie. She said her job had an entry-level marketing position open. It barely paid more than what he was making here, but he didn't really need the money. He was interested in it because the idea of running an ad campaign excited him. I was so happy to see him passionate about something. He looked over at me for approval when he got off the phone with her, and I had nodded. I ended up meeting Katie a couple of weeks after that, and she seemed to be a really nice person. It was a little weird that he would be working with a girl he'd had a one-night stand with, but I knew he loved me. I trusted him—like I should have from the beginning.

He gave his two weeks' notice to my dad the next day, but he wouldn't accept it. He told Jacob to go start his job as soon as possible. I was happy for him, but the selfish part of me wanted to soak up as much of my pool boy as I could before he left.

And since he started his training immediately for a job an hour away, he finally bought his own car. A four-year-old Toyota Corolla. Always the frugal one. I missed carpooling with him, too. *It's funny how you don't know you'll miss something until it's gone.*

My smartwatch buzzed, telling me that the pool was closed, and my shift had ended. *I could have shut it down thirty minutes ago,* I thought. There was nobody outside except the new pool boy, Cory, who had started cleaning. I stepped down my ladder and opened the lockbox with my phone inside. As usual, I had a few texts. But there was also a missed call and a voicemail from an unknown number. *Who calls people these days?*

One of the texts was from Jacob, telling me he was out front. Ever since he'd gotten his car, *he* had been picking *me* up. I smiled and texted him that I would be out in a bit. The other texts were random things from my mom, Jessica, and Rebecca. Then I played my voicemail.

Hi, Abby, this is Lauren Stefanski over at Franklin Middle. I hope you've been well. I was calling to let you know that after interviewing all of the candidates, listening to your voicemail, and doing a lot of thinking, I have decided to offer you the teaching position. Please call me back tomorrow if you're able and let me know if you would like to accept it. If you do, I would need you to start teacher orientation in two weeks. I wanted to hire someone with the passion that I heard in your voice, so thank you for following up with that call. Talk to you soon.

My knees were weak. "Yes!" I screamed for the whole world to hear. Poor Cory nearly fell into the pool. I couldn't believe it. My dreams were coming true. And I needed to tell the person who had helped make sure it happened. I broke the pool club rules and ran toward the club, ready to crash through the glass doors to get to Jacob sooner.

I opened the doors in a hurry, but something to my left caught my eye. There were red things all along the ground. Rose petals. I looked for Pat, but he was nowhere to be found. Curious, I followed the red trail until it led to the breakroom. I opened the door, and Jacob was standing inside, holding a single red rose. The only light in the room came from candles he had lit. There was a bottle of wine and a bowl of popcorn on the coffee table.

The door closed behind me. "What's this?" I asked, walking up to him and taking the rose in my hand.

"Just a special treat for my special lady." He kissed me, and we lingered there with our lips pressed against each other for a long time. "Though we may have to order takeout, unless you want me to pop another five bags."

I laughed and kissed him again. "No. This is perfect. You're perfect. And do you know what makes this moment even more perfect?" He arched his eyebrow at me. "I just got a call saying I got the job at Franklin! I got it, Jacob!"

"What!"

"Yes!"

He picked me up by the waist and spun me around.

"Well, of course you got it!" He squeezed me tight. "I'm so proud of you, babe."

I hugged him tight. "Thank you for pushing me to apply."

"This requires celebration!" He left the embrace of my arms, even though I wanted him to stay there forever, and popped open the wine bottle. I took a seat on the couch and looked at the television screen.

"Pride and Prejudice again?" I asked.

He shrugged and handed me my glass. "Well, we didn't get very far into last time."

"That's true." And I could tell we were going to pause it early again this time, too.

Jacob clinked my glass. "Cheers, babe. To both of our professional dreams coming true."

I looked at his beautiful face and thought of the amazing future he and I were going to share. "To all of our dreams coming true."

We both took a sip and snuggled up on the couch to watch the movie. Everything was as it should be.

Epilogue

Abby

Four Months Later

"So, tell me all about it!" Rebecca said. I held the phone to my ear as I was unpacking boxes.

"It's nothing amazing, but it's my own place, which makes it amazing enough," I said.

"Independence is priceless."

I nodded. "I love my parents. I do. But I am so glad to be out of the house and on my own."

"Damn straight! Oh, sorry," she said, away from the phone. "Andrew is telling me I'm being a little loud in the airport."

"I'm so jealous you're going to Paris. I wish I could have joined. I know Kelly is missing everyone."

"Yeah, she understands. You're still teaching, and you just moved into your own place. It's fine. But you can make it up to *me* by coming to visit us in California! Oh, you know what, Andrew? I'm going to be as loud as I want. There's literally a woman yelling on the intercom, so back off."

I laughed.

"So anyway, yes, we need to schedule you and Jacob coming out to meet us at our place. It is *beautiful* out here, Abby. Everywhere you look, you can take a picture. There are flowers growing everywhere. Even in cracks in the sidewalk! I can't believe I grew up thinking California was a terrible place just because my dad didn't like some things about it. And, oh my God, we found this artisan cheese place. Abby, let me tell you! You will die when you walk in there. They just let you sample all the cheeses. I might apply for a job there so I can taste test the product all the time."

I was smiling because I was so happy that little sheltered Rebecca had finally grown out of her shell. "Yes, we will definitely make a trip up there. Maybe during my spring break? Or in the summer?"

"Yes! Come visit in the early summer. It will be perfect for the vineyards and the beach."

"Sounds like a plan. I do miss you being so close, though. You seem like you're on the opposite side of the world."

"Yeah, I miss you and everyone else a lot too. It was scary at first. But I can't believe how happy I am that I took the plunge."

I heard a knock at the door. "Looks like my new roommate forgot their key," I said. I had thought about getting my own place and living by myself, but having a roommate was so much cheaper. I would have been open to getting a nicer place, but this was an okay first rental.

"Your roommate sounds like trouble already. Just don't do anything I wouldn't do," Rebecca said.

I walked toward the door, smiling. "No promises."

Rebecca laughed. "All right, girl, I'll let you go. We should be boarding in a few minutes. I love you! Talk to you soon."

"Love you! Have a safe flight! Eat all the cheese and tell

Kelly hello for me." We hung up the phone, and I opened the door. My heart fluttered at the sight of him. Who knew how long it was going to be before I was going to be comfortable living with a man? "What took you so long?"

Jacob came in the door, his hands full of boxes. "Don't get me started. I had to go to three different stores to find the coffee maker I wanted."

"You're ridiculous." I took one of the boxes from his stack and walked to the kitchen with it.

"Hey, you'll be thanking me once you taste the sweet brown bean water I'll start brewing for you every morning."

"Looking forward to it."

"Plus, there was one other thing I had to go to three different stores for before I found what I was looking for," he said.

"Oh yeah? Was it a microwave? Or a certain spoon with *just* the right handle?" I laughed at my own joke. He didn't answer, and I didn't feel like guessing anymore. So I placed the box on the counter and turned around.

He was down on one knee and holding out a ring.

I raised both of my hands to my mouth in shock.

"Abby Barber, I know it might be too soon to ask you this, but I want to be with you forever, and I'm tired of waiting. Will you marry me?"

My eyes started to cry. "Yes. A million times yes, Jacob Duncan." I walked over to him and held out my hand. He slid the ring on my finger. The center stone had a halo around it, and the band had side stones on it. He stood up and kissed me, and I jumped into his arms. He walked us to the bedroom as we kissed. We had only been together for six months, but we knew we were soulmates. Why prolong the inevitable? I wanted to marry him yesterday.

He dropped me on the bed and climbed on top of me. I took off his shirt and then he took off mine. He started kissing my breasts tenderly. I kept staring at the ring. My finger had always felt empty while dating him.

"It's a perfect fit. Who told you my size?"

"Jessica. But, I didn't have to change the ring at all. It's like it was made for you."

"What do you mean?"

He smiled. "That's my mom's ring. She was a four and a half too. I asked my dad if I could have it a couple of months ago. I thought he might get angry at having to give it up, but it actually made him smile."

I was grinning wider than I ever had in my life. "I love it. It's perfect. And I love you." He came up and kissed my lips. Then his kisses went lower, lower, and lower.

I had found the perfect man, and I was never letting him go.

THE END

Or is it?

So Jacob has proposed, but what happens after they get married? Join my mailing list with this link, and you'll get the BONUS EPILOGUE telling you all about it in your inbox immediately! If you are already on my mailing list, you will always receive the bonus epilogue on the day of publication.

. . .

My mailing list is how my fans find out about new releases, free stories, and behind-the-scenes insights into what locations or happenings in my life inspired me to write a particular setting, character, or situation. Join today!

Thank you!

Thank you so much for reading. I really hope you enjoyed this book. <u>I would be ever so grateful if you could leave an honest review for it by clicking this link.</u>

Other than telling your fellow romance reader friends about my book on social media, a review is one of the best ways to spread the word and help other readers find me. Just a line or two is all it takes to make a huge difference in my career.

Thanks again, and be sure to look out for my email on the release date for my next book, Falling for My Grumpy Boss.

Where to Find Laura Eagan

Follow me on Amazon <u>by Clicking Here</u>

Find all of my published books and their reading order <u>by going to my website, www.lauraeagan.com</u>

Falling Series

1. Falling for My Dad's Boss
2. Falling for My Brother's Best Friend
3. Falling for My Grumpy Boss (*January* 2024)
4. Falling for My Mafia Boss (*April* 2024)

What's Next?

Falling for My Grumpy Boss

Kelly starts her new job in Paris. But the world's most romantic city seems like it's filled with nothing but mean French people and heartbreak. Follow Kelly across the ocean as she navigates the cutthroat world of French fashion and does her best to tame her grumpy boss.

Coming out in January 2024

About the Author

Laura Eagan was born and raised in New Orleans, Louisiana. Like many other locals, she has had a hard time leaving. She is happily married and has two dogs.

She loves reading, eating, and traveling. When she's not doing those things, or doing chores, she can be found on her couch snuggling with her pups and watching a tv show.

You can join Laura Eagan's email list to learn of all future releases and any special discounts on her books, as well as receive a free bonus epilogue of the book you just read, <u>by clicking this link.</u>